Sanctuary

Glyn Smith-Wild

OBS

Supporting New Writers

Published in the United Kingdom 2012

OBS, 25 Tweed Close, Honiton, Devon EX14 2YU

A catalogue record for this book is available from the British Library.

ISBN-13: 978-1470091569

ISBN-10: 1470091569

To Sue.

My thanks go to my good friend Joan who was instrumental in this book being written and a continual source of encouragement and support throughout its journey to publication.

We are grateful to Larry Alen for the use of the photograph on the cover and to our cover artist Lloyd Lelina for his visual interpretation of the storyline.

Chapter 1

She was much later than usual getting home. Every few minutes in the last hour or so he had gone into the kitchen to watch out for her. Each time he looked the weather seemed to deteriorate further. It was going to be a rough night. The forecast said it could be snowing by the morning. This time, though, he had been able, through the steamed-up, rain-splattered window, to make out Mary fighting her way through the wind and rain across the dimly lit courtyard.

Ben was aware of his heart beating as he made his way to the door to let her in. Standing at the top of the stairs, he heard Mary put her key into the latch and watched as she opened the front door below.

'Hi,' he said with a big welcoming smile. 'You're late, but I think dinner has survived'.

His welcome had been offered in all innocence - he so wanted this to be a special evening - but when he looked at Mary he saw that her eyes were intense, glaring up at him.

'I didn't know you were cooking a meal,' she barked as she walked up the stairs towards him. 'I certainly didn't ask you to. So don't have a go at me for being late home. You sound like my mother. God can't I even have some time with my...'

'Whoa, whoa, whoa!' retorted Ben. 'All I said was...'

'Yes, I know what you said,' she continued, pushing him aside, 'I heard it plainly enough. I'm just a bit fed up with being treated like a kid.'

'I'm sorry, Mary. I didn't intend it to sound like that. Certainly didn't mean to treat you like a child. I'll just get dinner ready to serve. You go and freshen up, or whatever. I'll give you a shout when it's on the table.'

Ben stood back as she rushed past him.

'Stuff your bloody meal!' Mary almost screamed as she ran up the stairs to her bedroom. 'Just stuff it!'

Nonplussed would be an understatement. He stood there with his mouth half open, trying to take in the situation. She had walked straight past the dining table set with its crimson cloth, white linen napkins and the single red rose lying across its centre. She had not even noticed the ice bucket with the neck of the bottle of *Moët & Chandon* peeking out. He knew she sometimes had a short fuse, but he had never witnessed anything like this before.

Can't just be the weather, he thought. There must be more to it than that.

For such a large flat, the kitchen was remarkably small. Ben had been working in the limited space preparing a meal which included Chicken in a Masala wine sauce. He did not consider himself to be a good chef by any means and had chosen this recipe because it was simple to prepare, extremely tasty to eat and he knew that it was a favourite with them both. Not much could go wrong so long as he followed the recipe meticulously, he thought.

Being in a reminiscent mood as he cooked, he recalled that until he met Mary, his prowess with women had been noteworthy only by its failure rating.

He had always been intrigued by the opposite sex, and it was true they seemed to be attracted to him. It was the bringing together of these two facts that seemed to cause the problems. Everything would seem to be going along swimmingly and then the sudden, inexplicable ending. Not just once; no less than three times this had happened to him in the past.

It was by chance that he had met Mary. He had been selected by SRX Solutions to install a point-of-sale computer system at the hairdressing salon where she worked and she had been the one he had to train to operate the system.

She was stunning, her long chestnut coloured hair falling to her shoulders and the deepest brown eyes he had ever seen. He had been smitten by her at first sight. Unfortunately he hadn't felt his feelings for her were in any way requited. It was by chance that they discovered a common interest and had started meeting up at the local sports centre. He would play tennis, badminton or squash. She would spend time in the gym. They would often stop off to have a drink together on their way home and soon became good friends.

On one such evening, their discussions had led them to their common desire to get a foot on the property ladder. Neither of them could individually afford to buy a place they really liked. However, when they started to explore the idea of pooling their resources and buying something together it had excited them both and became a regular topic of conversation.

Five years ago she had finally agreed to share buying a maisonette in Reading. He had been overjoyed, not just at the thought of being able to acquire a better home than he had previously envisaged, but at the anticipation of this dark haired, olive skinned beauty living under the same roof with him. Perhaps he had found the perfect relationship; nothing emotional or romantic, just a business arrangement.

At first the relationship had been decidedly matter-of-fact. They had each agreed it should be that way and for more than a year it was.

As time went on Ben had begun looking forward to the evenings when she was at home. He had found himself looking at her more closely, watching her as she sat on the sofa, just a few feet away from him. Her fragrance would infuse the room. It wasn't her perfume; it was her own fresh, sweet pheromone, something distinctively hers. Her presence used to make him forget about anything else, and as time went on he had become more and more enchanted by her in a far from platonic way.

He had found himself fantasising about her as he lay in bed at night.

When they sat in their comfortable lounge in the evenings he had wanted so often to go over to her, kiss her, and take her to his bed. Nonetheless they had agreed from the start that this should not happen. The lines had been drawn. And Ben had decided, difficult as it was for him to deal with, that he would rather have a *status quo* situation, with her sharing the flat with him, than to make a false move, ruin everything, and lose her for ever.

Oblivious to Mary's changing frame of mind, he never once thought that she had amorous feelings for him, never considered that she reciprocated his thoughts for her.

One evening some months later when they had been in the kitchen washing up, he had been aware of her constantly bumping into him, pressing up against him to reach for a plate, briefly touching his arm as she went past him. He had turned around to ask her what she was up to, only to receive a long, passionate kiss, his head held firmly to her by the hands that still held the tea towel.

'At last!' Mary had said. 'You're a hard man to pin down, aren't you?' Ben had intercepted any further conversation, and had pulled her to him for another kiss. The platonic era was over. They had slept together that night, and most nights since.

Ben had just wished it could have happened much sooner. From that moment, at last, they each knew where they stood and their relationship had blossomed rapidly.

Ben brought himself back to today. It was five years ago today they had made the agreement to buy the flat and that was the reason Ben had decided to cook something special for them.

The aroma of the spices filled the kitchen. However, after her outburst, he doubted the meal would ever reach the table.

Chapter 2

It had been a terrible day for Mary. One of the most awful days she could remember. One half of her couldn't wait to get away from the salon. The other half was dreading what would happen when she did.

To make matters worse, Mrs Durham, her last customer on this Friday evening was more than twenty minutes late.

'I'm so sorry I'm late, Mary. I got caught up in traffic. Some kind of accident I think.' Mary was aware of a woman wearing a heavy full length coat bustling her ample form into the salon, catching her shoulder bag on the door as she did so. Her face was even more highly coloured than usual, her breathing asthmatic from her exertion.

Mary was not in the least bit interested. All she knew was Mrs Durham, her last customer on a Friday afternoon, was late. That meant she would be leaving late.

Mary prepared Mrs Durham for her usual full manicure.

'I would've cancelled, dear, but the choral society is performing in a contest in Birmingham this weekend so I feel I have to look my best.' Mary wasn't listening. Even so Mrs Durham kept on going, still trying to catch her breath. 'A friend of mine is driving me up to the NEC tomorrow morning. It feels like being on *X Factor*. At least I guess it must be the same kind of feeling. I'm awfully nervous but excited at the same time.'

Normally, Mary would have been enthusing about Mrs Durham's news. Today she was reluctantly offering a few grunts with the occasional 'Mmmm' thrown in. The woman just wouldn't stop.

'… So I'm staying up there after the performance, with my sister's ex. He's such a nice man. I just can't see what possessed her to leave him…'

Mary worked as fast as she could. Her two colleagues waved and grimaced to her, as they walked past her to let themselves out.

It was a ritual on Friday evenings when the salon closed, that the three of them would meet up at *The Prospect* just a few doors away from *Hair Today.*

'See you in a few minutes?' her colleague, Penny, said. Mary looked up and nodded.

'At least the weather looks reasonable,' Mrs Durham was saying, 'so we should be able get out and about. I don't really know the area at all, so it will be nice to …'

Forty long minutes later Mrs Durham was able to inspect Mary's work, and said she was more than pleased with the result. She paid for the manicure adding a hefty tip for Mary, apologising again for being late.

Mary quickly cashed up, turned off the lights and left the building, carefully locking the doors behind her. There were so many things on her mind that evening which had been plaguing her throughout the day. She couldn't stop thinking about the decision she had made. All day she had been going over and over the last five years since she and Ben had bought the flat in Reading.

Their relationship had progressed from the early days when they had both agreed that the arrangement should be purely financial. It had taken two years until their relationship had blossomed from the platonic to a full-blown love affair. It had been her own doing. Had she left it all to Ben, she doubted whether anything would ever have happened. She had tried all manner of things to get him to show some interest in her. She had masterminded the occasional "accidental" meeting between bathroom and bedroom after showering. The first time wearing just a towel wrapped around her, and as time went on, becoming more and more blatant. She would listen for him coming up the stairs and then leave the bathroom in just bra and pants, and once completely naked.

His reaction was to look embarrassed. That had not been her plan but that, it seemed, was Ben.

Over time, though, she had begun to see some changes in his attitude toward her. It had been the look in his eyes, the warm welcome when she had arrived home, and later she could see that the looks he was giving her held something more. Much more.

He can't resist for much longer, can he? she thought.

Ben eventually got the message when, one evening while they were doing the washing up, she had grabbed hold of him and kissed him. From that moment everything had changed and they had become lovers. Good lovers. She still had her own life, her own group of friends. Now she had Ben to come home to and to share her bed. For the last three years it had been almost perfect. Almost. On the other hand she could see little future in it. On the few occasions that she had tried to talk about making plans Ben had seemed to turn off completely. She had just had her thirty-fifth birthday, and would love nothing more than to think about starting a family, but she doubted that he would want to consider such things. She would like a ring on her finger, but suspected that was far from his aspirations.

Recently she had met someone who had entirely beguiled her with his charm, his wit, his seemingly overwhelming love for her. More importantly, he said he wanted the same things she did.

With all these thoughts spinning in her head she made her way the few yards down the road from the salon to *The Prospect*.

It was a typically miserable, cold and windy January afternoon. Post-Christmas gloom had set in.

The other two girls were already sitting in their regular seats in one of the bay windows looking out onto the bustling street outside where hordes of people were making their way home. It wasn't a great pub. The walls and ceilings were stained yellow by years of cigarette smoke, the furniture and fabrics were well worn and there was a pervading smell of stale beer coming from the floor covering. The whole place was in dire need of refurbishment, and the girls sometimes thought the same could be said of the staff. However, it was convenient and warm.

The three girls were the best of pals, working together in Ray's hair salon, *Hair Today*. On Friday evenings they would have a drink or two and a good natter about their plans for the weekend before making their way home.

Mary sauntered into the bar and joined the girls at their table.

'Here's Mary with two ells,' announced Penny, cheerily. Mary was often referred to in this way because, whenever she had to give her name to anyone, she always referred to herself as "Mary Willson with two ells", and it had stuck, in the same way as a nickname might.

Mary took her seat and glanced across the table at Penny. She was the pretty one, a quiet, reserved girl with her hair of burnt gold like autumnal evening sunshine, rosy complexion and pale green eyes. She was the senior stylist. Her life always seemed to be organised, departmentalised, in control. It was seldom she would show any annoyance or frustration. She was a good influence when there were problems at *Hair Today*, and had the ability to bring any upsets back under control with ease. I wonder how she would deal with all this, Mary thought to herself.

Her eyes then went to Georgina or "Grunge" as she had become known because of her outlandish taste in clothes and hair styles. She had moved south to study an Arts & Design course at Reading University and had come to work at *Hair Today* as a trainee stylist to help pay her fees. When she realised that she enjoyed her work at the salon much more than the college course, she had decided to work full time for Ray. Always ebullient, the joker, her hair could change colour two or three times a month; today it was mainly auburn with a large tuft

9

of orange standing up on the top of her head. This one she called *Volcano*. She attracted a lot of younger customers for Ray and was well thought of by all of his clients, although there were the occasional glances from the more staid customers when they saw some of the styles she was creating. The opposite of Penny, she was at times the cause of upsets at the salon because of her outspoken attitude. She was a typical Yorkshire lass and did not believe in holding back. If there was something to be said, she would be the one to say it regardless of the consequences. She offset this by being the comic as well. It was not unusual for the whole salon to be in fits of laughter from the things she said.

These two girls had become part of Mary's life. The three were good together. Mary felt sometimes that, because she was a few years older than either of them, she was looked upon as some kind of mother figure. Tonight she didn't want that responsibility. Tonight she was looking for their empathy, their support.

Things had been rather down beat most of the day at the salon and on this evening, too, there was an uncharacteristic hush in the conversation. At first nobody seemed to know why. Mary lifted her glass of white wine that had been bought for her. The usual gossiping, chattering and girl talk was missing. Mary was hardly aware of her surroundings let alone the conversation. She had felt like this all day.

She woke up when she realised that Grunge was talking to her.

'What?' she asked.

'You haven't heard a word I was saying, have you?' Grunge asked.

'No, not really. Sorry.'

'What's up, Mary?' asked Penny. 'You've been in another world all day.'

'Yes. I know. I'm sorry,' Mary said at last. 'It's just that I have this God almighty problem that I have got to sort out this weekend.'

'Well, are you going to tell us what it is?' asked Penny. 'You never know, it might help to share it.'

'Yeah, C'mon, Mary. We're all ears, and pretty nosey as well,' joked Grunge, in her inimitable way.

Mary flashed her eyes towards Grunge.

'Well, you all know how I feel about Ben. We've been sharing our flat since we bought it together nearly five years ago, and for most of the time we've been sleeping together as well. But, somehow everything's become a bit stale of late, kind of aimless. We don't seem to be going anywhere – no future, you know?' Mary started to explain. 'Anyway, I've been going out with another guy for just over a month now. Just as good friends at first. He's really good company, a great laugh, really captivating in fact. And it stayed like that for a while. But you know how it is. Things changed - slowly it seemed - our feelings for each other became much more intense, and then we realised that we were falling in love. I was just living from one meeting with him to the next, counting the days, hours, minutes, just like some silly schoolgirl.'

'Do we know this guy?' asked Penny. 'You certainly kept this quiet.'

'I doubt you know him,' Mary replied. 'He's not from round here. His name is Donald.'

'Donald?' Grunge exclaimed. 'You can't be serious about a bloke called Donald!'

'Oh, shut up Grunge. Just keep quiet and listen,' Penny almost shouted.

'Anyway, he's a bit older than me,' Mary continued. 'In fact he's almost old enough to be my father. His wife died last year, and he's such a nice guy. If you knew him, I think you'd see why I fell for him.

'How did you meet him?'

'It was strange really. It was when I went with Ray to an exhibition last year. We visited Donald's stand and he spent some time talking to Ray. All the time he was looking at me, almost studying me. I didn't think much of it at the time. Then he sought me out again later and found me in a bar. At least, that's how it looked to me. I saw him wandering around the exhibition, obviously searching for something or someone, and when he spotted me, he came straight over, asked if he could buy me a drink, and started chatting. The next thing I knew was that we had a date.'

Everything went quiet for a minute.

'The thing is, how on earth am I going to tell Ben?' she asked, looking intently at her friends. 'He's such a good friend, and we've been so good together for all these years. I feel awful. I've got to tell him this weekend. Donald's asked me to move in with him. He's got this lovely house in Wallingford, and says it's much too big for him on his own.'

Mary could see that Grunge was now listening intently to what was being said. She knew that she had met Ben on several occasions at parties, and it had become obvious that she had come to like him a lot. As the conversation went on, it was clear that Grunge was becoming really agitated, almost angry. Mary had seen her like this before, and knew that she would probably erupt soon.

And she did.

'So he needs somebody to keep the house clean, wash his pants, darn his socks. Is that it?' she eventually blurted out. 'This makes no sense at all. How could you even *think* of leaving Ben? You must be bloody mad!'

Mary snapped back, 'I might have known you'd say something like that. Can't you, just for once, try to understand? For God's sake, I love this bugger. I can't help it. I just love him. He's totally captivated me.'

Grunge just said, 'Mmm.'

Another difficult silence followed, and then Penny said, 'Actually, Mary, I think you're overlooking what a nice guy Ben is ...'

'I'm bloody not,' Mary retorted.

'No, hear me out.' Although Penny was quietly spoken there was a certain authority in her voice. 'What I mean is, you're not married to each other. All you did, originally, was buy the flat together. You have always had a remarkably free relationship, both you and he are out and about with anybody you like, no questions asked. I think you will find that he might just understand. I bet he has been close to this situation himself with some of the girls he's been around with, Katie Forrester for instance. She's had her eye on him for ages. So don't under estimate his ability to understand.'

'Don't mention that woman. She's always been there waiting to pounce. She really is some kind of predator. I just hope you're right,' Mary said quietly. 'It's just how to tell him that makes it so difficult. It's hardly the thing you just slip into a conversation, is it? *Oh, by the way, I'm a bit bored with our relationship so I'm moving out next week.* There's the financial part as well. I guess we'll have to sell the flat to be able to sort that out. It all seems so unfair.'

Nobody knew what to say.

It was Penny who spoke first. 'I think you've just got to pluck up the nerve to tell him as calmly as possible. Explain it to him like you have to us. You can't keep this bottled up any longer. Anyway,' she continued, 'I wouldn't be surprised if he has an inkling that something is wrong. Things can't have been exactly normal over the last few weeks, if your feelings for your new bloke have been as strong as you are telling us. To be honest, I would be surprised if he doesn't already know something like this is going on. You owe it to him to tell him as soon as you can find the courage.'

'I know you're right, Penny. I bet I've been a bit distant these last few weeks. Things on my mind. But he's never asked me what's wrong. Never moaned. That's half the problem. He's just so bloody nice!'

'Sorry about my outburst earlier,' Grunge butted in. 'Didn't mean to make things worse. It's just that my mouth takes over before my brain's in gear sometimes. I really hope everything works out for you. Anyway, I think it's my round. I'll go and get them in.'

'Hey. Don't worry too much,' said Penny when Grunge was out of earshot. 'Ben is never going to be short of female company. No doubt he'll miss you, however I think his philosophy is *Life goes on*.'

Mary wished she was more convinced that things were so simple. She had fallen desperately in love with Donald, had butterflies each time they were to meet. He seemed to be exactly what she was looking for. A relationship with a future, security, a family. She couldn't see any of these things in Ben, and yet they had had some great times together. He was a man of the present, living for today, having fun. Until now she had been satisfied, happy with that, but now she had the option of settling down, of growing up, and that was what she wanted.

The question remained, how on earth was she going to tell Ben?

Chapter 3

Peeling off her soaked clothes Mary threw herself onto the bed and, attempting to calm herself down by breathing deeply, she suddenly found herself weeping into her pillow.

The questions kept returning. How the hell am I going to deal with this? Why on earth did I behave like that? Poor Ben. He didn't deserve that and bless him, he's got much worse to come. I'll have to tell him tonight but how can I do that now after that slanging match? I've never treated him like that before. I've never treated *anybody* like that. Do I really care about him that much?

She lay there for some time, and when eventually, she began to feel calmer, got up from the bed, took a long hot shower, and went about using her beautician's skills to hide the aftermath of her tears.

'This,' she said aloud to herself, 'has got to be the moment of truth. I can't put it off any longer.'

Taking a deep breath she went back downstairs to find Ben looking extremely doleful, supposedly watching television, obviously not taking anything in.

She sat on the sofa alongside his chair, and for a while said absolutely nothing. Eventually with the increasing tension in the air she knew she had to say something.

'Ben,' she said softly, 'I'm so sorry about my outburst. You didn't deserve that.' As she went to continue Ben got in first.

'Yeah, I won't argue with that. Can I get you something to eat now? Or had I better not mention food this evening?' he asked. 'Dinner was pretty well ruined anyway, but I could knock up a snack for you.'

'Ben,' Mary began.

'Not now, eh? We'll talk in a little while. I'll just make some coffee. Seriously, would you like a snack?' he said, as he went off into the kitchen.

'Thanks,' Mary called after him. 'Something on toast would be about right.'

Everything went quiet again. The television purred away in the background. Mary couldn't see or hear anything above the hubbub in her head. How can he be so calm? I'd have been raving mad being treated like that. How come he's not reacting? Time after time she tried to practice how she would start what she had to say. None of them sounded right.

After a while, Ben returned with the coffees and her egg-on-toast with a simple side salad. He placed it on her lap, and for the first time looked into her melancholy, deep brown eyes, and smiled at her.

'Look. It's obvious we're going to have to talk. Clearly, something has happened that's had a big effect on you,' said Ben, the smile gone now and replaced with a look of deep concern. 'So now you can calm yourself down, and just tell me what's going on whenever you want.'

After a few minutes, Mary told him about Donald. How she had been seeing him for a few weeks, and how she had come to the point where she wanted to make a real commitment to him.

'Ben,' she said with tears welling in her eyes, 'we've had a wonderful few years together, and you're a really special guy. It's just that I don't think you've ever thought about the future - marriage, kids, that kind of thing. We've just enjoyed each other, and enjoyed living together, living for today. So you see, my feelings for Donald - it's different. It's really deep, really intense. I can't expect you to understand, I can hardly get my head round it myself, but that's the best way I can explain it.'

She had been looking at Ben while she was speaking, trying to gauge what his reaction was going to be. He wasn't looking at her. His eyes didn't seem to be focused on anything, and there was a blank, empty look on his face.

Mary wondered if Ben was going to ask her to stay. If he did, she knew it would be difficult to decide. There was even a possibility he would win.

For a while he said nothing and then he looked directly into those tearful eyes, got up from his chair, and walked slowly out of the room and back into the kitchen.

Ben leaned on the sink. His whole body was quivering. Part anguish, part anger. Part love, part hate. He had never experienced anything like this before. In a matter of minutes his comfortable, cosy life with Mary had come crashing down around his feet. It was like being in a collision with a buffalo. The breath had been knocked out of him. He just had not seen this coming.

He tried desperately to pull himself together, to stop the shaking. Instinctively, he reached into a cupboard, found the bottle of single malt whisky, and took a long slug straight from the bottle. It didn't help. He knew he must return to her. He knew he had to say something. But what?

What would happen if I ask her to change her mind? he asked himself. No, she's obviously made up her mind, and has made promises to this guy. I'll feel ten times worse if I ask her to stay, and she turns me down.

He wanted to say something like: "You have brought nothing but light and happiness into my life, more than I could ever hope for or deserve. I don't want it to end. You are part of my life."

What came out when he returned to the room, however, was more like: 'I'm so sorry to hear this, and while I am sad to see you go, I have only ever wanted for you to be happy, and if that means your being with someone else, then that is how it must be.' He could not remember the exact words, they were probably jumbled anyway. He said there was no hatred in him. Jealousy, maybe. Sadness, certainly. She would always retain a certain special place in his heart, whatever happened.

Ben Coverdale, he screamed at himself even as he spoke, you're a bloody idiot.

They were both near to tears by now. He moved next to her on the sofa, put his arm round her shoulder and pulled her towards him. Neither spoke.

Then, slowly, she turned toward him and kissed him.

'I had been dreading all of this,' she said. 'I should have known better. You really are something else.'

"So why don't you ask me to stay?" she wanted to yell at him.

Then she suddenly broke down, floods of tears running down her face and soaking into Ben's shirt. She just couldn't stop, couldn't control these emotions.

Ben sat silently, still with his arms round her shoulders, feeling the warmth of her tears falling on to him. He kissed her lightly on the cheek, tasting the salt of her crying.

Eventually her sobbing subsided.

'Can I ask just one favour?' he asked her.

'Go on,' Mary replied, hoping he might be about to say what she wanted to hear.

'I suggest we don't talk any more about this tonight. This has come as a complete blow to me. We can talk again tomorrow, when we'll have collected our thoughts and can make the decisions that have to be made without all this emotion.'

When they went to their beds neither of them could find the solace of slumber. They both lay tossing and turning, trying to get comfortable enough, to relax enough, to get to sleep.

The following morning Ben was awakened by Mary's expletives.

'Oh, shit!' she screamed. 'Look at the time. I'm supposed to be at work in half an hour! Oh shit!' She leapt out of bed, running into the bathroom, splashing water at the bits that needed it, and throwing on some work clothes.

She called back to Ben, who was still coming round, 'I should be back at lunchtime. I'm only working this morning. See you then.'

It seemed like old times, but Ben knew it wasn't. There was a finality about it that had to be sorted out later in the day. He decided another half an hour in bed wouldn't do any harm, and dozed back to sleep.

When he finally rose from his bed he tried to put his overnight thoughts into some kind of order. He felt different now. His attitude towards the situation had changed. He still felt completely let down, but instead of wallowing in his disappointment, he decided he had to take control. It was he that was being treated badly. She it was, for all the tears and emotions, who had decided it was all over. It was she who was off to make a new life with her sugar daddy. Why was he feeling so bad, so guilty about it? He had followed all the rules she'd laid down. When she had reset the boundary, he had encouraged the relationship to move on. He had gladly gone along with it. He had felt he was the luckiest man alive. And now she thought she could change everything again? 'Just let her go,' he heard himself saying. 'It's happened before and you managed to survive. What's so different this time?'

Who was he kidding? He knew this time it was different. This time he'd thought the love between them was much more precious, more permanent. Nevertheless, he was determined that he was not going to give her the satisfaction of seeing him upset. No more tears from him. He would be positive, in control. He would let her think it wasn't really having a great impact on his life. He had managed without her before, and he could manage without her now. Before she returned from work, he would have everything planned, everything documented, everything sorted. He thought of nothing else throughout the morning.

Ben knew the only way he was going to be able to deal with this was to make an absolutely clean break. Call it a day, a terribly sad day, water under the bridge, and many other clichés. He didn't feel he could bear to see her packing her things ready to move out and so he decided he would ask Mary to clear the flat of everything she wanted to take with her while he took a short break away.

By the time she came home at lunch time Ben had everything organised.

He asked her to sit down, and presented her with his plans. He would make all the arrangements to sell the flat, he told her, and they would share the profits. He would move into a smaller place until he knew what he was going to do. In the meantime, he was going to take a short holiday, and during that time, she could clear the flat of everything she wanted to take with her.

Ben could see Mary was astonished by his uncharacteristic assertiveness. He had never acted like this before. He hardly let her get a word in, and told her that, in his opinion, this was the only way to sort things out. To make a complete break. For both of them to start new chapters in their lives, to put this down to experience. Inside, he was despising himself for what he was doing. He could see her face. He knew he was hurting her.

But the real hurt was his. Until a few hours ago he thought he had everything. Now he felt he had nothing. She had taken it all away.

Chapter 4

Ben decided he had to get well away from Reading and everything it held for him at the moment. He needed to be able to blank out the current situation, as far as possible, from his mind. And the only place he could think of where he had a chance of doing that was France. Every time he went there he felt as if he was in another world, and that was exactly what he needed now. Later that day, having already packed his bags, Ben walked out of the flat, drove to Portsmouth and caught the overnight ferry to Caen.

His mind was still in turmoil.

There was none of the usual excitement of crossing the channel which was remarkably smooth for early January, and after breakfast on board of some soft, buttery pastries and a large, strong coffee, he drove his car off the ferry and headed south. He had no preconceived plans except for the fact that he would probably be heading for the Loire, his favourite area of France. He was in no hurry.

Daylight was just beginning to permeate the sky with hues of pink set on wispy, pale grey clouds. The French roads were even quieter than usual. Ben was always amazed how he could drive for miles seeing nothing more than the vast sweeping countryside. It was farming country, with isolated farmhouses dotted over the landscape and, as usual, there was hardly any human activity to be seen. The wintery countryside seemed almost deserted. This was part of the attraction. He could almost taste, almost smell France from the moment he arrived. It was always like this. Each time he came here, he felt at one with the place.

If he was honest there was little difference between the countryside in Normandy and that of some southern counties of England. The vineyards and sunflowers were found much further south. Nevertheless there was this inexplicable feeling, this ambience, which he had never experienced anywhere else. He was hoping that just being here would help him clear his head of the last couple of days.

Lazily, the sun revealed its face, creating long shadows across the undulating terrain.

After driving for a couple of hours, he arrived at the small town of Fougéres, and decided to stop for a coffee at a roadside café. He liked the look of the town, discovered a *Campanile* Hotel and booked himself in. After a refreshing shower, he sauntered back into the town. The colours, the sounds, the essence of the life of the town engulfed him. He was used to seeing well-dressed shop windows; Reading was, after all, a successful, bustling, shopping centre. Even so, here the colours stood out. The brightly lit fashion boutiques were displaying *haute couture* styles that would not be found at home, except maybe in London's West End. Even the way in which fruit and vegetables were laid out seemed to make the merchandise so much more appealing. And, of course, the *boulangeries* offering the most mouth-watering cakes and pastries anywhere in the world. Toys, chocolates, flowers, whatever was for sale seemed to shout out "Buy me!".

Turning off into the cobbled side streets, he was presented with a wonderful assortment of sights. There were old timbered houses alongside rows of shops built of grey stone.

After a while wandering the streets he stopped at a small café, almost full of locals. He chose the *plat du jour* and enjoyed an unhurried lunch of *Crêpe de Poulet* containing chicken, apple, mushroom, cream, and seasonal vegetables with a green salad, accompanied by a chilled French beer. He sat at a window seat inside the small restaurant and simply watched the world go by for over an hour. If it had not been such a chilly January day he would be sitting outside which would have been even better. I could live like this, he thought, but instantly reminded himself this was only a break for a week or so. Then it would be back to the world he knew and didn't love so much.

He knew he was fortunate to be able to just get up and go like this. He had worked hard to get to the position he was in. He and his two work colleagues, both, strangely enough, called Tony, had all been employed by the same software company in Bracknell, and had teamed up, outside of the company, to develop what had at first seemed a crazy idea. It had turned out to be a gold mine. He was not a 'techie' like the two Tonys, but had become an expert in e-commerce.

His two colleagues had developed the software and he was responsible for linking an admin section to it. Before long, all three of them had left their employment with SRX, formed a partnership, and had concentrated on developing their business venture.

The program they had developed had found a back way into the major internet search engines, and it was this facility they were selling to website owners who wanted their sites to be seen at the top of the listing on Google, Yahoo and the like. The customers signed up for a twelve month contract, paid a deposit, and then paid a monthly fee direct into the trio's bank.

It had worked better than they had dreamed it would, and the money just kept on coming. It was Ben's job to control the finances as part of his administration duties, leaving an agreed amount of working capital in the bank, and splitting the surplus between each of them.

Because of this Ben was seldom seen without his laptop. He had to keep a regular eye on things, to ensure customer satisfaction and to check on any payments that were bouncing for any reason.

Today was no exception. After another beer or three, he made his way back to the lower end of the town. As he wandered slowly towards his hotel he came across a dancing fountain.

Whilst it seemed so wonderfully out of place, almost hidden away, it was so beautiful to watch that he stood gazing at it for several minutes.

At the hotel Ben checked his emails, found that there was nothing urgent to attend to, lay back on his bed and dropped into a deep sleep.

When he awoke, it was time to think about eating again, and, feeling a bit lethargic, he decided to use the adjoining restaurant, where he had an excellent meal of braised duck with a selection of perfectly cooked vegetables and a particularly enjoyable bottle of Syrah.

Following the meal he decided to take a walk in the chill evening air. His meandering took him once again to the fountain, all the more striking to watch in the evening; the multi-coloured lights so much brighter in the darker surroundings.

Later, back in his room, whether it was the soporific effect of the wine, the effects of the travelling or just the relief of being away from the situation back home, he slipped slowly but surely into an unexpected depressed state of mind. This was something he was not used to and found difficult to cope with. Turning on the radio he heard Michael Jackson singing *She's out of My Life,* and immediately switched it off again, not wanting to make things any worse. His head was filled with Mary. The good times, the bad times. He kept pulling himself up, trying to change the images in his mind. Within minutes, she was back. He was being haunted by her.

His mind went back to one evening, fairly early in their relationship, when, while supposedly watching television, he had been mentally undressing her. Even as he vividly recalled the occasion, he felt guilty at his virtual invasion of her privacy.

That evening she had been sitting at the far end of the sofa, her feet tucked up under her, deep into a book. As she concentrated on her novel, her free hand played with her hair, twiddling strands into long strings. She often did this and for some unknown reason it used to drive him crazy with lust. He had continued to pretend to watch the programme, something about carbon dating of rocks found in some remote part of the Sahara while in his mind he had been slowly, mentally, salaciously disrobing her.

In his fantasy he had wanted to rip her pretty top from her, and then decided that wouldn't be the way. It had to be slow, sensual, exciting. He had imagined himself undoing the row of tiny buttons, one by one, and then peeling back the fabric, slipping it down her arms and discarding it on the floor. She had been wearing her flame red lingerie. Ben had seen it on many occasions draped over the clothes horse, but this time the bra was being filled by her beautiful, perky breasts.

He had reached round behind her back, deftly undoing the clasp, freeing her of the bright red fabric. Now, paraded in front of him, had been the handfuls of almond skinned breasts. He had spent some moments there, caressing, licking, and kissing until the dark pink nipples stood erect and proud.

Slowly, he had manoeuvred his way down her tummy covering her with his kisses, soon reaching her navel. It was pierced and had a single shiny pearl droplet hanging from it.

Further down her body, he had the more difficult task of removing her jeans that fitted so snugly to her hips and bum, like a second skin. Slowly, and with determination, he had been able to pull them off over her feet, adding them to the imaginary pile of garments on the floor.

She had not been wearing anything on her feet that night, so he had been left with just the flame red panties to deal with. No hurry now. The sight had been so intensely evocative. Then, when he was ready, he had slowly peeled them down her legs, over her feet, and to the floor. Her dark pubes were as neatly trimmed as her nails were perfectly manicured.

There she had been, an apparition, just feet away from him, sitting totally naked, reading her book. Now and then she would read something which amused her, and her body would shake gently with her inner laughter, and the sight of her jiggling breasts had been just too much.

During all of this, Ben had to cross his legs to hide the effect this living fantasy was having on him, but now the discomfort had become too much to bear, and he had to make tracks to his room where he could deal with the pain in his groin.

'You OK?' Mary had looked up from her book upon his return.

'Mmmm?' he had replied.

'Well, you went upstairs so quickly. And you do look rather flushed.'

'Do I? No, I'm fine. Just - er - something I had to attend to. That's all.'

Mary had offered him a lovely smile and returned to her book.

Tonight it was she that was invading *his* subconscious. He considered calling her, but persuaded himself that it was too late to do that. She would be with her new man, probably in bed with him. The thought of that scenario tormented him even more. There was, it seemed, nothing he could do. Mary must become history, just memories, just longings. How difficult was that going to be?

Awaking the next morning he felt refreshed and much more excited about the week ahead. Mary was not the first thing on his mind.

He had travelled to the Loire Valley a few times before, mostly on his own, on just one occasion with Mary. It was not that he wanted to re-trace his previous visits, more that he knew he felt comfortable there, and he could envisage himself sitting at pavement cafés, soaking up the atmosphere, albeit in his coat!

What he needed was a few days of indulgence before returning home to finalise the sale of the flat and prepare for a new life on his own. He became a tourist, exploring the Loire and Maine rivers as never before. Staying on minor roads, he could make his way along the rivers, stopping as and when he wished, ambling through villages and towns, taking mental pictures of the area. He ventured east as far as Chinon and west to Nantes, staying overnight where he felt it right. As the days passed, he found himself stopping to look in the windows of a number of *Immobiliers* in the towns which he visited, discovering the types of properties available in the area.

On the last day of his getaway he decided to eat at a small bistro tucked away in a side street close to the centre of Angers. He was unable to resist the aromas coming from the tiny restaurant. He was shown to a table, and having ordered *une bière pression*, was given the hand written menu. He studied it for a moment and then realised that he was in a spot of trouble. Not only was the menu difficult to read, but he had little idea of what the dishes were. There was a choice of three fixed-price menus.

While he stared at the piece of card in his hand, he became aware of a couple behind him speaking in English. He turned round in his seat.

'Excuse me, I hope you don't mind me asking, can you help me with the menu?'

'Of course,' the lady said. 'What do you need to know?'

'Well, basically, what everything is,' Ben said feeling embarrassed.

The couple helped him through each of the set meals, describing each dish.

'You should really try the Lamb Navarin,' the man advised. 'It really is superb. Look, why don't you join us at our table. It's nice to have a chat in English for a change.'

Ben moved to their table, and soon they were telling him of their life in France.

They had sold up six years ago, after a life of working in Bristol. He had been in insurance and had been made redundant.

She was a teacher. It had been a spur of the moment thing following a holiday in the Loire Valley.

'We did it all wrong, though. We didn't plan anything. We just sold our house and came here. The first two years were very difficult, what with the language, taxes and the different ways of doing things compared to England.'

'At one point,' the woman said, 'we very nearly gave up. We were on the point of calling it a day and going back. Fortunately, we persevered, and now we wouldn't dream of living anywhere else.'

They had bought a house with views over the river. She had found work teaching English as a second language, and he looked after the house and garden. Overall, they were better off now than when they both worked full time in Bristol.

The advice they had given him regarding the meal was good. The lamb dish, a kind of stew cooked with parsnips and carrots was mouth-watering. The conversation went on for well over an hour. They gave him many tips of what to do, and more importantly, what not to do if he ever decided to move to France himself.

The possibility of making this temporary experience a permanent one began to develop in Ben's mind. It was just a thought. He could work from here just as well as he could from Berkshire. If anything, broadband was more advanced here than in the UK, so there would be no problems with his work on that score. He now knew that property prices here were too good to be true. He could get so much more for his money. He had held on to a dream that had first implanted itself in his mind on his first ever foray into *La belle France* many years previously and now he could see the possibility of that dream becoming reality.

On his journey back to Reading the following day, his mind was whirring. He could not ignore his excitement at the idea of moving to France. First, though, he had to concentrate on the more immediate things. The flat had to be sold. He had to find somewhere else to live. And he had to get all thoughts of Mary out of his mind as well. It was not going to be easy.

Chapter 5

During the week Ben was away, Mary had busied herself with organising her move, sorting out the things she knew she wanted to take with her, and putting aside anything she did not.

She had intended to hire a Transit van and move her stuff herself with a little help from her friends, but Donald was having none of that!

'Leave it to me,' he had told her. 'I know somebody who can do that for you.'

Sure enough, on Friday morning two young guys arrived dead on time with a large van. Glass, china, and other breakables were carefully wrapped and professionally packed into chests. Furniture, not that there was much of it, was handled with kid gloves. Each item was labelled, carried so easily down the stairs to the waiting van, and taken on its way to her new home at Wallingford.

She followed a little later, having had a last look around the flat, firstly to make sure she had not forgotten anything, but equally from a sense of nostalgia. She was still trying to come to terms with Ben's reaction. It was not what she had expected. So cold, so business-like, almost cruel in its brevity.

'I've really enjoyed my five years here,' she said out loud. 'I just hope the next few years will produce as many happy moments.'

She wrote a note to Ben, telling him to dispose of anything she had not taken with her and signed it "all my love, Mary". Then she wrote it all again and signed it just "Mary". She did not want to give Ben any clue to her lingering feelings for him. This was, after all, the first day of a new chapter in her life. The past would have to be left to become just memories.

She drove the fourteen miles to Wallingford wondering what her new life would be like. It had all happened so fast. It was only a matter of weeks since she first met Donald and here she was now setting out to live with him. It was so unlike her to make such random decisions without going through all the good and bad points first. Donald had been so persuasive in his arguments that she had been carried along with the idea.

All very well meeting up for evenings and days out, or even the one weekend we spent together, she mused, but being with each other every day - and every night - it's so different. It's all happened so rapidly. It took Ben and me a while to get it right, so I wonder how long... 'Oh, stop it!' she said out loud to herself, 'You know it's going to be just fine. We love each other don't we? What else matters?'

Before she knew it she had pulled up in the driveway of Donald's house. Although Donald had described the house to her, this was the first time she had seen it. It was a wonderfully imposing place. Driving in through the large wrought iron gates, the long drive, bordered on both sides by well-manicured trees and lawns like bowling greens, brought her face to face with the double fronted red brick house, white-painted bay windows upstairs and down. There was an imposing entrance, the roof of which was supported on two fluted columns with some six or so wide steps running down from the entrance door to the gravelled drive. Climbing shrubs ran up the left hand wall, reaching to the first floor bay windows.

She brought her car to a standstill.

'He must have been watching the road!' Mary muttered to herself, for there waiting for her on the steps was her new partner.

The welcome was overwhelming. They had seen each other only four days earlier, but it was as if she had been away for a few months or even years.

31

She was whisked into the house despite her protestations about getting her luggage from the car.

'Oh, that can wait,' he said excitedly. 'I'm just so amazed this is actually happening. I just can't tell you ...' His speech faded away as he grabbed her to him.

He showed her into the lounge, took her coat, and they slumped down on the luxurious white leather sofa. To Mary the room was huge; something more suited to a film set than a place where she would be living. She could get the whole area of her flat into that one room, she thought. Donald's excitement overwhelmed her and she found the sad recollections of the events of the last few days evaporating away.

He asked whether she would like an aperitif, adding, 'I've prepared a little something for later, which I hope you'll like.' Mary said a white wine would be nice.

'Dry, medium, sweet?' Donald asked.

'Have you got a Chardonnay?'

'Wouldn't you like something a bit more special?'

Mary looked up at him and said, 'No, a Chardonnay is fine. It's probably my favourite white wine.'

'Really?' retorted Donald. 'I can see we have some educating to do! I'll get the Chardonnay,' and he walked away leaving her to her own thoughts.

Mary didn't appreciate his remark. She had her own likes and tastes, not just of wines, but a whole host of things, and she hoped she was not going to have to compromise too far at this early stage of the relationship. I can see I've got to practise some assertion here, she told herself.

The meal that was served for her sometime later was wonderful. Escalope of veal, served with a light, delicately balanced herb and white wine sauce, and vegetables that had been cooked to *al dente* perfection.

'When did you learn to cook like this?' Mary said as she enjoyed the feast.

Donald looked just a little abashed, and confessed that in this instance he had got a friend who owned a local restaurant to prepare the meal for them.

'You said *you* had prepared it!' Mary jested. 'What a cheat!'

She meant it to come out as a joke. Donald didn't see it that way, and started to defend himself, and the more he said, the more ridiculous the situation became.

'Oh, stop it, Donald. I was joking!' Mary had to say after a few minutes. 'It was nice of you to go to that kind of trouble. I feel honoured. And the meal is lovely.'

'To be honest, my darling,' Donald explained sheepishly, almost in a whisper, 'my culinary skills do leave a lot to be desired. And I have to admit I have been eating out rather a lot lately - for the sake of my health!'

At least he's joking as well, now, Mary thought, but her mind suddenly raced back to the first reaction from Grunge when she had let on about her secret.

Stop it! she told herself. You've only been here a few hours! You can't start having any doubts just yet. She turned to Donald, who was still looking a little embarrassed, and said, 'Well, as it's confession time, I've got to warn you; I'm not exactly *Masterchef* of the year. Certainly don't have any Michelin stars up my sleeve.'

She looked closely at his face. Did he show some disappointment? No, she must have imagined it.

By the end of the evening they both became much more relaxed, and after Donald had fetched Mary's luggage from the car for her, they retired to the indulgence of the master bedroom. Mary's eyes opened wide.

This was another enormous room, more like a suite in a five star hotel than just a simple bedroom. The king size bed was the focal point. In addition there was a pale blue velour three piece suite, a small desk, and a huge, wall mounted television. Everything in the room was controlled from a "doofer", the curtains, the lights, the television. God, I could live in here, Mary thought. Never mind just sleep.

She busied herself in the en suite bathroom with its white marble tops, hidden lighting and luxurious pale blue carpet, and regaled herself in a new pink and white nightdress she had bought during the week. It was rather more revealing than she usually wore, but she thought Donald would approve.

She threw herself onto the king size bed, and waited while Donald carried out his ablutions. And waited. And waited.

Eventually he appeared wearing striped pyjamas, buttoned neatly, the trouser half looking as though they had been pressed! And then he proceeded to carefully fold his discarded clothes, placing them in a neat pile on a chair at the far end of the room.

Mary was wondering what was going on. Did she have to rip off her sexy nightie to make him look at her? Should she spread eagle herself, hands holding the headboard?

Eventually, he strolled over to the bed and admitted, 'Mary, you look gorgeous. What a lucky man I am!' Then he climbed into bed beside her and switched off the light.

He's turned the lights off, Mary screamed to herself. He's turned the bloody lights off!

The ensuing love making was brief. Nothing special, but OK nonetheless. Then Donald turned his back to her and, snoring gently, quickly drifted off to sleep. Mary lay in her luxurious bed, wondering where all her friends were, and what they were up to. She tried, but couldn't stop herself from thinking about Ben - she wouldn't be surprised if Katie Forrester had made her move on him by now.

The weekend that followed was leisurely, and, if nothing else, informative.

After a late breakfast on Saturday Mary persuaded Donald to show her round Wallingford.

'I've never been there before,' she said.

They set off, Mary done up in her warmest coat and scarf to keep out the biting wind. Donald, she thought, looked more set for the Alps in his jet black glasses and padded jacket.

She found the narrow streets with their variety of small shops, pubs and restaurants utterly charming, and they spent a long time in the Lamb Arcade nosing around the antique shops. They had an unhurried lunch sat in a secluded corner of a small, elegant bistro and managed to get through a bottle of Australian Shiraz between them.

The afternoon was taken up by more sightseeing and Mary was impressed by the Castle Gardens. She had to cajole Donald to let her see what sports facilities there were.

'I must keep in shape,' she said.

'I didn't realise you were a sporting girl,' he replied reluctantly. 'OK, I'll take you to the leisure centre. They will be able to tell you what's available.' He was right. The staff at the Castle Centre were eager to help, and told her all she needed to know about the facilities in the town. She signed up straight away, while Donald stood hidden away in a corner pretending to study the notice boards.

'What's your favourite sport, then?' he asked as they walked away.

'Oh, I just use the gym,' she told him. 'I'm also involved in the training of a netball team in Reading. I hope I can carry on doing that. It's fulfilling, and the team is doing well in the local league.' Donald didn't reply. Instead he took her down to the river, where they walked, arm in arm, for some time. It was cold and cloudy, and the wind was still bitter so the walking kept them warm. Donald, still wearing his dark glasses, took her to a cosy little café on the water's edge. Mary chose a table by a window looking out on to the river while he went to get his pot of tea and toasted tea cake, and a hot chocolate and a blueberry muffin for her.

Walking toward her, he put the tray on a table toward the back of the café and beckoned her to join him there. She dutifully left her window seat and went to join him.

'I thought you wanted to keep in shape,' Donald quipped looking at the tray on the table.

'Oh, I don't have to worry about what I eat,' she told him. 'I'm one of the lucky ones.'

Sunday was a lazy day. Late up again, a walk down the lane to get the Sunday papers, and a trip into town for a lunchtime carvery. The weather was overcast with heavy clouds threatening rain, yet Donald was once again wearing his obligatory dark glasses. Mary began to wonder if he had a problem with his eyes but said nothing.

The rest of the day was spent just lolling around in the luxury of her new home. In the evening Donald lit a log fire in the lounge.

Chapter 6

Arriving back home, Ben spent most of his time organising everything that had to be done, trying in vain to eradicate Mary from his mind.

He had registered the flat for sale with local Estate Agents, and had advertised it on the Internet. Now it was just a waiting game. He knew he was going to move to somewhere much smaller and could not take all the clutter he had collected along the years with him so he started clearing out cupboards, being ruthless as to what he threw away.

Mary had taken what she wanted, and had left a note to the effect that what she hadn't taken, she didn't want, and would he dispose of it for her.

For the time being he had put the thoughts of a life in France on the back boiler. It was something he would return to when the time was right.

On his third day back, he was sitting in the lounge, working with his laptop when he happened to glance out of the large picture window to see a girl with flowing blonde hair walking down the road opposite towards his flat.

Katie! Now here was somebody who could help him take his mind off Mary for a while.

Was she coming to see him? He doubted it.

He could hardly help but notice her when she had come to work for SRX Solutions as a receptionist. She was spectacularly beautiful with her long blonde hair, sparkling blue eyes and a body that would score a ten by any man's standard. Ben had always considered her to be way outside of his league.

However, he and Katie did go out for a drink occasionally and shortly after he and Mary had bought the flat, they had started to become close friends. Too close in fact. He knew at the time that to get any more intimately involved with her would be a mistake, and could well ruin the enjoyable lifestyle he one day hoped to have with Mary. The last time he and Katie had met they did go to bed together, however something happened which was entirely foreign to him. He found he just couldn't make love to this beautiful girl. She had behaved so obscenely that in normal circumstances he would have been powerless to resist. On this occasion it seemed to have no effect on him at all.

'Jesus Christ,' Katie had exclaimed, coming up from a perfectly performed blow job. 'What the hell has a girl got to do to get you going?' He had admitted to her his thoughts, his feelings, in respect of Mary. 'So what?' had been her response. 'All I want is sex. Nothing else.'

There was nothing Ben could have done about it. He just couldn't perform for her and so, much to Katie's exasperation, that was the last time they had gone out with each other.

Katie! Now she was crossing the road. She *was* coming here.

She was most men's fantasy girl. Those long blonde tresses which blew in the wind as she walked so jauntily, so confidently. And she had the looks to go with it. Her pale blue eyes could melt any normal man in minutes. Her body was svelte, and her cute bum and long shapely legs finished the picture of perfection.

The doorbell rang.

Ben almost tripped in his rush to get to the door. And there she was, looking up at him and smiling the way only she could. From anyone else, it would simply be a friendly smile. From Katie it emerged as a smouldering invitation.

God, he thought as he gaped at her, I wonder how many times that smile has got her into trouble, how many times it has been misinterpreted.

'Hi!' she said cheerily.

Ben seemed to freeze, continuing to stare at her.

'Can I come in, then?' she added.

'Sorry. Yeah, yes, of course you can. I'm just surprised, you know...'

Still he stood there, seemingly barring her entry with his arm still holding the door open.

'So, can I come in?' Katie repeated, and eventually he made way for her to come in, and took her up the stairs into the lounge.

'Drink?' he asked.

'A white wine would go down well.'

Ben brought her wine and a beer for himself.

'Sorry to hear about you and Mary,' Katie said with a sad look on her face. 'Came as a bit of a shock. I thought you two were a permanent feature.'

Ben was hardly listening to what she was saying. His mind was racing ahead of the conversation, imagining the reason for her visit. Could it be that now Mary was no longer on the scene, they could get together and complete what they had been denied last time they tried?

'What? Oh yes, well I thought so as well of course,' he stuttered.

'What went wrong then?' Katie asked, shining those eyes into his.

'You tell me. I thought things were good, really good. There you go, it seems she wanted much more from the relationship. Marriage, family, that kind of thing,' he explained. 'And she simply found someone who wanted the same things as she did. Someone who she could "commit to" as she put it. As I didn't want that kind of thing at the moment, who was I to stand in her way when she had found what she wanted.'

'So you just let her go?' Katie sounded astounded.

'No. It wasn't as simple as that. I thought the world of her. We were - I don't know - warm together. We were good friends, the best of friends, we trusted each other, and I thought our two lives settled so easily into a pattern which was good for both of

39

us. She was right, though. There was never any talk of the future from me. I didn't know she wanted that kind of thing.'

'That's so sad,' Katie said softly.

'Yeah, it is. You see, originally we only really got together to buy this flat. We both wanted somewhere to live, and we both liked each other enough... Look, I don't want to talk about it.'

'Even so, you let her go that easily?'

'I thought about asking her to stay but I figured she had made up her mind and there was no point. Anyway, if she could decide to get up and go now, she could just as easily do it any time in the future. Look, I'm doing my best to forget about her. I've made a decision. Whether it's the right one I don't know. All I know is that I've got to live with it. Now, please can we change the subject?'

There was a break in the conversation, so Ben got some more drinks and a few roasted peanuts. His heart was still beating faster than usual as he envisaged himself and this gorgeous girl, bodies entwined in passionate love making. Therapy. That's what it would be. Therapy. Surely that was what had brought her to his flat this afternoon.

When they were settled again he asked, 'And what about you? We haven't really seen each other since...'

'Yes, least said about that the better,' Katie butted in. 'I'm doing OK. I've been going out with Dave.' Ben looked blank. 'You know him - Dave Atkinson. You've met him a few times at...'

'Dave Atkinson?' Ben echoed. 'Please tell me you're joking, Katie. He's a load of trouble. You know he is. Anything nasty going on round here and you can bet he's involved in it somewhere. What in God's name made you ...?'

'Hey, hang on,' Katie interrupted. 'That's how he used to be, I agree. He's changed an awful lot lately. Not exactly an angel, I'm sure, but he says he loves me, and that counts for a lot.'

Ben recalled that Katie had always needed to be loved. She once told him that her then current man had told her that if she had a few grand in the bank, and bigger tits, he could really love her. He remembered how that had upset her. But Dave Atkinson? How desperate can you get for love?

'And you feel the same way?' he asked.

'Yes, as it happens. I do,' she said, sounding increasingly annoyed.

'Then, dear Katie, I wish you the best of happiness... and luck,' he added. 'I just hope that I'm wrong and you're right about him. I wouldn't touch him with a barge pole.'

'I'm not asking you to. Actually,' Katie informed him, 'he's asked me to marry him.'

'And?' Ben enquired.

'And I've said yes.'

'Then he's an extremely lucky man,' said Ben in disbelief. 'I hope you will be happy. I really do!'

Ben was deeply concerned by this announcement but nothing he could say this afternoon would make an iota of difference. For all her apparent confidence, Katie had always seemed rather vulnerable and easily swayed. However, the decision had been made and it really was no business of his anyway.

Before they parted later in the evening, Ben said, 'Look, I know you've made your mind up, and I really do wish you well. But listen Katie, if you ever need help of any kind - if it turns out that I'm right and you're wrong about this guy - you must call me. I don't really know where I might be because I don't know what my plans are for the future, but you can always get me through my web site. You promise?'

'Yes,' she said reluctantly. 'I promise. But I'm sure it won't come to that. I just wanted you to know, that's all. And I was hoping you'd be a bit more supportive and enthusiastic.' And with that she kissed him, a nice warm kiss Ben thought, and disappeared into the evening.

He got himself another drink, and just sat and dwelt on what he had been told.

Chapter 7

Ben had enjoyed a happy enough childhood in London. He had done sufficiently well to get a place at one of London's more prestigious private schools for boys, nevertheless whilst he had the intelligence to excel, in practice he did far from well. He had not really enjoyed his school-days at all and had come away with a rather meagre set of qualifications.

During his final year at school his mother had died. She was, in his opinion, a perfect mother, loving, caring, always supportive, appearing to be on his side against his more austere father. They had always been extremely close, and Ben had always felt his mother had understood him remarkably well. Ben had serious difficulty in coming to terms with her death. He felt devastated, abandoned and angry.

'How can you leave me now? Now, when I need you most,' he had sobbed.

On the day of the funeral, he had travelled in the hearse with his father, and had walked behind the coffin into the church. He had sat in the front pew with the coffin positioned just to his right. The service had started, and after the first hymn *How Great Thou Art,* the vicar started his scripted summary of his mother's life, making it only too obvious that he was reading every word. As far as Ben could recall, this man had never even met his mother. Who was he to be recounting her life? Ben had been unable to bear it any longer. Calmly, he had risen from his pew and walked out of the church.

'What a farce!' he had muttered out loud once outside the church. 'I've never even met some of these people before. Where were they all while Mum was so ill? Now they all turn up to "pay their respect". Well, I don't want to be any part of their sham. They can bury Mum as deep as they like, but that is not where she is. She can't be held in a wooden box!' He had been aware of someone following him and, looking over his shoulder, he saw an aunt who he had not met since he was a little boy.

'Ben!' she had called after him. 'Come back into the church. You owe it to your Mum – and your Dad.'

Ben had been so furious that at first he had been lost for words then, holding back what he really wanted to say, he had said calmly: 'I'm sorry Auntie but I can't bear to hear these people, many I have never even met, saying how wonderful she was. I can't bear to see her dropped into the ground in her wooden box. I am dreading the thought of having to live with my father without Mum being there. So I am not coming back into the church, I am not going to be there to see her buried, and I am certainly not coming back to the house for the wake. My memories of my mother are private and precious, and nobody is going to take them away from me.'

'Nobody wants to do that, Ben, but …'

'Auntie, I have made up my mind. Now, please, go away and leave me alone. Please just go away!'

Later in the day, when everybody else had left the house his father confronted him. He told Ben that he was disgusted by his behaviour. 'Nobody finds these things easy,' he said. He went on to say that Ben owed it to his mother to be there, and that in his eyes he had behaved like a wimp, running away when he should have had the courage to see the day out like everybody else. Throughout the tirade of insults fired at him, Ben had stood absolutely still, looking stolidly into his father's eyes. When it was over he had turned and silently walked away up to his bedroom.

'I'm sorry if I let you down, Mum. I just couldn't stand to see you put into the ground. I didn't want to remember you like that,' Ben had whispered as he prepared for bed, and as he drifted off to sleep, he heard a soft voice replying.

'I won't be contained in a box, Ben. I am not to be found in a lump of stone or a plaque on a wall. You will find me where the sparrows are twittering, where the blackbird sings his evening song. You will find me in the trees, the stars, the clouds and where the ocean crashes on the shore.'

With his mother's words still in his mind, Ben had had a remarkably peaceful night.

He had left his father and his home at the first opportunity and moved to Reading to start work at SRX Solutions, a computer software company in Bracknell. Only then had he realised just how painfully shy he was. It would only take a word from the pretty girl who brought round the tea trolley to make him blush profusely and he was sure everybody in the office must have noticed. Slowly, painfully slowly, he had started to gain the confidence he needed. When he was invited to sit with some female colleagues in the canteen, he would make himself accept. He had become well-liked by a number of the girls there, and began to get to know some of them through the social activities which were such an important part of the life of the company. A good social life for the employees meant, according to company policy, a much happier, and more productive, workforce. Nonetheless there had always been this incapacity to say what he wanted, to explain what he was feeling. And it remained to this day.

'If only,' he told himself now. 'If only I had been bold enough to tell Mary how I really felt about her, perhaps none of this would be happening.'

He started to berate himself for being such an fool. He was already beginning to realise how much he was missing her, how much he loved her.

Chapter 8

It should have been something of a celebration.

Mary, Penny and Grunge were once again sitting in their favourite window seat in *The Prospect* at the end of an unusually busy week in the salon. Sadly, this was to be the last time the three of them would be meeting up like this on a regular basis.

Mary had handed in her notice two weeks previously, and today was her last day.

Ray had not taken her leaving the salon well. She was probably one of the best stylists he had ever had working for him, and now, with her beautician training, was an extremely valuable member of his staff. She had significantly increased his clientele, and had attracted just the kind of customers he wanted, wealthy, middle-aged women who enjoyed spending money on themselves.

The fact that she had only given him two weeks' notice just added to his problems, and he had shown his displeasure with her ever since she had told him of her intentions.

There was something troubling Mary that was plain for everybody to see.

'I thought you'd be really excited,' said Penny looking at Mary's sullen face. 'It's not everyone who has the opportunity to branch out on their own, especially when you don't have to fork out the dosh yourself!'

'I know,' Mary said, 'but I'm going to miss you lot. I've really enjoyed my time here, and I'm sorry to have let Ray down so badly. He hasn't forgiven me, has he?'

'He was just peeved you gave him so little notice, that's all,' said Penny attempting to reassure her.

'Yes, I know. I wish I could've given him more notice. Once again everything was arranged so quickly. I know Donald meant well. I'd been moaning about the travelling, the parking and so on, and then when he just announced he'd "solved the problem" and told me all the details, what could I do?'

'I think I'd have told him to consider my feelings a bit more, and maybe discuss things with me before making decisions about my life.' Grunge was speaking her mind once again.

'He's a really persuasive man, and he was sure he was doing the best for me, bless him,' Mary said.

'Maybe he was,' replied Grunge, 'but you can't go through the rest of your life allowing somebody else, whoever it is and however much they say they love you, directing your life like this. You've got to stand up to him girl, or he'll completely dominate your life.' Grunge looked at Mary's face. 'OK, I've said my bit. I'll shut up now.'

'No, you're probably right, Grunge - and I don't often say that,' Mary replied. 'You see, he has this way about him, I don't know - not exactly domineering, but extremely persuasive. He can always win an argument just by making you admit he's right and you're wrong, even when you know it isn't true. It's difficult to stand up against that. Perhaps I should enrol in some assertion lessons.'

'I agree with Grunge. You'll have to find a way of overcoming this. Use your God given, wily, feminine ways. If he's as generous as you make out, ask for a few things *you* want, and try to have a compelling argument to use against him. Get in first on a few things,' suggested Penny. 'What's your new salon like, anyway?'

'I told you before that it was already a going concern, had been there for a few years. But it was beginning to lose what customers it had due to a lack of keeping up with the times. It needed bringing up to date so it could attract new clients. I think Donald bought the business relatively cheaply. He's spent a lot of money on refurbishment and new equipment,' Mary told them. 'At least I had a say in the equipment, and it wasn't cheap, either.'

'Good for you!' chipped in Grunge. 'He's obviously rolling in it. What does he do?'

'To be honest, I don't know,' Mary admitted. 'He doesn't say much about it. He's some kind of financial consultant, and works with some pretty large businesses. As I understand it, he made his money in South Africa before he returned to the UK with his wife a few years ago. He's often in London, and has spells when he flies all over the place, but most of the time he's at home in his study, working away with whatever he does.'

'Who cares?' Grunge said with a wry smile, 'As long as he wants to spend some of his money on you!'

'Has he told you how his wife died?' Penny asked.

'Not really,' Mary told them. 'I think it was cancer or something like that. I've never brought up the subject, and obviously he doesn't want to. There are no photographs or any other signs of her in the house - bit strange, really. The only time he mentioned her was to tell me earlier on in our relationship that she had died a few years ago. Can we change the subject?'

Which they did, discussing all manner of things including who might replace Mary at the salon. They had seen one or two girls coming in for interview, but Ray was not forthcoming about whether or not they were suitable, and the mood in the salon being as it was, nobody wanted to ask.

'I reckon,' put in Grunge, as usual never lost for words, 'that he'll end up with two people, one as a stylist and another as a beautician.'

Penny agreed. The chance of finding a suitably qualified replacement for Mary was pretty remote.

'Anyway,' she said, 'it would ease our work load a bit if he did. It's getting a bit frantic at the moment.'

It was late into the evening when they finally split up and made their own ways home. They had decided to eat while they were there, and as Donald was away for a few days, Mary was not under any pressure to get back home. They said their farewells, not knowing when, if ever, they would get together like this again.

It was a week or so later that Mary sat in the huge lounge and considered how much her life had changed since the move to Donald's house.

During the first couple of weeks she had found everything exciting, strange, different. She had been cosseted at every move, hardly allowed to lift a finger, and she felt awkward and, often, a bit useless.

However, as time had gone on, she was involved more and more in the household operation, expected more and more to "pull her weight", and told much too often that, "That is not how Margaret would have done it," with the addendum of, "but I don't suppose it really matters."

She had always expected to do her share of everything, now she felt that gradually she was being expected to be a full time housewife as well as running the salon. She tried to understand, even though she frequently heard Grunge's prophetic voice warning her about her having to darn his socks, and wash his Y-fronts. She tried hard to shut the voice out, and to get on with her new life the best way she could.

Her biggest problem was not seeing her friends as often as she would have liked. She was beginning to feel very alone. Admittedly, the salon that Donald had acquired made life easier in that she didn't have to travel, but Mary found the two stylists there were not the easiest people to get to know. She often caught them whispering in corners, and presumed she was the topic of their near silent conversations.

It's probably the fact that I have come in as their new boss, Mary tried to convince herself. If the truth were known, she didn't really like the "boss" part of the job. She would much rather be one of the girls.

Donald had also tried his best to dissuade her from going to the gym. He said he was worried about her being out on her own. Mary was convinced that it was more likely he just wanted her at home. Now, just over a month after moving in with him, he was even trying to stop her from continuing her netball training. It was not turning out at all as she had hoped. She felt trapped.

Today, however, was certainly the worst day of her young life. Her period was three weeks late - something that had never happened before. In panic, she had bought herself a pregnancy testing pack and, whilst she somehow already knew the result, had now seen confirmation that she'd been caught out. The test was pronounced positive. She was pregnant.

Mary had dreamed of motherhood. It was something she really wanted. She should be ecstatic. She wasn't.

She knew it couldn't be Donald's. He was almost paranoid about taking precautions. He did not want a family at his time of life. Rather different, she thought, to the impression he had given her before they got together.

Mary's heart sank as she realised she was carrying Ben's baby.

What kind of idiot am I? This surely will be the end of this relationship. Donald's moral standards won't be able to handle this. I slept with someone else while I was making plans to move in with him! What a bloody fool!

The knowledge that she was carrying Ben's baby took over her whole life. She thought of little else, day and night. Considering all the options she could think of. Should she terminate the pregnancy, abort the tiny person growing inside her? Ought she to tell Ben? She knew she dare not share her dilemma with Donald, that was for sure, though she knew she would eventually have to find a way. But not now, not yet.

A month later, still living in panic mode, still having found no solution, simple or otherwise, she made a rather feeble excuse to her colleagues at the salon that she was feeling sick. Well, that's true enough, she thought when she put the phone down. As surreptitiously as she could, she left the house in the normal way, at the normal time with the normal "peck on the cheek" from Donald. 'I might be a bit late this evening,' she said as she left the house. 'I've got something to deal with.'

'How late?' quizzed Donald.

'I've no idea really. I'll probably grab something to eat, so don't cook for me.'

'Are you sure? I could prepare a salad or...'

'Thanks, but don't bother.'

'It's no bother...' but she was gone.

'In a rush as usual,' Donald muttered to himself.

Mary made her way to Reading. She had no plans. She was still having difficulty coming to terms with her situation. She just felt she had to talk to someone, and wondered if Penny or Grunge from Ray's salon would be around to listen, and maybe give her some advice.

When she got to Reading, she spent over an hour just walking up and down Broad Street and Friar Street, going over things a million times, still making no sense of it all. Her hope was that by telling someone else of her predicament, it might just result in her being able to decide which way to go.

She called in at the salon. The girls were still there, although there was a new face, a stunningly beautiful black face belonging to Collette. Her friends came over immediately, leaving their customers to talk among themselves.

'Hi!' 'Hi!' 'Hi!' from her friends and big hugs all round. Even Ray came out from his office and gave her a kiss on the cheek.

'How *are* you?' 'Why haven't you been in touch?' 'How's it all going?' The questions kept coming.

'Look, I can't disturb your work like this,' Mary eventually said. 'As it's Friday. Shall we meet at the usual place after you've finished?'

51

'Great idea!' they said in unison. 'See you around six?'

'You're on,' Mary said, and set off out to have some lunch and to roam the town for another few hours. This time her wanderings took her down towards the river through St Mary's Butts. She went to walk past the old church but decided instead to take a look inside. Outside, the architecture was strangely different, unique even, with its chequered multi-coloured stone. In all the time she had lived in the town, she had never ventured inside any of the churches.

Inside it was cool and dark, with the unique aroma which was to be found in old buildings. However the thing that struck her most was the peace. How could such a building produce this feeling of calm? She stood just inside the door, and, as her eyes became adjusted to the dimness, took in the ancient beauty of the place.

There were just three other people in the church, a couple sitting near the back and an older lady sitting more toward the front. Mary made her way gingerly down the central aisle until she was about half way, and quietly shuffled into a pew to her right. She sat there and simply let the tranquil atmosphere drift over her. She felt safe and comfortable, and found she was able to contemplate on the events of the last few weeks much more pragmatically.

Time seemed to disappear. It was unimportant.

Suddenly she was aware of a presence to her left. She turned her head. Standing there was a small, bespectacled, elderly lady, her silver grey hair in tight curls, and a wonderfully ruddy complexion.

'I don't want to disturb you, my dear,' she said in no more than a whisper. 'I just wondered if you need to talk with anyone. We have a lot of people come in here, some just to pray, some to get out of the rain, but others who need a friendly soul to talk with.'

'No, I'm fine,' Mary lied. 'I have just come in for some peace and tranquillity. There seems to be a lot of that in here!'

'Yes, my dear. Many people say that. It's not just the building, you know. It's the spirit of the people who worship here that creates this peaceful feeling. I've visited many churches, and you only find this atmosphere in some, not all. It's the people, you see, not the building. Anyway, if you're OK I'll leave you in peace, my dear. Sorry to have disturbed your meditation.' And with that she was gone. Mary was not conscious of her departure any more than she had been aware of her arrival.

Mary looked at her watch, and realised she had been there for almost two hours. She was loath to leave and go back to the reality outside although she had to admit she was much more relaxed now than she had been two hours ago - some sort of inner peace had taken over.

She eventually left the church and emerged into the smoky reality of Reading on a busy Friday afternoon. Slowly she made her way back in to town, passing the shopping mall. She did not feel in need of retail therapy but stopped off for a cup of tea, and just spent the rest of the afternoon aimlessly wandering from street to street. She now had two things on her mind. Not just her personal situation, but also the overwhelming effect that her visit to the church had had upon her.

'Very strange,' she kept whispering to herself. 'Very strange!'

The three girls were already in the pub and the welcome was overwhelming.

The new girl, Colette, was obviously part of the group in the same way Mary used to be.

Drinks were ordered along with some crisps, and then there was all the catching up to do. It was a long time before the attention turned to Mary, and it was another few minutes before Mary told them of the events that had led her to come and meet them today.

'I don't expect you to be able to help in any way,' she told the girls, 'I just needed to tell somebody who is not involved with it all. I feel absolutely stupid letting this happen. How do I tell Donald? And can I ever tell Ben?'

'You've got to tell them both sooner or later,' said Penny in her quiet matter-of-fact way, 'and the sooner the better I would think.'

Up until this point Grunge had hardly spoken a word, but she couldn't hold out any longer.

'Have you considered just how lucky you are?' she started.

'What?' Mary said in utter shock. 'How can you say that? I'm in the most God awful mess. How can that be lucky?'

''Cos you've got a little bit of Ben growing inside you, that's what! I tell you something, I wouldn't mind carrying his baby. He's one of the nicest guys I've ever known.'

'How do you know him? In your dreams?'

'No, Mary. After you had decided to leave and he came back from his trip to France, he and I went out together several times. There was nothing in it, just the two of us enjoying a few nights out.'

'What? You and Ben? I just can't imagine that.'

'Just shut up Mary, and listen.'

At this point, much to Mary's relief, Penny and Colette left the table and made their way to the bar, obviously not wanting to get any more involved.

'Mary, the guy was crazy about you. He never admitted it in so many words, never brought you up in conversation - that was always me. But every time we did talk about you, he had this tell-tale look on his face, this almost embarrassed expression about him. He just wanted to hide his feelings about you, but he couldn't. Not from me. I simply enjoyed his company. I didn't want anything else and as you so rightly say, we were a bit of an odd couple. That doesn't mean I couldn't see what was going on.'

Mary was speechless.

'So,' continued Grunge, 'do you see what I mean? You may have made the stupidest decision of your life, and walked away from him. But you've still got a part of him with you. Not everybody has that chance.'

Mary had difficulty in getting her head round all of this. It was not something she had expected to hear. 'That may just possibly be true,' she said. 'I somehow doubt he feels that way anymore. He may have given you that impression but, believe me, he showed nothing of that on the day we parted company. Quite the opposite, I would say. I imagine by now he's found somebody to take my place easily enough. Possibly even Katie!'

'I don't think so,' was the blunt reply.

'I wouldn't be so sure, Grunge. I drove past our flat just a few days after he came back from France and saw Katie crossing the road and going towards the flat. And I didn't imagine that. I saw it with my own two eyes.'

'Yes, he told me about that. Believe it or not, Katie had called on him to say goodbye. She was getting married.'

'Who to?'

'That doesn't matter. The fact is it was a farewell call. So the other girl in Ben's life also disappeared, though I don't think that was such a big deal really, as far as Ben was concerned.'

'Are you absolutely certain? I thought it was almost inevitable they would get together after I left. He always fancied the pants off her.'

'He's never shagged her. Did you know that? Oh, Ben and I had some really deep heart to heart chats sometimes. You, you silly cow, were the only one Ben ever had eyes for. Crazy isn't it?'

'Do you know where Ben is now?' Mary enquired.

'No, I don't, not exactly. And to be honest, Mary, even if I did, I don't think I'd tell you. You just don't deserve him, with or without his baby. I think, after what you've put him through already, you should leave him to get on with his life, wherever that may be, and with whoever he chooses.'

'If you do see him, you won't tell him about the baby will you?' pleaded Mary.

'Of course I won't. I'm not the one to tell him, am I?'

'Do you think I should then?'

'That's your problem, Mary, not mine. Anyway, I think I've said enough, probably too much. Let's go and join the others and have another drink.'

As they were moving away from their table, Mary took hold of Grunge's arm, and said quietly into her ear 'Thanks, Grunge. I guess I needed that. I do appreciate your honesty, even if I find it hard to accept.'

Mary stayed a little longer with the girls, and asked them not to pass on what they had heard to anyone else. As it happened, Penny and Colette seemed much too interested in each other to be bothered much by Mary's predicament.

As Mary drove home that evening, she dwelt on the happenings of the day, and strangely, although she was no nearer finding answers to her problems, she was conscious she was less troubled in herself.

When she arrived home, Donald was on the phone, and was obviously on one of his long calls. He acknowledged her arrival and made a grimace at the phone, suggesting it could take a while.

Mary made some coffee and took one in to Donald. He looked up at her and mouthed "Thank you," and carried on with his conversation.

It was some quarter of an hour later that Donald appeared.

'How did your day go?' he asked.

'Oh, pretty good really,' Mary replied. 'Hope you don't mind, but as I was in Reading, I met up with my old pals and we had a drink. It was nice to catch up with all the gossip.'

Donald just grunted, and turned on the television.

During the next few days, Mary often found herself day-dreaming and talking to herself about things. Except she realised she was not talking to herself. She was, in fact, talking to a small, bespectacled elderly lady with curly, silver grey hair who offered no answers but listened with a friendly smile. Every time this happened, Mary felt some of the calmness she had experienced in the church flowing through her again. More than once she was aware of one or other of her staff looking at her and she just carried on with her work regardless.

She also kept remembering - almost word for word - Grunge's outburst. It had made her take an alternative view of her circumstances, and she had to admit that maybe - just maybe - Grunge was right.

Chapter 9

The flat did not sell as quickly as Ben would have liked, although there was a stream of people coming to view it. The estate agent suggested if Ben wanted a really quick response, he might consider reducing the price.

Ben did not see any reason for dropping the price. As far as he was concerned the asking price was more than reasonable for the property. It had been a show flat before they had bought it and it was well appointed throughout. It comprised two floors, with spacious lounge and dining areas plus a fully equipped, though somewhat confined, kitchen on the first floor. The second floor was taken up by two large bedrooms separated by the bathroom. The bedroom to the front of the flat had the same wall to wall picture window that was to be found in the lounge. Throughout, the carpeting and curtains were far superior to what he and Mary would have been able to afford. Over the years, they had also added their own personal touches to make it less like a show flat and more a warm and comfortable home. The location was good too, within walking distance of a railway station linking to London Paddington in just half an hour, and a slightly longer walk down to the town centre. For luxury and location like this, he saw no reason at all to lessen the price.

He was beginning to lose patience, so took over the task of showing off the flat to potential buyers himself, rather than leaving it to the estate agent people. To them, he felt, it was just another property. To Ben it was special, unique, and he enjoyed pointing out some of the features he was sure the agent had neglected. In no time at all a nice young couple liked it enough to offer the asking price.

Now there was another interminable wait whilst the solicitors went about trying to justify their fees.

Ben could not recall when he actually decided that moving to France was definitely for him. The conversation he had with the English couple in Angers had a lot to do with it. He had felt their enthusiasm as they told him of their life in France. The fact that property was so much cheaper there, the wonderful food and wine not to mention the climate, had confirmed his decision. His moving there became more feasible by the day since his return home. Now it felt right. He would never have an opportunity like this again. He knew it was something he had to do.

He went through the flat with an even finer tooth comb, throwing out anything he had any doubts about needing in the future. And at the same time he started considering the practicalities of moving to France, reading books, surfing the internet, and visiting estate agents who were selling property abroad.

He had watched many a television programme such as *No Going Back* and *A Place in the Sun* and tried to think back to the problems people taking part in such programmes had encountered. As far as he could recall, most of the problems stemmed from lack of real preparation, so he listed foreseeable problems as and when he thought of them.

The benefits were easy to list. Things in Reading, and the UK generally, had declined so much in recent years that he no longer wanted to stay where he was. Just a few years ago, he was perfectly happy to go into town on a Saturday evening, meet up with some friends and maybe end up at a party somewhere. Now, regardless of the fact he was relatively fit, he felt uneasy in the town in the evenings. There were the hoodies who gathered in shop doorways and on street corners, the open trading of a wide range of illegal substances, and an overall feeling that you should be looking over your shoulder all the time; a feeling of intimidation, of danger. This feeling of threat was exacerbated later in the evening when the binge drinkers were thrown out of the town centre pubs and clubs. Inevitably, fights broke out and all too often innocent bystanders were injured in the fracas.

Looking around the town in daylight was not much better. Yes, there had always been graffiti, but now it was everywhere. There were the beggars, too, sitting with their scruffy mutts outside shop doorways. Ben wondered why it was so many of them had dogs, was it to maximise the sympathy vote? If it was, it didn't work for him. Even walking through Prospect Park, it was not unusual to see discarded needles lying on the grass while kids were playing ball just a few yards away.

Why would anybody want to live amongst this? The pros for his emigration were overwhelming.

When it came to cons he came to the conclusion there were a few major quandaries that would have to be addressed.

How well he would cope on his own. What if he missed Mary more than he thought he would? What if he found it difficult to make new friends over there? And the language! That must be at the top of the list. If he was to make a success of what he wanted to do, he had to improve on the little bit of French he remembered from school. He enrolled for French classes at the local technical college, bought books and a *Linguaphone* course. He meant business. He consoled himself that if it all went pear-shaped, at least he would have a better command of a foreign language which wouldn't be such a bad thing.

After just two sessions of the Intermediate Course, he had to admit he had overestimated his recollection of GCSE French. He humbly decided he had to go back to the basics, and enrolled as a beginner. Even then he found that whilst he could express himself in simple phrases, when it came to understanding what the leader of the group was saying, he was in trouble.

He had to overcome this problem and contacted a lady who was advertising her services in French conversational sessions.

Madame, as she insisted on being addressed, would not speak a word of English during the lessons, which was exactly what he needed but was, at first, acutely frustrating, as he understood little of what she said. Even so, after just a few sessions he found that, because he had to, he began to understand the language much better and they started to have more meaningful conversations. As the weeks passed he found he was beginning to come to terms with the challenge and actually began to enjoy the language much more.

'Only when you start to think in French,' he was told by the teacher at the evening class, 'can you really consider you are getting to grips with the language.'

So he still had a long way to go, but gradually he started to feel much more confident and decided it was time to explore other factors where, in his opinion, people had often let themselves down.

For one thing, he wanted to make sure he understood the complexities of buying and selling property in France. He garnered a wealth of information on the internet and realised immediately that a lot depended on finding the right people to guide you through the unfamiliar processes. At first glance, buying property in France seemed a lot more straightforward than purchasing a house in the UK, but the thought of trying to do it without help seemed absurd. He had read of many people who had landed in serious trouble by trying, and he didn't want to join them.

He familiarised himself with the different ways of buying, the different taxes and fees which are sometimes, not always, included in the original sale price, and resolved to make absolutely sure, right from the start, that he always knew what the final, total price would be.

Having done his homework on the theory, he knew that none of what he had learned could be put into practice until he tried to find the property he dreamed of.

There were other things to sort out first. His two colleagues were unaware of his plans, and obviously needed to be consulted, and of course, the flat was still awaiting contracts to be signed.

His business was taking up a lot of his time and he had to find somewhere else to live when he moved out of the flat.

All in all, he found he was so busy with everything going on, that by day he hardly had time to miss Mary. The evenings were a different matter, being on his own and having more time to think, he tended to drift off on memory tours. On the whole, though, he felt he was coping pretty well for most of the time and tried to convince himself that life without Mary might not be such a problem after all.

Some of his friends thought he was becoming a recluse, as he had not been seen out and about as much recently and resulted in visits from a range of people who were 'just passing' and wondered how he was. 'You must be missing her', was a common line to which he would lie 'Well, yes. But we were just friends, you know, not really a permanent couple, though most people thought we were'.

He was sure they all meant well but the reminders were not helping at all. He was frequently invited out, but made excuses that, for one reason or another, he just couldn't make it.

There was just one exception, one particular caller, who always managed to take his mind off Mary. That was her strange colleague, Grunge. The first time she came to see him her hair was a multi-shade of blue and she was wearing her usual quirky clothes. Nothing matched, most items seemed to be a few sizes too big and all in all she looked a bit like a cardboard box dweller. Where on earth, thought Ben, does she find all that stuff? He had met her before at parties and Mary often told him about the antics she got up to at the salon.

Grunge had noticed that he was missing from the social group, and so had decided to try to do something positive about the situation.

To Ben she was a breath of fresh air. There was no sad puppy look in her eyes as there had been with some of the other visitors. He didn't imagine for one moment she was thinking 'Poor bloke. I wonder how he manages to cope on his own'.

On her first visit she stayed for a whole evening, and the only time Mary came into the conversation was when Grunge told him that she was leaving the salon. Apparently her new bloke, Donald, had said the commuting would be too much for her and was setting her up in her own salon he had bought for her nearer to her new home.

She told him that both she and Penny had pleaded with her to think about it seriously but Mary had been adamant and was thoroughly convinced she was doing the right thing. Ray, the owner of the salon, she said, was extremely put out that she could let him down so casually, and had made that perfectly plain to her.

The rest of that evening was spent on much more trivial things, and at one point they had both laughed so much that tears were running down their faces. She was a great girl. Far from fanciable, as far as Ben was concerned, but so much fun that he hoped such evenings could be a regular occurrence. She was just what he needed.

It became something of regularity. They went out for drinks to some pubs he would never have thought of frequenting, had meals at places he had never heard of, and they generally had some fun times together. And yet there was not a single suggestion of romance of any kind. They just seemed to hit it off and were good company for each other.

After what seemed an eternity, Ben received news that contracts for the sale of the flat were ready to be signed.

Ben had already decided to take on a furnished, one bedroom bedsit for the time being. He put together things he needed to take with him to the new bijou flat, and arranged for most of his furniture to be put into storage. The couple buying the flat had agreed to take the carpets, curtains and a majority of the white goods which made things easier for him.

Over a weekend, he moved into a completely new environment. It reminded him of the first 'place of his own' he had rented when he first came to live in Reading. It wasn't dissimilar in its shortage of space, and want of comfort. It would do for now. Contracts were exchanged, keys were handed over and the considerable profit accumulated over the five years was split between him and Mary as agreed.

He now knew exactly what funds he had from the sale, and could start looking at properties available in France.

What exactly did he want from this venture? Was it just somewhere to live, where he would not have to do much serious work on the property to make it habitable? Or on the other hand, did he want, perhaps, a second property which could be rented out as a holiday cottage?

The latter would give him a second income, but would take time. He felt up to the challenge.

His search began.

The internet was a good starting place, providing a good feel for prices in different areas. He knew where he would like to live if he could find something in his price range there.

It was an enjoyable and eye-opening research project, taking up many evening hours and confirmed the pleasantly surprising prices.

He made a short list of his favourite properties and details of the selling agents. He knew the only way to find out how truthful the descriptions were was to take a couple of weeks off to visit the area again and see first-hand what was available.

Only if and when he was convinced about the move would he share his plans with friends and colleagues, until then, as far as anyone was concerned, he was simply off on holiday again.

The evening before he left, he allowed himself to reminisce about his life. He went to bed unusually early and just lay there wondering about Mary. Was she happy? Was she missing him? Did she even think about him? He permitted himself to re-live some of the good times they had spent together. Whereas previously such recollections only afforded pain, tonight the memories brought unfamiliar inner warmth, almost a peace.

Perhaps then, he told himself, he would be able to cope with life without her, and just live on the memories.

As he floated into sleep he was surprised that once again his thoughts turned to Katie. Her decision to marry Dave had to be a mistake, didn't it?

Chapter 10

Katie had not had an easy life. Her father had openly told her on more than one occasion that she was a mistake.

At the age of six, she had been removed from her parents as she was considered to be at risk if she remained with them. She was allocated a place at a children's home, and once she had settled to the idea of being part of a much larger family, she adapted to it really well.

She was, however, easily influenced and fast became part of a group who made life exceedingly difficult not only for the management and staff, but for many of the other young residents, especially the smaller and weaker ones. Katie's gang terrorised them, and she and her friends were constantly being grounded or put into detention.

At the same time, her education had been painfully slow, as she carried her bullying ways with her into school. It became a regular occurrence for her to be sent home, and in the end, at the age of ten, she had been expelled.

She had been sent to psychologists, psychiatrists, behavioural experts, but it seemed that nothing anybody suggested had any effect on her.

It was by chance that she had been noticed by a couple who were visiting the children's home to discuss the possibility of becoming foster parents, and who, for some unknown reason, had simply taken a shine to her. The first time they had seen her she had been sitting on the floor of the lounge area, leaning against the wall, pretending to read a book.

During the interview, the couple had mentioned the girl, and were told not to judge this particular book by its cover.

Beneath Katie's angelic looks, the blonde curls, the blue eyes, there lurked, they were told, something bordering on a monster.

However, the couple had made a point of stopping to say "hello" to her on their way out, which had come as a complete surprise to Katie. She had grunted a reply to their greeting but was not at all eager to continue with any conversation. As they had walked away she stared after them, muttering, 'What a pair of geeks!'

It had been a long drawn out affair for the couple, Sheila and Roy, to become foster parents and at times had become almost unbearably intrusive and personal. Nevertheless they had persevered, and paid many visits to the children's home to pursue their application. At each visit they had sought out Katie, and each time they saw just a slight glimmer of recognition in her eyes. After a while they could actually have some form of dialogue with her.

They were still being warned not to get too involved with Katie, as she "spelled trouble with a capital T". Even so, Katie held a certain fascination, maybe a challenge, for them. During one visit they asked permission to take Katie out for a day, were advised not to, however if they really wanted to, there would be no actual opposition. Secretly, the home's managers would have agreed to just about anything that might be of benefit to the girl.

Sheila and Roy had found Katie, and asked whether she would like to have a day out with them the next weekend. 'What?' had been Katie's curt reply. 'You want to take me to the frigging zoo? I don't think so!'

'Who said anything about a zoo?' Roy had chipped in. 'You decide where you would like to go or what you want to see. It would be your day.'

'Why? Fancy me, do you?' Katie had said, looking straight at Roy and attempting a sexy pose.

Sheila had taken over the banter. 'Look, Katie, it's only a suggestion. We just thought you might like to get out of here for a few hours, that's all. If you don't like the idea, it's no big deal.'

'All right, then,' Katie had said. 'But don't let me down like the others have, that's all.'

The following Saturday Sheila and Roy had picked her up, and the trio had gone off for the day. They took her to the shops where they bought a few bits and pieces of clothing and underwear for her. Not too much. They didn't want to imply they were trying to buy her affection. They had lunch at MacDonald's, much to Roy's disdain, and in the afternoon they went for a walk along the river, making numerous stops to watch ducks and other wildlife that inhabited the river banks. Later, they had stopped for refreshments in a little café, where Katie made a real pig of herself with the selection of cakes on offer. As the afternoon had rolled on, Katie had become much more talkative and animated, and was upset when they had announced it was time to take her back. To their surprise and delight, she had told them when they returned to the home, that she had really enjoyed her day out and the best bit had been the walk by the river, and could they do it again soon.

Over a long, and sometimes difficult, time, a really loving relationship had grown between them. One of the landmarks was when she had confided in them that she was "rubbish with money" and asked them to help her to manage her meagre finances better.

Another was a few weeks later when Katie had announced, 'Today, it's my turn to take you out! I've been saving up for this,' she had told them. 'Thought it was time I did my bit, yeah?' She had taken them further out of town for a walk down country lanes, and across fields, stopping occasionally to climb a tree or to clamber over gates or banks. She had shown all the signs of somebody thoroughly enjoying herself. Later she had taken them to a pretty little village pub and bought bar snacks for them. 'You'll have to pay for the booze, though,' she had said. It had been a memorable day for all three of them.

After what had seemed a lifetime, Sheila and Rob had gained their recognition as foster parents, and it had been a natural transition for them to apply to foster Katie. Firstly they had put the suggestion to Katie, who by now knew them well enough to talk about anything and everything.

'Why haven't you got kids of your own?' she had asked.

'I can't have children,' Sheila had replied. 'That's why we applied to become foster parents. We would really love to have children in our home. It would somehow make it complete.'

'Then we met you,' Roy had added. 'Somehow we both knew from that first day that you were the person we wanted to share our lives with.'

'Oh, per-leez! You'll have me crying in a minute,' the girl had mocked, and then with a huge smile added, 'but I'm glad you persevered. I was a bit of a brat at first, though, yeah?'

'Yeah,' Roy had echoed, 'you could say that.'

Two days before her thirteenth birthday, Katie had left the children's home and started a new life with Sheila and Roy. Even this turned out to be more difficult for Katie than she expected. Now she was no longer surrounded by her gang of friends, she had felt lonely and vulnerable in her new school and often came home in foul moods, swearing she was never going back there again.

Sheila and Roy had supported her in every way they could, but it was a long time before Katie had become totally comfortable with her new life.

As years went on she became an extremely attractive young lady, and wherever she went, she was surrounded by boys like bees round a honey pot. She had been sexually active long before she should have been and she loved it. She was the ultimate flirt, utterly cruel sometimes, leading a boy on and then dropping him like a lead balloon for no apparent reason. She had a new power now, sex, and she used it mercilessly. Many were the times she would arrive home late in the evening with the tell-tale smirk on her face - another one bites the dust!

The other quality, if that was the right word, she had acquired from the circumstances of her young life was that of being able to look after herself in just about every situation. She was tough and could manage her way through any predicament.

Sheila had taken on the mother's part of "having words" with her about the risks of sex.

Katie had smiled at her and said, 'Sheila, I probably know much more about sex than you do. I'm no fool. No boy is going to get me into trouble. There's no way I want some screaming brat ruining my life! I'm just having fun, that's all.'

'OK,' Sheila had said. 'Just be careful.'

'No worries,' had been the reply.

Katie had left school at sixteen with just 2 GCSE's in art, and to her surprise, English, and then gone through numerous boring jobs, stacking shelves, serving coffees, waitressing, none of them lasting more than a few weeks. Then she got her first break. She had been sent by the Job Centre to an interview for a post as a receptionist in a small hotel, and to her amazement had got the job.

Suddenly she had found something she enjoyed, and was good at. Management, staff and customers all loved her, and she was in her element. She kept the job until there had been a change of ownership, and the new management brought with them many of their own staff. Katie lost her job. But she now had some good references, and used them when she had applied for another receptionists post at SRX, a computer software company in Bracknell.

Once again, she had excelled, and it was there she had first met Ben. She flirted outrageously with most of the younger males, but it had been Ben that she had her eye on. He had been, as it were, a challenge for her, because he didn't react to her like the others.

Must be gay she had told herself, although she was assured by the other girls that he certainly wasn't gay. So she had just continued her mischief at every opportunity.

There had been a great social life amongst the staff there, and it was through these social gatherings that she had come

70

across Dave, who, at the time was going out with another of the girls in the office. She thought he was gorgeous. It took her some time and effort to get to know him.

It didn't help that he kept on disappearing for weeks or even months at a time, and then appearing on the scene again. She was prepared to wait. Absence, it seems, does make the lust grow stronger.

Once they had become an item it was not long before the date was set for the wedding.

Chapter 11

Ben set off on an unpleasant March afternoon, drove to Portsmouth and boarded the ferry once again to Caen. The crossing was rough and when he arrived early the following morning, the weather had deteriorated further. The lashing rain and the gale force winds made driving more hazardous than he would have liked.

This time he had planned on driving straight down to the Loire Valley, but decided, in these conditions, it would be much wiser to stop overnight somewhere, and hope the weather would improve the following day.

He turned off the main road and, for the first time in his life, stayed at a *Chambre d'hote* which he came across close to the town of Mayenne.

The house was owned by a friendly couple in their late thirties or early forties, who instantly made him welcome in their home. It was an attractive old house with an acre or so of land on which they grew a variety of vegetables, some of which were brought to the table in the evening in the form of a local casserole. His room was comfortable, the furnishings typically French. The bed had solid mahogany head and foot boards, matching the design of the wardrobe and two chests. Already, Ben was enjoying the benefits of his hard work with his French. Once or twice he had to ask the couple to speak a bit more slowly, but on the whole he found it reasonably easy to hold a good conversation with them.

He told them the reason for his visit, and they were eager to impart to him some more knowledge regarding the various taxes and fees involved in buying property, and also some valuable insights into how difficult it can be, especially for a foreigner, to sell property, something Ben had to admit he had not previously taken into consideration.

All the more reason to get everything right from the start, he told himself.

It was an enjoyable experience staying in a French home, and he made a mental note of all the little touches that made his stay so pleasant; the little dish of chocolates and a bottle of local beer on the small desk in the corner of the room, the history of the house translated into English.

The weather on the next day was little better, still overcast and grey. He would have been much happier to see the clear sunshine he normally associated with central France. Having lost his sense of urgency to reach the Loire Valley and, as Fougéres was not far away, he decided to take a detour, to see it again.

The sky remained leaden as he drove west along the deserted road from Mayenne to Fougéres. The town still appealed to him. Being in no hurry he spent several hours exploring and discovered the enormous medieval castle, almost hidden away in the valley at the northern end of the town. He took a guided tour with an English speaking guide and found the detailed historic commentary fascinating, even for someone who had not enjoyed history at all whilst at school.

Later, he looked in the windows of several *Immobilieres* to see what property was available in the area. He was pleasantly surprised at what he saw, and noticed there were several properties in a group of villages nearby. Having time to spare, he drove the few kilometres west of the town. Leaving his car, he walked through the first village. There were a number of properties with *A vendre* signs being displayed.

He wondered just who would possibly want to take on some of them as they appeared to be not much more than shells of old barns. He wouldn't mind carrying out relatively minor DIY tasks, but he shuddered at the thought of taking on anything like that.

However, there were other properties that were more appealing, and he wondered whether he should venture further and take a look inside some of them. It seemed strange to him that there were so many properties in the same area for sale.

It was whilst buying a pastry in one of the *boulangeries,* that he learned that most of the properties being sold belonged to British owners. Apparently, everything was being bought up as soon as it became available, and re-sold at a hefty mark up. The place, it seemed, was fast becoming a ghetto, overrun by the British, and not to the native population's liking, either.

That was it, then. The last thing Ben wanted was to become part of a colony of Brits. Anyway, nice as some of the cottages looked, this was much further north than he had intended. He retraced his steps to his car, picking up some more *pâtis* to eat on his journey and headed south with the intention of reaching Angers before evening.

The journey was uneventful, and as he drove further south, the weather began to lighten a little, but the skies were still grey. The arable landscape of Normandy was now being replaced by vineyards. Later in the year, he knew, there would be field after field of sunflowers, each of their heads following the sun's course across the sky. Now he was becoming excited and as he passed through the small towns and villages dotted along his route, he tried to imagine what would transpire during the next few days. Some of the smaller towns looked rather sad and dilapidated, many of the houses built of grey stone with windows firmly shuttered facing directly onto the road.

His heart was beating faster as at last he approached his favourite Loire Valley town, Angers. As he approached the outskirts of the town, the sun was trying its hardest to disperse the remaining stubborn clouds.

Ben felt at home here. It was a vibrant place, no doubt in part due to the fact that it was a university town. Groups of students could be seen outside cafés or sitting on the walls surrounding the large square in the centre of the town.

There were countless bars, cafés and restaurants open, each competing for trade, and as the lacklustre day turned into a beautiful spring evening, each had a good share of the business. He could see by the number of people sitting outside which were the most popular establishments. There was a general hubbub of sound punctuated by laughter throughout the square from people enjoying their early evening eating and drinking.

Ben's priority was to find somewhere to stay.

Looking around he noticed one of the more popular restaurants had accommodation, and a sign outside said *chambres disponibles ce soir;* vacancies tonight. He made an instant decision. It would be nice to stay somewhere where he could observe and soak up this vibrant atmosphere.

He was warmly welcomed into the small hotel and shown to a room which, whilst it could not be called luxurious, was adequately comfortable and would suit him perfectly. He explained to the lady proprietor that he did not know how long he would be staying.

'*Pas de problème!*' he was told.

Tired after a day's travel, he took a leisurely shower then checked his emails, responding where necessary. When he was ready, he sauntered down to the restaurant, ordered a *Pastis* and took his time in selecting a meal from the wide ranging menu, with some assistance from his waitress.

It did not surprise him to see how full the restaurant was. The atmosphere was electric. The waitresses were surely the most attractive he had ever seen, and their uniforms were not the usual white blouses and black skirts. They were dressed almost as burlesque dancers in their corseted outfits of the brightest hues imaginable, almost dancing as they served, bright eyed and wearing the most wonderful smiles. The lights inside the restaurant were dimmed, with cleverly positioned spots of light being directed onto large prints of Toulouse-Lautrec works, and scenes from *Moulin Rouge* and *Folies Bergere.* The whole place had a sensual, almost promiscuous atmosphere, and it was obvious from the fact that almost all the tables were taken this early in the evening that it was a favourite with the locals; always a good sign.

One of the many things Ben had always admired about French life was the unhurried way they had of eating. A meal out meant a whole evening's entertainment, not the hurried, double booking regime he was used to back home. Whole families, often three generations, would be at the table together. No particular celebration necessary, just a family get together enjoying the food, the wine and the atmosphere set before them. It was noticeable, too, that any children at the table were treated much more as adults than in England. They were involved in the family conversations and, even at their young age, really appreciated their food. In this particular restaurant there was no Children's Menu, simply children's portions of the main menu.

The aromas from the kitchen, the vocal hubbub, the audible busyness of the chef and his staff in the kitchen all made up the pleasure of the evening.

Ben's meal was delicious. He ordered a steak, and explained to his waitress he was British, and therefore would prefer his meat cooked just a little bit longer than the French norm.

'*Je comprends trés bien*,' the girl smiled.

When, much later in the evening, he finally finished his meal he went back to his room. Satiated and just a little tipsy from the wine, he drifted into a deep, peaceful sleep.

That night his dreams, once again, centred on Katie. Probably it was because my waitress reminded me of her, he told himself upon waking the next morning.

Chapter 12

Ben slowly emerged from his slumbers early the next morning and wandered down to the restaurant to enjoy his *petit-déjeuner*.

Strong black coffee came served in a soup bowl, or that is how it appeared to Ben. The croissants were buttery and succulent.

Ben had made a short list of agencies he had found on the internet, and thought it would be wise to start locally. His first call would be with one of the *Immobilieres* just across the square from where he was staying. Having finished his breakfast, he went back to his room, checked his emails of which there were few, and decided to reply to them later in the day. He had much more urgent things to attend to right now.

Bracing himself for action, he grabbed the file containing the property details he had downloaded before leaving the UK, smartened himself up a little, and made his way across the square. He was greeted warmly by a smartly dressed man, slightly older than himself, probably early forties, Ben thought, who seemed eager to help him.

Ben showed him the details he had with him, but was told, 'I am sorry, Monsieur, both of those properties have been sold already.'

'But I only downloaded these details a few days ago,' replied Ben. 'Are you saying the sales of both of these properties have gone through?

'I am sorry, that is the situation. Of course we have other similar properties we would be pleased to show you.'

Yes, thought Ben, having perused some property details in the window, I bet you have. Nothing that I can afford, though.

The young man left him for a few minutes and returned with details of four properties which he thought would be worth considering. Ben had a quick look at the details in front of him, and whilst he understood most of the blurb, he was not able to make sense of some of the more technical stuff. After a while he discarded one of the four properties which was way above his intended budget, and asked when he could view the other three.

'If you can wait for one minute, Monsieur, I will see if there is somebody available to go with you this morning.'

'That's kind. Thank you,' returned Ben.

While he was waiting, he took the opportunity to look around the walls at more properties currently being displayed. What puzzled him was why some of these had not been offered to him as well. Were there only certain types of properties offered to foreigners? For the time being he would not pursue that and returned to his seat.

Within minutes he was told that Nicole could take him to these three properties in just a few minutes, if he didn't mind waiting, and a cup of coffee was brought to him.

About a quarter of an hour later he was being driven out of the town, along some picturesque country lanes, to the first of the properties. Nicole was a pretty dark-haired girl with a typically French short hair style. She was in her mid-thirties, Ben guessed, had a fascinating accent, and spoke English well.

Arriving at the first viewing, Ben stared in disbelief. The setting was perfect; the property was set in a small orchard. They had, however, cleverly photographed it from an angle that implied it was a complete building. This was hardly true. The place was just a ruin. True it did have a roof, as was pointed out by Nicole.

'But not much else!' Ben retorted.

'A lot of English people look for these properties,' Nicole said rather firmly. 'You look for something that is more habitable, yes?'

'Certainly am,' said Ben. 'I want to be able to move in straight away, even if there are minor restorations to be made,' he told her.

'Then the next one on the list might interest you,' she told him.

Another short journey brought them to the second property. This one was in a rather unspectacular suburb, and was dowdy and dark, facing on to the main road that ran through the town. Even so, he felt it was worth looking at in more detail. Inside, the drab décor would need a complete makeover, but at least it had a slate roof, and there was a bathroom, if you could call it that.

'This is more habitable *vous ne pensez pas*?' he was asked.

'It's a bit better,' replied Ben, 'but it's not what I am looking for. I would like a bit more land with it and more out of town, perhaps,' he told her.

'So you definitely do not like this one either?' Nicole asked. Ben could sense a lessening of the friendly accord which was prevalent when they first set out.

The third house was further out of town and did have some land with it. It also had a large paved patio - and a swimming pool! It was rather splendid, but after inspecting it, Ben knew, before he was told, that the price was way above what he wanted to pay. He would have stretched his budget if it had been exactly right for him, but it wasn't.

Nicole now blatantly showed her annoyance at what she considered to be the wasting of her time, and said rather tersely, perhaps he could call back another day to see if there were any other properties that suited him. With that they drove back to the office in an embarrassing silence, and she bade him good day.

Nearing lunchtime Ben decided to have a beer and a bite to eat back at his hotel so he could mull over the morning's disappointment. He thought it would have been a rather more pleasant experience than this. Maybe he had built his hopes too high, and told himself to be patient. He was sure to find what he wanted if he took his time.

While he was supping his second beer, the restaurant's proprietor came and sat with him at his table, introducing herself as Madame Delphine and initially wanted to find out if the room was to his liking.

'It's fine,' Ben told her. 'Certainly comfortable enough for me.'

'That is good,' she replied in her delightful *Anglais* accent, and then asked him why he was here. Ben told her of his plans and of his disappointing first attempt at finding something he liked and could afford.

She told him the *Immobilier* he had chosen, was not the best for his requirements by any means. 'They are only really interested in larger, *plus cher* properties,' she said. 'And I should tell you, some of the other agencies are not happy to sell to English people at all. The area is becoming too full of second homes, or holiday apartments and gîtes. So you will find yourself fighting a bit of *une bataille*!'

'Can you recommend an agency that might look more kindly towards someone who wants to reside here?' he asked.

'When you ask about properties,' she told him 'it is important you tell them you intend to live here permanently, otherwise they will think you are yet another person looking for a second home or holiday home. You won't get the best treatment from anyone who thinks that. You see,' she continued, '*les étrangers* buying properties in the Loire Valley have pushed up prices so much, that many local people, especially young people, cannot afford homes for themselves. And, of course, for much of the year the properties are empty.'

'Yes, I understand. The same thing is happening in the UK where people from the cities are buying up cottages and houses in the loveliest areas, and the local people can't afford to buy something themselves because the prices are rising all the time,' Ben told her. They carried on talking for some time until the lunchtime customers started to take their places at the tables.

'Of course, you do not have to buy through an *Immobilier* in France. Perhaps you can find something you like and purchase it directly from the owner. Look for "*A Vendre*" signs while you wander around the towns and villages. You never know ...'

Ben considered what she had said, especially the advice she had given him to take some time wandering around the area, to branch out a little into the villages, and see if he could see something he liked *A vendre.*

After checking his emails, and feeling a little drowsy after his beers, Ben dozed into a half-sleep for more than an hour.

He awoke, rather annoyed with himself for such an indulgence, and decided to take Madame Delphine's advice and drive around the local villages.

That evening he was no further forward. There was just nothing anywhere approaching his dream cottage.

There was nothing more he could do that day, so he had a shower, changed into some comfortable, smart casuals and went down to enjoy another delicious meal, surrounded by lively groups of people and families. Oh, how the French enjoyed eating!

He sat there eating, drinking, and watching the world go by.

As it began to get dark, Madame Delphine was by his side again.

'How did you get on?' she asked.

'Not well at all. I just can't find anything bordering on what I'm looking for.'

'You actually know what you're looking for?'

'Well, sort of. I have a picture in my mind, you know.'

'Have you crossed over the river?'

'No. Not yet. I've stayed this side today. Would that be a worthwhile thing to do, to look on the other side?'

'*Certainement.* There are many pretty villages just a few kilometres away that might have what you are looking for. But will you find anything for sale? *Je ne sais pas.'*

Ben was totally taken aback by the friendliness shown by this woman who he had only met two days before. He finished his wine, and decided to take a walk around the city in the twilight.

The place was vibrant, whether it was pavement cafés and restaurants, or the more colourful tiny bars hidden away in the side lanes, it was wide awake. The smell of sweet waffles mingled with the savoury aromas of French cuisine. Music emanated from many of the bars but there was none of the rowdiness that such places would exhibit in the UK. People were merely enjoying themselves. Groups of students gathered in the square, drinking and eating, chattering and laughing. There was no sense of the intimidation that he was used to back in Reading.

Ben felt at home here. This is definitely for me, he thought. I feel a sense of belonging, and that's before I find somewhere to live! Tomorrow, he promised himself, I will do things differently.

He meandered through more tiny lanes, down towards the beautiful St. Maurice's Cathedral, looking all the more impressive in the floodlights. He climbed what seemed to be hundreds of steps up from the centre of the town to the front of the building. Eventually, and somewhat reluctantly making his way back to his hotel room, he settled in for a good night's sleep.

Chapter 13

Three more frustrating days passed in Ben's search for his home in France.

He was beginning to get despondent not knowing what to try next. He had approached two other *Immobilieres* yet nothing was forthcoming from either. He was told that so many properties matching his requirements had been sold to *étrangers* in the last few months, that it was difficult for the agency to find enough of them to satisfy demand.

Perhaps he would have to consider other areas, which he would regret, as he had really set his sights on this location. However, he must be realistic.

Arriving back at his room later that afternoon, he started to search the internet again, moving west towards Nantes, and east towards Saumur. Both lovely cities he had visited in the past, but as far as he was concerned neither offered the same lively atmosphere he had found in and around Angers.

His search did not bring about anything positive, but he decided he would visit Nantes the next morning and start searching there.

Feeling rather depressed, he went down to the restaurant for some food and wine, hoping the atmosphere there would help lift his spirits.

No sooner had he ordered his wine than Madame Delphine came, almost running, over to him, obviously excited about something.

'Ben,' she said, almost out of breath, 'You must come and meet a good friend of mine. He thinks he might be able to help you with your search.' She whisked him away to a table inside the restaurant, where a smartly dressed man was sitting at a table accompanied by, Ben presumed, his wife.

'Ben, this is François, and this is Michelina.' Ben shook them both by their hands and sat down at the table with them, as did Madame Delphine.

'François,' she explained, 'has friends and acquaintances all over the place, and really knows what is going on.'

François spoke immaculate English. 'That makes me sound like a scandalmonger. I'm not! I don't spend my time with busybodies. It's just that I'm a Notaire,' he said. 'But there is something I *do* know that I think might be of interest to you.'

Ben was immediately perked up by the sound of this.

'Have you visited Sainte-Justine in your search?' François asked.

'The name rings a bell,' Ben replied, 'but, to be honest, I've visited so many places in the last few days, I can't say for certain I've been there.'

'It's on the north side of the river, about ten kilometres. Well, I have a friend and client there. He has a small farm, like so many others in small villages. You know, a few cows, goats, chickens - just enough to make a living,' François started to explain when he was interrupted by Michelina whose English was not as good as her husband's.

'He is a *charmant* old man,' she said, struggling for the right words, 'and he, er, is working very hard. He has a mother – she is *ancienne* - who runs the place, and likes to think she runs her son, Jean-Pierre, also.'

'Anyway,' continued François, 'up until recently he rented out a farm cottage to a young couple. Now they have moved to Rennes to work, and he is looking for tenants for the cottage.'

'I don't want to rent though,' Ben explained feeling suddenly deflated.

'I know, Ben,' he said, 'but I think he could be persuaded to sell. He doesn't really want to bother with new tenants. He has told me that already, and the money from a sale could go towards some urgent repairs on his own property. If you would like me to, I'll come with you, show you the cottages, and if you like them, introduce you to Jean-Pierre.'

'Cottages?' Ben had clung on to the plural.

'*Oui*,' interjected Michelina, 'they are *deux chalets*, but only one is habitable at the moment. It is *tres joli*, and has some land. It sounds like what you look for?'

'It certainly does. When can I see it?'

'I'll get in touch with him tomorrow, and see if we can see the cottages on Thursday, if you are free then.'

'I'm free any time you like. I'm getting really excited about this.'

'That's done, then. Now, we'd be happy if you would join us for something to eat.'

Madame Delphine left them at that point and Ben was persuaded to tell them all about himself, and why he wanted to leave England to live here. He felt it was bordering on an inquisition at times, yet it was meant in a friendly way. Ben was more than happy to fill them in on the reasons for his property search, if, for no other reason, than to impress upon François that he was serious in his intentions and wanted to live in the property himself, not to kit it out as a holiday cottage.

The evening was a great success.

In return for Ben sharing his life history with the couple, he was treated to a range of information about Saint-Justine. François, it turned out, also knew the town Mayor, and would be able to personally introduce Ben to him. It seemed that the attitude of *La Mairie* was usually kindly towards anyone who would be improving the state of some of the older properties, and François was certain his venture would be looked upon sympathetically.

Saint-Justine had, he was told, undergone something of a face-lift in the past few years, with a number of rather nice properties being built. Some of them were for 'aliens', as he put it, but most were for people who worked in Angers. The overall effect had raised the general appearance of the town, and the Mayor was happy.

While they were talking, Madame Delphine walked past their table to ask if everything was to their liking. She smiled when they said how much they were enjoying their meal and walked away.

'Tell me,' asked Ben, 'why does everybody, including your good selves, always address her as Madame Delphine, and not just by her first name?'

Madame Delphine had in days gone by, he was told, been a well-respected dancer at both *Moulin Rouge* and the original *Folies Bergere.* 'In fact,' François told him, 'if you look closely at some of the posters on the walls of her restaurant, you will find her name listed as Delphine Treasure. She was apparently absolutely stunning.'

'She still is,' said Ben. 'I can almost see her on stage, now you have told me. It also explains the waitresses and the Lautrec prints. It all makes sense. How wonderful to actually meet a *Folies* dancer.'

'Not just *a* dancer,' François said, '*une danseuse principale*. I agree with you though. You can still imagine her in all her finery, can't you?'

'Now, don't get too carried away.' This was Michelina adding her bit to the conversation. 'All this fantasising might not be good for a man of François's age.'

The evening continued in a light hearted vein, and Ben learned a lot more about the area and the people who lived there.

Throughout the following two days, he spent his time exploring Angers itself, and on the second day, becoming impatient, he decided to take a preview of his possible new home town.

The description that François had given was pretty accurate. After crossing over *L'oceane,* the fast toll road to the west coast, the road to Sainte-Justine narrowed and was fringed on both sides by thick woodland. After passing a sports centre and a small industrial estate, the main street leading into the town was lined with expensive, attractive properties. The properties nearer the *centre ville* were older, mostly painted white and seemingly in pristine condition. The town itself was spotlessly clean. No discarded Coke cans or crisp packets here.

The only problem Ben had was that he could not find any sign of the cottages that had been described to him. He could see no signs indicating properties for sale or to let. He walked through the small town several times and relaxed by having a drink at a smart little *tabac* and felt comfortable there. He gave up trying to find the cottage. You'll just have to wait, mate, he told himself, returning to Angers later in the day.

That evening, François 'phoned, and arranged to pick Ben up at ten o'clock the following day.

Ben found it impossible to sleep that night.

He had a picture in his mind of the two cottages. That was not new. He'd had such a picture in his mind for a long time. Now, though, it was much more real, much more penetrating. He tossed and turned for hours, it seemed, just trying to imagine more and more details of the property, despite telling himself this was a complete waste of time, and all it was achieving was a lack of sleep.

The next morning he awoke, excited as a kid at Christmas, just wanting it to be ten o'clock. It was all too thrilling, just too good to be true.

He took a shower, and put on some smart casual clothes.

Breakfast was the usual croissants and coffee. Afterwards he still had nearly an hour to kill before François was due to collect him, probably the longest hour he had ever experienced. As soon as François arrived they headed off to the village.

Ben told François he had been to have a look at the village, but hadn't been able to find any cottages matching the description he had been given.

'No, I don't suppose you could,' François replied, smiling. 'They're pretty well hidden away. I think you'll like them when we get there.'

They drove the few kilometres from Angers and turned off on the road to the village. Travelling down the smart road to *Centre Ville* they continued right through the centre and out the other end, where the road narrowed. Ben could now see ploughed fields to either side of the road. A further kilometre down the road they took a turn into a lane that was not much more than a farm track and stopped after a few hundred metres.

'This is why you couldn't find it, perhaps?' François joked. 'You see what I mean, now?'

Ben didn't reply. There were overgrown hedgerows on either side of the narrow lane, with the odd spindly tree poking its way out. They left the car in the lane and walked up another few metres. On the right was a sadly neglected wooden gate, sagging from its hinges, easily missed amongst the jungle of the hedgerow. It took both of them to lift the gate to get it to open.

Beyond the gate was an area covered with gravel, a mass of weeds growing through it. In the centre of the expanse of gravel it was just possible to make out that at one time there had been a small circular flower bed. Ahead of him sat an attractive little cottage, with small windows, a red-tiled roof and what was once a white pebble-dashed frontage. A mass of brambles and ivy encompassed a substantial part of the walls and a large tree to the left afforded shade to the garden. Entry to the cottage was gained through a small front door hidden under a porch.

It was in need of considerable TLC, but even in its present state it was, as far as Ben was concerned, almost perfect. His heart was beating fast as he tried to suppress his excitement. The only noticeable difference between this and his dream cottage was that, in his dream, the cottages had been in a better state of repair, and the gates had been of wrought iron.

Across at ninety degrees to the cottage was an even more dilapidated building. It was bigger than the cottage, and built in a similar style. There was the red-tiled roof, but holes in the walls where there were once the same small windows as in the cottage. The same mass of brambles and other climbing weeds had taken control and had made their way through the apertures that had once been windows.

Ben was dumb struck. He was not aware of François talking to him. He took some steps into the front gravelled area, and made his way, not at first to the cottage, but to the other building, and looked inside.

The door refused to open, so Ben pushed aside some of the climbers and peered in through one of the openings. Inside there was virtually nothing. It was pretty rough. The walls were of bare stone, and looking up he could see a few chinks of light through the roof, but he was not deterred by that. It meant he had a blank canvas to work with. So much better than having to pull the place apart and start again.

It was only then he heard François' voice. 'You're not disappointed are you, Ben?' he was saying. 'Come and see the cottage.'

'I'm not disappointed at all, François. This is so close to what I want, I feel as if I'm dreaming.'

'There's a lot of work needed on that building, Ben. Many years ago it used to be a dairy, and has never been lived in as far as I know.'

'No problem. It would suit me just fine, but let's look at the cottage.'

François unlocked the front door with some difficulty and they walked inside.

It was as he had guessed it would be; somewhat dark, owing to the small windows and the overgrown greenery outside. Secateurs and some changes to the décor would soon help solve that problem. The interior was deceptive. It was much larger than he had expected. The front door led into a sizeable living area, some six metres square. The ceilings were low, and beamed. Not low enough for Ben to have to stoop although there may be a problem for people taller than him. The furnishings were old and rather dowdy, but that was immaterial. He would be bringing his own furniture.

Turning left from the front door he saw a large kitchen and dining area, about half the size of the living area, the fittings old and sad.

Narrow stairs led him upstairs where there were two good sized bedrooms, each having views of the surrounding countryside, plus a bathroom and toilet.

He could see no signs of leaks or damp anywhere, no smell of dankness or decay, all of which was a pleasant surprise considering how long the cottage had been unoccupied and how old the place was.

Yes, I could happily live here, he said to himself.

'Well?' It was François interrupting his thoughts again.

'Sorry,' Ben said. 'I was miles away again. This is amazing. I was just telling myself that I could happily live here. How sure are you he will sell? More importantly, what will be his price?'

'You haven't finished yet, Ben. Come and have a look at the grounds.'

"The grounds". That sounded so imposing. Without hesitation, Ben went outside again. It was not a spectacular day. There was just a little pale sunshine, yet even in these conditions, he had fallen in love with the place.

They went to the rear of the cottage, and there before him Ben saw a sprawling wilderness. It couldn't be classed as a garden, however it was as big an area as the two cottages occupied.

'Room for a pool, perhaps?' François was querying.

'I doubt I'd want that,' replied Ben. 'I'd be much more interested in producing my own fruit and vegetables. A few chickens, perhaps. That kind of thing.' Then looking around again he asked, 'Are those buildings included, do you know?'

'Absolutely. Everything in this area comes with the cottage.'

The buildings he spoke of were two old barns of different sizes, one with a roof, the other not much more than four walls with a few rafters remaining in place.

Ben decided to ignore these two buildings for the moment. Enough to know they were there, and might fit into his plans in some way in the future.

Clearing the tangled wasteland would be a massive task he told himself, but the end result would provide a nice area in which he could grow some of his own food.

He climbed through brambles and weeds up to his waist, down to the far end of the area, marked by what was once a fence. There he discovered to his delight that on his side of the fence ran a little stream burbling its way below the undergrowth. He could already picture this as an area where he could relax on a summer evening with a book and a glass or two of wine.

He made his way back, with the widest of grins on his face, to where François was waiting.

'This is just about perfect,' he said. 'When can we meet the owner?'

'I can arrange that now if you like, providing he's at home. You'll have to meet his mother as well, though. She has to know everything that goes on. I'll just give them a call.'

Once again Ben waited with bated breath. He just wanted to know whether or not they would sell the place. He would be more than disappointed if they wouldn't.

François spoke politely and precisely to whoever was on the other end of the phone, and there were several interruptions from him of *"oui", "non", "d'accord"* and *"je comprends"*.

The call took some time, but eventually François said they would be welcome at the farm now, if that would be OK.

Ben had another glance around at the cottage and the old dairy building, and then made his way with François towards the car. 'We'll leave the car here, Ben. It's only a few metres up the track.'

They made their way further up the lane, which became even more deeply rutted, towards a rather beautiful, albeit dilapidated, old farmhouse. It was built of creamy coloured stone with a roof of red clay tiles, the walls almost covered by ivy and other creeping plants. They had to tip-toe through a courtyard which was strewn with all manner of old implements, machinery parts and rather pungent evidence of the few animals which were kept there. A solid wood door led them straight into an enormous kitchen and eating area. Dominating the room was a wooden table that must have been some three or four metres in length, with a few chairs at one end. Piles of papers, magazines and bags of who-knows-what covered the majority of the table at the other end.

Coming through the door at the far end of the room was Jean-Pierre, his weathered face almost resembling a walnut, his skin as red as a tomato. Behind him hobbled his stooped mother with her mass of grey hair, wearing a heavy, long skirt of some woven tweed and around her shoulders, a knitted shawl. Ben guessed she must have been in her nineties.

Ben was introduced to and warmly welcomed by the pair and shook the old man's huge, rough and gnarled hand.

The ensuing conversation was then between them and François, and although Ben could keep up with most of what was being said, the speed at which they all spoke, and what he supposed was a strong local dialect, made it difficult to be sure of everything being said. Every now and then, the two hosts would look over at him and then continue their chatting. Ben just hoped François would enlighten him on the details of the conversation sooner rather than later.

There was a lengthy period while Jean-Pierre and his mother talked earnestly with each other. At first Ben thought he could detect some level of disagreement between them, but it didn't last long. When they had finished their discourse, they turned back to François, and with two toothy smiles, each shook his hand.

'Ben, you will be pleased to know they will be happy to sell the cottage to you,' François announced. 'All we have to decide now is the price. I'll let you know more of the details of our discussion in a minute. Are you happy to leave the bargaining with me, or do you want to be part of it?'

'I think I'll leave it in your hands,' Ben replied. 'I'm sure you know much more about this than I do.'

Jean-Pierre's mother had disappeared, but soon emerged again holding in her hands a rolled document covered in years of dust which was dispersed into the room's atmosphere with one enormous gust of breath from her.

The document was laid out on the part of the table which was not covered with other paraphernalia. Jean-Pierre, in the meantime had produced a bottle of wine and four glasses of varying sizes and styles. The glasses were filled and passed round. What the wine was Ben could only guess, not the most beautiful nose or taste, but eye-wateringly powerful it certainly was.

François was now studying the plans with the couple, and making copious notes.

Then there were discussions about all manner of things. Ben learned later that when buying or selling property in France, if there are offspring or relatives who might have an interest in the property, they have to agree to the sale. In this case there were no such problems. The discussion seemed to go on for a long time. Eventually Ben could make out that they had got around to discussing the price.

Ben had noticed that François only referred to "the cottage" in all his negotiations, implying that he had no real interest in anything else, and it seemed that the haggling was because the owners were pointing out the value of the land in addition to the cottage.

François eventually took Ben to one side.

'I need to know how much of your plans you want me to tell them,' he said. 'I am saying you are only really interested in the cottage to live in, but they are saying that there are other buildings there, too, and the land as well. What do you want me to tell them? If I tell them of your plans, then you will almost certainly pay more.'

'I'd much rather be honest with them,' Ben told François. 'I would rather haggle on a price which allows for my plans.' François was happy to take on board what Ben had said and went back to the negotiating table.

Some time and a few glasses of wine later, a deal seemed to be struck.

François informed Ben of the negotiated price, at which Ben was pleasantly surprised, but he asked François to go back with another deal. He told him he was concerned about the state of the track leading to the cottage, and that he would certainly have to resurface it. If they could reduce the price just a little, he would continue the resurfacing right up to their farm gate.

François took the suggestion back to Jean-Pierre, and after a short discourse with his mother, the price was reduced and hands were shaken all round.

The last proviso was that Ben's plans had to be run past the Mayor, to ensure Ben would be allowed to do what he proposed. François doubted there would be a problem, nevertheless he instilled in the old couple that it had to be done.

If the Mayor approved in principle, then the deal would be done, and the legal procedures would be put into operation, which, Ben was assured, were much faster and simpler than in the UK.

Another phone call from François confirmed that the Mayor was in his office the next day, and he would be pleased to discuss the situation with Ben and François.

Chapter 14

'Monsieur Le Maire offers his apologies. He will be here as soon as he can. He expects to be about one hour,' the receptionist told them.

Ben was not at all put out by this, and suggested to François that he might spend the hour at the cottages. He made his way the short distance to the top of the village and up the track to his future home.

Firstly he had another glance inside the cottage he would be occupying, and confirmed his original thought that it was suitable enough for him to live in without any major work having to be done. However, he was more interested in the other building - the old dairy, which would hopefully provide him with some additional income. He wished he had brought a tape measure with him, but sized it the best he could by pacing the floor area. There were signs that both water and electricity had been connected at some time in the past. Not all that surprising, he said to himself, seeing that it was once a dairy. He doubted, though, that those connections would be usable now. He would have to look into that. There was no sign of a connection to a septic tank anywhere, and made a note to ask about that as well.

He was tremendously excited about the concept of developing this shell into a comfortable holiday home.

His next stop was the pair of older buildings behind the cottage. He ventured inside the larger one first rather hesitantly, and to his surprise found it was remarkably dry, regardless of the fact that there was some light showing through the roof here and there. There were weeds and brambles growing inside, but the thick stone walls were in good condition, and the roof structure of huge wooden beams seemed to be sound as well. He had no immediate plans for these two barns, but he was sure they would play some part in a future project. The smaller of the two was a different matter. The stone walls were intact, but other than a couple of roof timbers, there was no roof at all. He measured these two structures in the same rough way he had the dairy, and then turned his attention to the grounds.

He had never considered himself to be a gardener and had no idea where or how he would start. I'll have to do a lot of homework on the subject, he told himself.

Again, he made his way through the undergrowth to the dilapidated fence at the far end, turned around, and looked back at the properties from a new perspective. It couldn't be more perfect. It was just what he was looking for. More, in fact, than he had ever hoped to find.

He took his camera from his rucksack, and started clicking at all he could see. The photographs would help him remember everything more clearly when he got back home.

Before he knew it the hour had passed and he was on his way back to *La Mairie* to join François and the Mayor.

When he arrived at the smart glass and wood-clad building sitting alongside the church, François was standing outside in conversation with a smartly dressed gentleman who was introduced to Ben, and hands were shaken.

François addressed the Mayor by his first name, but the greeting between the Mayor and Ben was rather more formal, though nonetheless cordial.

Ben had been practising what he wanted to confirm with the Mayor - that his plans for not just living there but also turning the dairy into a holiday let were acceptable to him.

It became obvious that the Mayor was eminently proud of his village, and always looked upon property improvements in a good light.

'So many of our villages have older properties just left to decay,' he said. 'I have tried to encourage not just new development in Sainte-Justine, but also the renovation of older buildings, so your enthusiasm about looking after those buildings meets with my absolute approval. Obviously I will need to know if you want to make any structural alterations. Other than that, I'm happy with what you want to do.'

'There is one thing I would like to sound you out on,' Ben said. 'There are two old barns behind the cottage. As they stand at present they are pretty well redundant, and I won't be needing barns. How would you react if I wanted to use the existing building materials to build another cottage in their place?'

'In principal, I feel the same about that, but you would have to go through the appropriate channels to get final approval. I would not put anything in your way, and would be happy to support such an application, I can assure you,' he replied. Then, looking at his watch, he added, 'Look, why don't we adjourn to *Maison Catherine* just down the road and continue our discussions there?'

It didn't seem there was any point in disagreeing, as the Mayor had already left his seat, and was informing his receptionist that we were going down the road. She obviously knew what "down the road" meant and did not venture to ask when he might be back. Ben guessed that this was probably a fairly regular occurrence.

They wandered their way on foot "down the road" to a small restaurant, and took a table towards the back of the dining room. Ben noticed a *réservée* notice on the table. So this must be a *very* regular occurrence, he smiled to himself.

The conversation turned to business between the Mayor and François for a while until the Mayor suddenly turned to Ben and said, 'How rude we are, François. We are here for Ben's benefit today, and here we are talking our own business. Please excuse us, Ben.'

Ben assured him it was not a problem and was then inundated with more information about St Justine. How it was developing into a predominantly younger persons' town, with excellent sports facilities, a good primary school, a small shopping centre with plans for a much larger shopping facility just to the east of the town. He even told them about the recently built water works, which apparently produced the cleanest drinking water in the area, if not the whole of France.

He was told he would seldom have to use his car in the town, as there were well used walking and cycle tracks criss-crossing the town.

Ben knew much of this before the meeting. However, it was good to see the authorities so enthused about the commune they were in charge of.

By the end of the lunch, which Ben noticed with an inward smile, was paid for by François, he had learned a lot more about the village.

'How do you feel about it all now?' asked François once they had left *Maison Catherine.*

'Absolutely over the moon!' he replied.

'That's good. Then I suggest we go to see if John-Pierre and his mother are at home, and make them a formal offer, if that is all right with you.'

'Brilliant!' Ben replied eagerly.

They made their way back to the farm, passing the cottages on their right as they drove up the track, to find both parties were at home.

Hands were shaken, wine was poured, and they sat once again around the enormous table. Ben left most of the talking to François, but was able to interject here and there.

François was able to tell the couple that the Mayor was in favour of what Ben had in mind, and all that had to be done now was to agree a final selling price. Whether there was a hidden suggestion in the way François was negotiating Ben did not know, but he was surprised when the final price turned out to be even less than had been mentioned previously. It was now some 20 per cent less than he had originally budgeted for and John-Pierre had said there were two fields adjoining the land which he would be happy to sell to Ben in the future if he needed more land. One piece was the field on the far side of the stream at the end of the garden, and the other was a larger adjoining field situated behind the dairy.

It was confirmed, as Ben had thought, that the original water, electricity and drainage connections to the dairy would have to be re-installed as they were too old to be safe. That did not come as any surprise to him, and considering the lowering of the price, seemed more than acceptable.

'So all that remains now,' François said as they left the farm, 'is to arrange a deposit, and sort out how you want to finance it. I'm away for the weekend. However I can meet with you some time on Monday. That means you'll have to stay here for another weekend. Is that a problem?'

'No problem at all,' was Ben's cheery reply. 'It will give me a chance to get my head round all this. It's all happening so quickly.'

It was agreed the final touches would be sorted out after the weekend, and with a shaking of hands, François and Ben went back to the car and drove off down the track from the farm. Suddenly, Ben asked François to stop the car. He got out and walked back up the lane to the gate leading to his cottages, where he had seen an old strip of wood laying on the ground by the gate. He picked it up and, turning it over, he saw engraved in old black lettering, "La Sanctuaire".

'Perfect,' he said allowed. 'The Sanctuary. Yes that's what it will be. My Sanctuary!'

Chapter 15

Katie's wedding was a truly grand affair, not exactly what she would have chosen if she had been given her way, but she was relishing every second of it.

The whole event had been planned by Dave's father and Auntie Grace.

Dave had agreed with Katie that they would observe all the traditions, and he had gone to his family home the night before the wedding whilst she stayed at his house in Reading. Katie spent the morning of the big day at Ray's salon being pampered by Penny and Colette. Ray had agreed that Penny would go back to the house with Katie to help her make the final preparations. Katie knew how brilliant Penny's hair design skills were, and Penny enjoyed the task of making Katie's long golden hair look sensational. They were ready in plenty of time and had a glass or two of wine before the white Rolls Royce arrived to pick them up.

Penny was not going to be a bridesmaid, that role was being played by Dave's sister, Summer. Again it was not really Katie's idea, but the family had insisted and Katie had acquiesced. Penny had agreed to call at the family house in Wheathampstead to collect Summer and drive to the church with her.

The Atkinson's home was a huge Georgian house set in what must have been a few acres of gardens and woodlands. It was not unusual to see a Rolls Royce in the drive way. Dave's father was a senior scientist at Harwell Atomic Energy Research Establishment, and was not short of a bob or two as Dave had put it before she first went there to meet his father and Auntie Grace.

Today Katie looked amazing. She knew the wedding was going to be a formal affair with all the men in top hats and tails, but she wanted to make a statement, and she did so exquisitely. She and Auntie Grace had looked through all the designer catalogues, showing all the typical dresses, with yards of lace and huge trains.

Katie ignored all the advice such as *that would look beautiful on you, dear* and chose a beautifully simple, close fitting dress in ivory satin with the palest of blue trimmings and embroidery, from a wedding shop in Reading. It fitted her like a glove, emphasised everything that needed emphasising, and hid the bits that needed to be hidden. Penny had done a perfect job on her hair. She did not want it up as most brides seemed to like. She was proud of her hair, much preferring it down, around and over her shoulders. Penny had understood perfectly what she wanted, and had decorated it with ribbons and flowers of the same shade of blue to match the trimmings on her dress.

The resulting simplicity was a triumph amongst all the formality of the men and many of the women surrounding her. She had never looked or felt more radiant.

Her only regret was that her foster parents were unable to come. Earlier in the year they had decided to go to New Zealand to visit part of their family who had emigrated there a couple of years previously. She would have loved them to be part of this special day. She had been unable to trace her only uncle, so the ceremony had been changed. She was not going to be accompanied down the aisle by the person who was to give her away, an expression Katie had never liked anyway, but was to walk down with her husband to be. At the altar she would join her bridesmaid, and Dave would link up with his best man, an old school friend.

She was also disappointed, yet hardly surprised, that Ben had not come. She had sent him an invitation to the only address she had for him, but in truth she had no idea where he was.

The ceremony was held in the beautiful St Helen's church in the village, picturesque with its tall spire, and the service went wonderfully smoothly, without any mishaps that Katie noticed. She was hardly conscious of what was going on, she was so excited, so high on adrenalin.

Nobody spoke to air a reason why they should not be joined in matrimony. The vows were taken, rings exchanged, register signed, and the bride was kissed by her new husband, rather intensely, Katie thought. After the wedding the guests morphed into paparazzi and hundreds of photographs were taken. The official photographer was meticulous in forming every conceivable combination of family and relatives. Eventually everyone made their way to the reception at an hotel in Harpenden.

The hotel management had done them proud. The wedding breakfast was to be served in a large white marquee in the hotel's garden. As guests arrived they were offered a choice of drinks, and as the weather was fine, made their way into the garden. The varied menu had something for everyone, vegans, vegetarians and carnivores.

Once the guests had been informed the meal was ready, they all made their way to their appointed tables to sample the hotel's cuisine.

The best man's speech was hilarious. Katie couldn't help feeling a bit sorry for Dave having to listen to a catalogue of his misdemeanours and sexual antics in front of all his relatives. Despite the occasional shocked looks from his family, he took it all in good part. She was delighted to hear that they had received a telemessage from her foster parents, sending their love, and saying how sorry they were to have missed such an auspicious day.

The reception, back in the hotel, progressed in the normal way. She and Dave had to start the dancing and as neither of them were good dancers they were relieved when some of the guests wandered out to join them, including a great uncle and aunt who must have been in their late eighties, who made it all look so simple. Katie just looked on enviously, as they took to the floor. It appeared they could cope with almost any rhythm with consummate ease, and in fact they stayed out on the dance floor for most of the night, with brief breaks for topping up their drinks.

Katie spent her time, when she was not being asked by all and sundry to dance, just looking round the room, studying the guests, part of the family with whom she was now involved.

Dave's father was doing the rounds, especially with the younger female guests, and as the evening wore on, was becoming more and more blatantly flirtatious. You could see some of the girls move away when they saw him making a bee-line for them.

Katie wondered about Auntie Grace. Perhaps she's his wife's sister? Considering his behaviour this evening, it was more likely she was not related at all, and was called Auntie Grace for the children's sake. She certainly appeared to be a few years younger than him and seemed totally oblivious to his philandering.

Katie looked over to her bridesmaid, Summer, who had not spoken a word to her since they met in the church earlier. I don't know about Summer, Katie mused. More like a miserable afternoon in November! Since they had first been introduced, Katie had not once been able to make any eye contact with her. Her head was always bowed, and she really did look like the most miserable child you could meet.

It was then that Katie set eyes on Dave's Uncle George and Auntie Betty, a really pleasant couple, but her gaze was soon diverted to their son Adrian and his girlfriend Melissa. How gorgeous can a guy get? Katie sighed. Dave was pretty good looking, but this guy was something different. He stood a couple of inches over six foot and was dressed in an immaculate light grey suit with a superb choice of shirt to match it. Melissa was a stunner too with her long auburn ringletted hair falling down to her shoulders. They were so tactile they appeared to be conjoined at some point of their anatomy. There was much touching, caressing and kissing at every opportunity.

'Lucky cow,' Katie whispered under her breath.

'Who's a lucky cow?' Dave had crept up behind her, and grabbed her round her waist.

'Oh, hi!' she replied. 'Me, you idiot. I'm the lucky cow! Who did you think I meant?'

'Don't know,' he replied, then grabbed her arm to take her to meet some of his friends.

For the rest of the evening, Katie could hardly keep her eyes off the two lovers, watching their every move, and getting more and more excited by them both as the evening wore on. She half expected them to end up in the middle of the dance floor ripping each other's clothes off and putting on a show for everyone. The more she watched, the more aroused she became. This was a feeling that Katie was only too familiar with. She felt the tell-tale signs of the heat rising from her body, the blushing spreading up to her neck and cheeks.

During an "excuse me" dance, Katie made a bee line for Adrian, but had to wait her turn to hold this gorgeous creature against her. After the dance, he bent to kiss her but she made a point of putting one hand behind his head and turning her head to face him just as he was about to plant a cursory kiss on her cheek, and they kissed full on the lips. Katie made it linger just a little longer than it should, and gently caressed his lips with her tongue before letting him go. Poor Adrian was rather shocked and quickly made his way back to his Melissa.

Oh well, Katie sighed. Mission accomplished I suppose. Then, as she rebuked herself for her lustful feelings, she found herself dancing with her father-in-law.

She, too, was a bit wary of him. She remembered that at their first meeting, he had pulled her aside when Dave was not around, and had told her she would be much better off marrying him than his son. 'He's a wastrel,' he had told her. 'Claims he's got lots of money, yet has got absolutely nothing to show for it. But I could really make you a happy, wealthy young lady.' She had managed to smile sweetly at him, and offered her thanks.

Here she was now, in his arms in a slow smoochy dance, being held much more closely than she would have liked. She was pleased to be rescued once more by Dave.

'I think it's time to cut the cake, sweetheart,' said Dave as he swept her away from his father's clutches. 'Sorry about him. He does get a bit carried away after a few drinks.'

The bride and groom placed the silver knife into the cake and posed for more photographs.

'I think we should go and get changed, Dave. I'm getting too warm in this dress.'

He agreed and they disappeared discretely to their hotel room without anyone noticing.

Once inside the room, Katie rid herself of her dress, and grabbed Dave's arm as he was making for the bathroom.

'Fuck me, Dave - please! I'm so bloody horny.'

She lay back on the bed, pulled her knees up to her chest, removing her matching ivory and pale blue knickers and holding the pose. Dave stared at the inviting, almost pornographic sight meeting his gaze and moved over towards the bed, tearing off his suit jacket as he went.

Upon reaching the bed, he went to kneel between her legs, but she got hold of him by his hair, and pulled him up towards her face.

'Not now, Dave. Just fuck me! For God's sake, just fuck me!'

Dave did as he was told, surprised that she did not want the foreplay that was normally such a major part of their love making. He didn't have to be told twice and moved up her body to kiss her. She returned his kiss intensely and then went about tearing off the remainder of his clothes. Dave had caught her mood, her urgency, roughly pushed her legs apart and entered her causing her to scream. Normally she issued plaintive little sounds when they made love, but this was different. She made so much noise that Dave thought the whole hotel would be able to hear them. He was in charge now, and he was doing exactly what she had asked.

It was fast, furious and almost brutal; all over in just a few minutes. It was exactly what she needed. Her orgasm was violent, and Dave had to put his hand over her mouth to quell the noise. She held his head in her hands, and kissed him passionately. 'That was wonderful,' she said, still panting from her exertion. 'I guess we had better get back downstairs before they miss us.'

They changed into more comfortable casual clothes, but as Katie grabbed her panties to put back on, Dave snatched them out of her hands.

'Oh, no you don't,' he said. 'No knickers for a week. That was the deal we had. No knickers for a week after we were married.'

She tried her best to grab them back to no avail. This time Dave had won and she accepted defeat warning him that he may well regret this move. Dave just laughed, and stuffed her panties in his pocket before they went downstairs with give-away grins on their faces. They reappeared amongst their guests, and started to circulate again.

It was much later when the guests started to leave. Katie had another kiss from Adrian as he and Melissa left. Her lusting was over now, and the peck on the cheek was quite adequate.

It was early morning before they eventually got back to their bedroom, and they both drifted off into a peaceful slumber without any further sex. It was the following morning when they made love. No urgency now. They decided to forego breakfast, and just languished in each other's arms until eventually they made the effort to get up.

They were not having a proper honeymoon now. That was to be saved until later in the year, when Dave had more spare time. For now they were spending just a few days in St. Ives in Cornwall. Dave's father had lent them the Jaguar, and they took a comfortable, leisurely drive through some of the most beautiful countryside to a modest little hotel on the sea front of the Cornish town.

They were shown to their room which was a bit on the small side yet well appointed, clean and comfortable.

'Bit small,' Dave said as they unloaded their suitcases.

'Who cares?' Katie replied. 'It's what you do in it that counts, isn't it?' With that she grabbed hold of him and fought him on to the bed.

'Let's start as I mean to go on!' she said, and Dave wasn't going to argue with her.

Chapter 16

When Monday arrived, Ben was feeling apprehensive about his meeting with François. It was now that things could go wrong. There could be misunderstandings that might cause all manner of problems in the future. The more he thought about it, the more anxious he became and by the time he arrived at the Notaire's smart offices he was beginning to feel sick with nerves.

He was shown into François' office. At once his nerves were dissipated by the welcome he received.

'Ben, how nice to see you again. You haven't changed your mind over the week-end?'

'Oh, no,' Ben replied. 'I'm more enthusiastic than ever. I've been over to St. Justine again to have another look.'

'Well, that's good. So we can get down to business then,' François said ushering Ben to a comfortable chair.

'Firstly, Ben, it is quite usual in France for the Notaire to act for both parties in property matters. It simplifies things and reduces costs. So are you happy for me to act for the sellers as well as for you?'

'Seems to make sense to me. I have often wondered why we can't do the same thing in the UK.'

'Good. OK, there are a number of things that I will go through with you. I want you to be absolutely clear what is happening and how things are done over here. It's quite straight forward but rather different to how you do things in England.'

There followed a long list of things that had to be done. Very little of it affected Ben. The great majority of it would be completed by the Notaire.

After a while François asked 'How will you be financing your venture?'

'I have enough in my bank to cover the deposit, so that's no problem. In fact I could just about pay the total price from my bank, but I need considerable funds to carry out all the work, so I will be taking out a mortgage to buy the property.'

'Then I would recommend that you obtain your mortgage from a French bank. We might be more selective who we lend money to and how much we lend,' he told Ben, 'but our interest rates are certainly much more competitive than yours.'

Ben agreed to transfer sufficient funds into a client account with François so that the deposit and other expenses could be paid as they arose, making things much simpler for all parties.

'What about a survey?' Ben asked

'Generally, few buyers bother with them in France,' Ben was told. 'I can arrange for a survey to be carried out for you, but I must warn you it is a seriously expensive service over here. What I will do for you, is to write in a clause into the contract, that if anything major is discovered within, say, three months, then the vendor will share the expense with you.'

Ben considered that he had seen the properties for himself, and was pretty well aware of their condition, and gratefully agreed to François' suggestion.

Other matters such as insurance, registering new ownership and a number of other things would be taken care of by François, and he would keep Ben informed of developments all the way to completion.

'You must attend the completion ceremony,' Ben was told. 'Not just because we need your signature on a number of documents, but also so that you can experience the event. It is more like a celebration in France, and almost always ends with a few glasses of wine. You'll enjoy it.'

'I was beginning to give up, you know,' Ben said. 'But thanks to you, I can go back to England knowing my best interests are being looked after. I just can't thank you enough. I think it may well have been a disaster if you had not come to my rescue.'

Ben was entirely confident to leave the whole matter in the hands of François and a day or two later, after thanking Madame Delphine for her enormous help, and for introducing him to François, he left to return to England.

Back in Reading, Ben had about three months to get everything organised for his final, permanent move to Sainte-Justine.

Firstly, he had to talk with his colleagues to let them know of his intentions. So a meeting was arranged and although they seemed a bit put out, they were not totally surprised. In a roundabout way, they had heard that he had split up with Mary.

'You can't let us down, now,' was the immediate response.

'Who's saying anything about letting you down?' Ben retorted. 'I'm not letting you down. I have no intention of leaving our little partnership. I'd be an idiot to do that! Hey, I've just been away in France for three weeks. Have you noticed anything different? Have I let you down in any way? No! I've been doing my bit all the time - signing up new clients, supporting existing ones, just as I would if I had been in Reading. I want to carry on in the same way, but working from France, that's all.'

'I'm not sure that's possible.'

'Oh. It is. I've looked into this, and if we form a Limited Liability Partnership,' he told them, 'then this would mean I could work in France, and be taxed as a partner in the UK. I'm sure our accountants could set it up for us.'

His next meeting was with his Bank Manager to arrange a transfer of funds to François' account, and to advise him of his intention of moving to France.

He was with a major international bank, and it seemed such transactions were becoming increasingly commonplace with so many people moving abroad.

'And are you requiring funding for this venture?' the manager asked him.

'Yes I will be, but I've been advised that I would do better to get a mortgage over there than here. What's your opinion?' Ben asked.

'Good advice, Ben. I can arrange for an account to be set up over there for you, and we could give them a good recommendation, and advise them of your excellent borrowing record over here. That way, you stay with us, and get the best deal over there. How's that sound?'

His manager said he would arrange for all the necessary application documents to be sent over from France, and he would liaise with Ben's Notaire in France in order to confirm that he was to become a French resident.

Ben was beginning to disbelieve how smoothly everything was going. He was expecting all sorts of complications, and maybe there would be some along the way, but the initial steps seemed too simple to be true.

During the ensuing weeks, Ben had to juggle his time to deal with everything that was going on. There were emails from François, letters from accountants, bank managers and solicitors.

The only real relief from it all was when he met up with Grunge in town one day, and they set a date for another evening out. It turned out to be another new experience for Ben - a new bar-cum-restaurant that had opened in "Wokingham of all places" as Grunge had put it. A decidedly strange place called "The Dungeon - Meet New People - Make New Friends" had been built in cellars underneath two shops in the High Street. It was dark as you entered, but once your eyes became adjusted it was an extraordinarily interesting place.

The obvious difference was that enormous pine wood tables had been used, and as customers arrived they were all seated at the same table. The subsequent tables were filled up only when all the seats at the first table had been taken. This meant you sat alongside someone who you had never met before, and probably never would again. The orders were taken, but instead of taking a table number, you were asked for your first name, so when your dish was ready, everybody sitting around you knew your name. Furthermore, it stated on the menu that you were encouraged to introduce yourself to the person who came to sit next to you. It seemed a bit weird to Ben, but it was, he supposed, a way of meeting someone new.

His conversation with Grunge, who used her proper name Georgina, for once this evening, was regularly interrupted by people sitting around them. Not something you expect and it took some getting used to.

She so wanted to tell him the truth about Mary, however a promise was a promise and she kept her lips well and truly sealed on that subject.

Ben told her about his moving to France and of his plans for his future.

'Oh, how exciting,' the girl opposite said. 'I love France. Where are you going to live?'

Ben told the girl, grudgingly, of his plans.

'I hope I'll get an invite to visit you there,' Grunge said, and Ben promised her that she would be top of his list when he'd got things organised enough to accept visitors.

They had a number of evenings out thoroughly enjoying each other's company, knowing it would never be more than that. This was a case of opposites attracting, although Ben did notice that her appearance softened slightly the more she went out with him. Strangely, he regretted the change. He enjoyed her the way she had always been, and he hoped he had not played any part in her mellowing.

He had to make two additional short trips to Angers to meet with François who wanted to make sure he was doing exactly what Ben wanted and, whilst there, to set up his new banking facilities and sign the mortgage documents. With just a few minor exceptions, which were easily resolved, François was doing a great job.

The next visit to France would be to sign the final documents.

He would have been counting the days if it were not for the fact that he was so busy doing other things. It felt as if there was more to do in England than there was in France regarding this move. Things were moving on and most of the forms regarding the Limited Liability Partnership, and the final touches to the new agreement the partners had drawn up, had been signed and sealed.

Things seemed to be moving much faster in France which was mostly down to having François on his case. Sooner than he had expected he received a call from the Notaire's office to say that the final documents were ready to sign whenever he wanted.

Ben's last few days in England were frantic, trying to get finalisation on the things being arranged, but eventually everything was sorted and Ben was able to book his single ferry fare from Portsmouth.

Early one Friday morning in the middle of May he set off on his new venture. He had sold his car and purchased a Transit Van into which he had loaded everything from his bedsit along with the furniture which he knew he would need immediately from the storage depot. The remainder of the furniture in storage was being picked up by Pickfords later in the day, and would arrive at his new home on Saturday afternoon, if all went well.

Only a few people knew what he was up to. His colleagues, obviously, and Grunge, but other than that, he had not had time to arrange a farewell party, not that he would really have wanted to anyway. This was his life, and if the truth be known, whilst he was excited about what was facing him, he felt strangely alone as he set off. More alone than he had anticipated, but the adrenalin caused by the excitement of the moment soon overcame his feelings of isolation. He remained totally oblivious of what was happening all around him.

Chapter 17

On the day that Ben departed for France, Mary had arrived home as usual from a busy day at work. It had been an enjoyable day. She was beginning to get on better with her associates at the new salon. They had begun to accept her not so much as their new boss, but as part of the team. The atmosphere was much more relaxed which had, as a consequence, seen much happier clients - and more of them.

Donald had greeted her with a hug and kiss, and told her he was taking her out for the evening if she cared to get ready.

'There's no rush,' he assured her. 'The table is not booked until eight. Hope that's all right?'

'That's lovely,' Mary glowed. She looked around her wardrobe. After four months her pregnancy was beginning to show. She knew she was running out of time to tell Donald the news of the baby yet still she had not plucked up the courage. Each time she got close to it, he would say something nice or give her a cuddle, and each time she would back away from telling him.

She had laid awake on many nights thinking of ways in which she could find the courage to do what she knew she would have to do soon. The little old lady had listened to her, without offering any help except to tell her "not to worry, everything will work out for you in the end".

'Yes, but how?' she would ask her, but there were no more details forthcoming.

On this evening, she busied herself in finding something special to wear, and had a long soak in the bath so that she was thoroughly relaxed for her night out.

It was a beautiful evening, so she chose a long flowing dress which did well at hiding the little seventeen week bulge she was becoming so aware of, but which, thus far, as far as she knew, Donald had not noticed.

Donald told her how lovely she looked, and they drove out into the countryside to a beautiful old thatched tavern, which Donald had visited, he told her, on several previous occasions.

They were greeted by the owner, who seemed to know Donald well, and taken to their table looking out over the beautifully kept gardens to the river. Drinks and a plate of savoury tasters were served. Donald asked her how the salon was progressing and she was able to tell him that she felt much happier there now. She told him about some of the customers that had been in today and some of the funnier anecdotes of recent times such as when Mrs Connors, in the midst of having a wash and blow dry, was interrupted by her ten year old son who came running in to tell her that their dog was eating the new kitten, and could she come home? It was seldom they had conversations like this and they were both beginning to relax in each other's company.

Their starters were served, and Mary realised why Donald was so partial to the place. The flavours and presentation of her starter, a salmon and prawn soufflé, were absolutely divine.

'You like?' Donald asked.

'It's out of this world,' she said. 'I can't wait for the main course.'

'I thought you'd like it. They're working hard to get their first Michelin Star,' he told her.

'I'd have thought they have an excellent chance with food like this,' she enthused.

The conversation continued. As usual, it was all about her. He hardly ever talked about himself, his wife, his past, his present. It was always about her. She had told him a lot about herself, but he had a way of making her divulge a little bit more each time they had evenings like this. This time she was asked

116

again about her family. Did she have any brothers or sisters? Were her parents still alive?

She had told him all of this before, but she told him again that she was an only child, about her father being killed in a road accident, and that she and her mother had never seen or spoken to each other since the accident.

When they were at home, most evenings were spent watching television, and he did not like to be disturbed by conversation when he was concentrating on a programme. Then, when they were out, they talked at length - about her, always about her.

Later in the evening the subject changed to travel. Where had she been? What was her favourite country? Whether she enjoyed foreign food, culture, people. She was relieved when the main course was brought to them. She had chosen a fillet of chicken breast in a white wine sauce with courgettes, mushrooms, tomatoes, leeks and herbs.

But this time it did not stop the conversing. This time he was intent on the conversation continuing. Until unexpectedly his mood changed and looked at her intently.

'Mary,' he started, 'I'm so happy you're more settled now. I was concerned that things might not work out for you. It all looks so much better now. If you're more content, then so am I.'

He was fidgeting with something in his pocket as he spoke.

'So,' he continued, bringing a small black box into view 'I would like to...'

'Donald, no!' Mary said in an urgent whisper. 'Please, don't do this! I can't do this! I'm so sorry.'

'What do you mean, you can't? I could understand don't want to, or not ready to, but can't? Why can't?

The little lady with silver curls appeared in Mary's mind. This is your chance, girl. Handle it carefully, she advised.

'Because I'm pregnant,' Mary announced quietly.

'You're what?' Donald retorted loudly enough for heads to turn towards their table. Then he lowered his voice enough for it not to be overheard. 'That's impossible. I always take precautions. You know that.'

There was no other way to tell him now, thought Mary, so just announced, 'It's not your baby, Donald. It's not your fault at all.'

'Not mine? Then who the hell is the father?' He was in danger of being overheard again, but could not avoid it, such was his bewilderment.

Mary did her best to explain that up until the time she agreed to move in with him, she was having regular sex with Ben, and she was at a loss as to how the precautions she had been taking had let her down. She could see she was wasting her time. Donald just could not handle this. Angry red veins appeared on his forehead, his eyes took on a wild look. He looked as if he might explode or have a heart attack at any moment, but she could also see tears welling up in his eyes, whether of anger or sorrow it was difficult to tell.

He stared across the table at her, motionless, for what seemed like minutes but was probably only seconds, and then got up from his seat, flung his napkin on to the table, knocking over his glass of wine, and stormed over to the reception bar, spoke with the Maitre D, and left without a backwards glance.

Mary was stunned yet not totally surprised. At that instant she could not feel any emotion at all. She just sat there staring at nothing, hearing nothing, feeling nothing. Totally frozen to the moment.

She looked at the plate in front of her, and toyed with a few mouthfuls of the delicious food. What amazed her was that there were no tears, no anger, no panic. She felt she should be crying, but her overwhelming feeling was of relief that at last she had told Donald the truth.

The friendly waiter came over and whispered to her that Donald was not feeling at all well and had decided to go home, but he had said that he wanted her to stay and hoped she would enjoy her meal. They would call a taxi for her whenever she wanted to leave.

Mary thanked him, and decided to try to play it as cool as Donald had. She continued to pick at her meal, in a vain attempt to try to get to terms with what had just happened.

There you are, my dear. It's done now, said a voice in her head.

But what on earth do I do next? Mary asked herself.

Mary continued to fiddle with her food tasting nothing, still unaware of anything or anybody around her.

There was a thundering in her head that would not go away, and she decided that although she could not imagine the outcome of her decision, she had to leave and take her taxi home.

Donald had to stop his car on two occasions on his way home to be physically sick. When, eventually, he arrived at his front door he felt exhausted and drained both physically and emotionally. He could not countenance what had been announced that evening; could not understand how she could have done this to him, and more importantly, could not conceive of any way forward with their relationship.

He took himself to bed, where he just wished he could weep, but he could not, wished he could die but knew he wouldn't, wished it had all been a bad dream but knew it was not.

Upon reaching the house, Mary was terrified of what might be awaiting her.

Donald's car was parked awkwardly in the drive. There was no sign of life. No lights were on, no sounds could be heard.

She crept inside, made herself a cup of hot chocolate, found herself a throw to wrap round her, and slumped into the long, comfortable sofa in the lounge, and sooner than she had expected, drifted into sleep.

It was Donald who woke first the following morning. He threw on his dressing gown and made his way downstairs, trying to regain some semblance of normality for the day ahead. As he passed the lounge, he saw Mary lying on the couch, wrapped in a throw, and he just stood and watched her breathing slowly, oblivious of his presence. Her hair was a mess, signs of mascara were evident on her cheeks, but he just stood and gazed upon her.

He must have stayed there for several minutes, before eventually making his way to the kitchen to grab himself some breakfast.

He was about to sit down, when something made him look up. Mary was leaning against the doorway into the kitchen, looking horribly pale, and, could it be, frightened, like a rabbit in a car's headlights? Neither of them spoke. Neither of them knew what to say.

Eventually it was Donald who made the first move, as he got up from the table, and made his way to where she was standing. Mary stiffened, and stood up straight, not knowing what to expect. Abuse? Perhaps even a slap? She stepped slightly backwards, but Donald caught hold of her hands, and held them tightly.

'Donald, I can't imagine how you must feel. It was probably the biggest mistake I've ever made, and it *was* a mistake. It really was,' she said.

'But you were still sleeping with him while you were going out with me!'

'Yes, I know. This happens all the time doesn't it? A guy falls in love with a married woman, and he knows that every time they say goodnight, she is going home to sleep with her husband. I know I wasn't married to Ben, but it's the same thing really. How could I tell him I no longer wanted to share his bed?'

'Let me ask you this, then. Did you love him more than me?'

'Donald, at this moment I don't really know. I did wonder if he would ask me to stay with him, but he didn't. He didn't say so in so many words, but his attitude was "You've made your bed ..."'

'... So you must lie on it. Yes, I know the saying. But if he *had* asked you to stay, would you have?'

'I don't know, Donald. I wondered that at the time. The situation didn't arise, so I didn't have to decide.'

'I don't know where we go from here, Mary. Maybe in a while I can come to terms with it. I think I might, just might have been able to if it were *my* child, but the thought of playing father to someone else's child - I just don't know whether I can, I just don't know.'

'You're right. It's going to be difficult to put this all behind us.'

'No, we can't "put it behind us". We have to accept what has happened, and live with it. For God's sake, Mary, don't try to hide anything else from me. You are going to have a child. You can't pretend it's not happening. No. Somehow we just have to live with the situation.'

'I didn't know what to expect today, she said. 'I didn't think you would want me here for another day.'

'Perhaps if I hadn't seen you asleep on the sofa, and the state you were in, I might have thought differently. But seeing you there, so obviously unhappy, well...'

'I'd better tidy myself up a bit. I do look a mess, don't I?' Mary said as she caught sight of herself in a mirror.

As she walked away, Donald was deep in thought. He never envisaged, never planned that he would actually fall in love with this girl. That hadn't been the idea at all. He needed her. He still needed her, so as much as he ought to kick her out, he knew he couldn't.

He doubted whether he could accept the situation, but he most certainly had to live with it. She *had* to stay.

Chapter 18

Having arrived late afternoon in Caen, Ben began his journey south to his new home. François had told him that all the final papers were ready to sign, and the "ceremony" could be carried out on Saturday.

This time he had no intention of stopping over en route. Hopefully he would be staying for one more night at Madame Delphine's restaurant so that he would be all set as early as possible the following morning.

As he drove through the now familiar French countryside that evening in May, he felt something unfamiliar within him. He told himself it was the excitement, the nerves, the adrenaline due to the feeling of the unknown developing before him, but none of his explanations was adequate. There was something else. Had he forgotten something of importance? Had he neglected to sign any documents before he left? He was sure it was neither of those things. For once in his life, he had made a list of things that had to be done a few weeks earlier, and everything on that list had been checked and double checked before he left. He tried hard to put the feeling behind him, and just concentrate on the matters in hand. Just enjoy the moment. Imbue the developing sunset with its continuously changing hues of pinks and blues.

It was late in the evening when he arrived at his destination, and he was exhausted. Driving the van had been much slower and more tiring than driving that distance in his car. Madame Delphine saw him walk into the restaurant, and greeted him warmly.

'Yes,' she said in answer to Ben's request for accommodation. 'François said you were driving down tonight, so I put a room aside just in case you needed it.'

'That's fantastic! I'll just go and change. It's not too late to eat is it?'

'Of course not. I'll put something together for you. Something nice!' she said, patting him on the shoulder.

Ben grabbed his overnight bag from the van, went to his room, showered, dressed and went back to the restaurant in record time. He was famished, having only stopped for a coffee and baguette on the way down.

Madame Delphine came to his table with a glass of his favourite wine as soon as he showed up.

'You must be so excited, yes?' she said.

'That's putting it mildly,' Ben returned. 'It's been the longest few weeks of my life, waiting for today. But here I am, and tomorrow, hopefully, everything will be completed, and I can move into my new home and start a new, exciting chapter of my life.'

'Everything will be OK. François has kept me up-to-date with everything each time I have met him. He is a competent man. He has never let me down, and I've been using his services for many years now.'

'And I'm sure it will be reflected in his bill!' Ben joked.

'I'm sure it will!' laughed Madame Delphine as she went to the kitchen to organise his meal.

Still tired from his journey and feeling more relaxed with the meal and wine inside him, Ben was asleep almost before his head hit the pillow.

It certainly was a ceremony.

Ben didn't know whether this had been put on especially for him, or whether it was the normal procedure for the exchange of contracts.

Not at all like the cold impersonal procedures back home; this was truly informal. As well as Ben and François, and, of course Jean-Pierre and his mother, François' wife, Michelina, was there, and, to Ben's utter surprise and delight, so was Madame Delphine.

The *Mairie* was a modern structure, fabricated from timber and glass. Like all the other new buildings in this village it had been designed to blend in with the older structures. It sat pleasantly adjacent to the pretty white painted church with just a small sign on the side facing the road informing that it was *La Mairie*.

Inside, a table had been prepared in one corner of the room, with an assortment of pastries, both sweet and savoury, as well as a selection of fine wines. Ben, being the cynic he was, couldn't help wondering whose bill this had gone on. It was a wonderfully friendly meeting between vendor and purchaser. It seemed there was no hurry to get down to business; it was all greetings, hugs and kisses. Ben realised he had got to get used to this.

Eventually, papers were produced by François' secretary. Once everybody was ready the two parties gathered round the table and the legal business began. It was thorough though not, it seemed, as complex as in England and ended with a cheque being handed to Jean-Pierre who immediately handed it to his mother.

Upon completion there were more kisses and hugs. Ben was made to feel so much part of the lives of these people whom he had only met a few weeks ago, that he became unbelievably emotional and had to suppress tears welling up in his eyes – that, he knew, would be so un-British!

As he left to fetch his van, he was tapped on the shoulder by Jean-Pierre who handed him a wicker basket full of all manner of food. He could see eggs, cheese, fruit and vegetables as well as a couple of bottles of red wine. He was staggered by the gesture, and thanked Jean-Pierre, only to be told that it wasn't really from him, but his mother, who by this time was nowhere to be seen. More tears to be stifled.

Ben took the basket, which was much heavier than he expected. He had to wonder what else was hidden under the top layer that could weigh so much.

By the time he finally got away, it was lunch time. He was too excited to eat, so he drove his van straight to his new home, planning to get organised before the furniture arrived.

It was a beautiful day, warm sunshine clothed everything in its yellow glow, and *La Sanctuaire* looked even more welcoming than he remembered it. He had never really noticed the seasons before. He knew summer followed spring, but he could somehow *feel* the spring here. He just stood and looked at the cottage with a great feeling of contentment. The overgrown hedgerows were no longer dull browns and greens as he had seen them on previous visits. They were now a kaleidoscope of the lemons, purples and pinks of the wild flowers vying for their share of the sun. There was a noticeable aroma of things growing, an earthy smell with an almost imperceptible perfume from the spring flowers. Everything had just gone so well, so smoothly, that he almost expected something to go wrong soon.

Ben looked around at his new home. How good it looked. This was the moment he had waited for. *La Sanctuaire*. His new life started here. Finally he took the few steps toward the cottage, proudly took out the key, gently unlocked the little front door, and entered the living room. François had done him proud. Not only had the electricity been connected for him, even the telephone was working. He could sense the dust, and a slight mustiness in the air so he went round the cottage opening all the windows. His next task was to take out the smaller items of furniture that had been left by the tenants; chairs, small cupboards and the like. These he took over to the dairy cottage until he decided what to do with them all. He hoped the furniture removal men would help him with the heavier stuff.

125

There were, however, some items that were so intrinsically French, the antique oil lamps, two old lithographic prints of Paris, a gilt-framed mirror and an enormous hand painted water jug which he would be keeping to maintain character in his cottage interior.

After countless times of climbing and descending the narrow stairs, carrying armfuls of items across the courtyard, he rather wished he had stopped for lunch, as he was fast realising just how hungry he was, but he kept going until he had removed everything he could. He managed to get one of the old iron-framed beds ready for himself, realising that this would not be one of his most comfortable nights. The mattress was old and lumpy but it was clean, and did not smell of damp or anything unpleasant.

All he had to do now was to wait for the removal men to arrive. He dared not go down the road to find something to eat in case they arrived while he was gone. Instead he stayed on in the cottage, making notes of all the things he had to do to transform it to his taste, soon realising the list was much larger than he had anticipated.

Having moved out so much of the furniture and fittings, he became aware of the true state of the decorations, woodwork and fabrics. It seemed nothing had been done for many years. In fact it was going to need a sizeable makeover to bring it up to a standard he could live with. It was only cosmetic, he told himself, so he could take as long as he wanted. No rush.

It was beginning to get dark when the removal men arrived. They had apparently lost their way more than once, and did not seem too happy about their journey at all. The difficulty they had in manoeuvring their vehicle through the gate did not make matters any better. Ben tried his best to pacify them, but to little avail.

When he asked them to help him out with the old furniture, he thought at first they were going to refuse, but after promising them substantial beer money, they agreed. Then Ben had an idea which brightened them up even more.

'Do we have to unload everything tonight?' he asked. 'What if I can arrange accommodation for you, and we do all this in the morning?'

'Well, that sounds good to us,' was the reply. 'We'll phone the guvnor, and he can make changes to the return ferry times. There's no way we are going to try to drive back tonight. Great idea.'

So while Ben called Madame Delphine, the men telephoned back to their depot, and told them they would have to delay their return. Madame Delphine said she could manage to fit the men in, but they would have to share a room, to which they agreed. The men simply had to wait for a call confirming a ferry booking for the following day.

All that had to be done that evening was to get the men down to Madame Delphine's restaurant, which took just a few minutes, and get them fed. The smells of herb-laden dishes emanating from the kitchen enticed Ben to stay. He had a light meal and a beer, and then made his way back to *La Sanctuaire* after agreeing with the men, who by now were enjoying their meals, that he would pick them up early the following morning.

Ben drove into the courtyard, the first time he had experienced it in the dark, and felt just a little uneasy. It wasn't so much the darkness but the absolute silence which took him by surprise. It almost hurt his ears. I guess I will have to get used to this, he said to himself.

The daytime smells had now been replaced by a chill, dank clamminess. He left the van lights on while he unlocked the front door, and then, having turned the van lights off, he made his way inside.

He immediately cursed himself for taking almost everything over to the dairy. 'This is going to be a pretty bleak night,' he muttered. There was nothing to do other than go to bed, which he did without too much regret as it had been a

127

highly eventful day. Having got to the bedroom, he swore yet again, as he realised that his bedding was in the van! He ventured back downstairs and out into the courtyard, unlocked the van doors, and started to rummage around to find the few things he needed for the night. 'I bet if Mary had organised things...' He left his thoughts unfinished. That was the first time he had really thought about her since arriving here and he wanted to brush it away.

He found the few things he wanted. It was as he was climbing down from the back of the van he thought he saw something scurry across the courtyard to the dairy building. In the darkness it seemed rather large, but he told himself it was probably his imagination running wild. Even so, he hurriedly made his way back into the cottage and upstairs to his minimalist bedroom.

The darkness and the silence kept him awake for some time. Occasional animal noises from the farm up the lane and the eerie sound of what he thought might be owls didn't help, nor did the unyielding mattress on his bed. It was all so alien to him. He had been on holiday in the countryside before, but nowhere like this. He couldn't wait for the morning to come.

It seemed an absolute age before the first signs of light peeked through his window accompanied by the sound of a cockerel crowing nearby. He had not slept much at all, but felt more comfortable with the start of daylight. He turned over and went back to sleep, waking some two hours later. Now he realised that he had left it much later than he had planned. Dressing quickly he made his way to Angers to motivate the crew.

He found the men tucking into their breakfast. 'Where's the egg and bacon, then?' they shouted when they saw him arrive. 'Don't know how you can survive on breakfasts like this!' Ben ignored their comments and joined them at their table hurriedly drinking his bowl of coffee whilst enjoying the fragrance of the recently baked buttery croissants he so loved.

'I'll be back for a proper meal later on. I think I'll deserve it!' he said to Madame Delphine as he left still eating the remains of a croissant he had taken from the table.

Back at the cottage, the men moved swiftly and efficiently, helping Ben to move the beds and the other larger pieces of furniture over to the dairy, and then moving his own pieces into their respective rooms. It took most of the morning, but finally he was installed in his new home. Now he felt more comfortable about things, even though thoughts of the dark, spectral, nights to come still worried him slightly.

The men left soon after mid-day. Having found the basket of goodies that Jean-Pierre had given him the previous day, Ben sorted through it, helping himself to enough things to make a tasty snack and a glass or two of the powerful, home-produced wine. Then he made a start on forming some semblance of order in the cottage, moving this piece to there, and that piece from there to somewhere else, like a life-size game of chess, until he considered it good enough for now.

He started to list the things he would need to buy to make a start on improving the appearance of the place. It turned out to be a protracted list; paint, plaster, timber, a range of tools and a ladder. Good thing I've got the van, he told himself, and decided he would visit *Mr Bricolage,* the large DIY store in Angers, the following day.

Chapter 19

Ben managed to juggle his DIY assignments with his normal day-to-day work. He checked his emails three times every day, and dealt with them as he felt necessary. He also made many trips during the ensuing days to *Mr Bricolage,* each time returning with a van load of tools and materials.

He decided the quickest and easiest way to breathe some life into the interior of the cottage was to paint almost everything white. Hopefully it would reflect what little light came in through the tiny windows. Where beams were exposed he employed some antique oak varnish. White gloss was applied to all of the other woodwork, and slowly his work took effect. The rooms became much lighter, and the place looked clean and cared for once again.

Most of the ground floor was laid with grey slate tiles, which gave authenticity to the building, and kept the cottage pleasantly cool during the warm days. However, they all needed a face-lift, which was painstakingly hard work, scrubbing and scraping each tile individually.

During the cooler parts of the day, early morning or late evening, he worked outside trying to make something of the garden area to the rear of the cottages. He had bought a small Rotavator, and put it to good use, clearing away great piles of brambles, nettles and other unwanted weeds.

During the increasingly warm afternoons he would work on his laptop in the relative cool of the cottage. His business was continuing to do well – much better than he had ever dared hope for, and at the end of every month the net proceeds were divided, one half being reinvested in the business and the other half being split between the three partners.

At the same time he needed to find some builders who could help him do something special with the dairy. After a while trying for himself and getting nowhere, he decided to ask the advice of François who, once again, had the answers.

'I must warn you, they're not the cheapest. But they are reliable and will do a good job for you.' Then he added, 'Ben, you will have to get used to the laid back approach of small business in France. It is just the way things are here. Urgent is not, apparently, in their dictionary. My advice is to always add at least fifty per cent to the time they tell you it will take, and possibly about the same amount to the bill!'

François was right. They didn't turn up on the day that had been agreed, or the next. But eventually they arrived, and Ben showed them his scribbled plans for the building.

There were a few nods and *"d'accords"* and then the boss suggested they take a look at the building. Most of what Ben wanted was, he was told, acceptable. When the boss took him inside he explained to Ben, that as the building was situated on a slope, it would be possible to lower the floor at one end fairly simply, because the foundations of the building went a long way down.

'That way, you see,' said the builder, not attempting a word of English, 'you would be able to put in a mezzanine floor at the far end of the building, and one, or maybe two, extra bedrooms.'

'Wow!' Ben exclaimed. 'That would never have crossed my mind. That would be brilliant. But I expect it would cost a lot of money?'

'*Mais bien sûr!*' But of course, said the Frenchman 'However, if you want to use it as a holiday cottage, you need as many rooms as possible. Is that not right?'

'Absolutely. You will work out a price for me?'

When Ben eventually got the quotation, he was rather surprised. It was a lot more than he had expected, and if

François's words were to be taken literally, it would eat up almost the entire mortgage he had arranged. He thought it through, and decided that as his own business was going so well, he would go ahead with it.

He made an appointment, and took the plans to the Mayor for his approval, and left them with him. He was delighted that after only two weeks the plans were certified, providing there were no structural changes made to the exterior.

Work started in early July, and the whole place quickly became a building site.

Ben was amused by the serious way in which the builders took their elongated lunch breaks. No sitting in vans with a Thermos and a pack of sandwiches. Here, they made room to put up a makeshift table, placed a table cloth on it, and set out the table with plates, cutlery and, of course, the obligatory wine glasses! It was a communal affair, and the men, for most of the time, were engaged in animated discussions about anything and everything.

Occasionally, as Ben wandered past, he was invited to join them and have a glass of wine, but usually he turned down their invitation as he felt he would be intruding in some way. On the few occasions when he did accept their invitation the conversation was light-hearted and jovial. Often comparing English women with their French counterparts, complaining about their wives, moaning about the high rates of taxation, much the same way that builders world-wide do.

As the building progressed, he was frequently taken over to the dairy to be proudly shown the progress, and each time he came away impressed by the quality of the work they were doing.

Regardless of everything that was going on, he did sometimes feel isolated. The cottage seemed so secluded, and he was still struggling to get used to the almost total silence late in the evenings and the animal noises early in the mornings; the crowing cockerel, the cows being taken to the sheds for milking, the occasional sheep or goat bleating away.

He was making every effort to get to know people. He made regular visits to the local *Tabac* for a beer or a snack, and he had joined what turned out to be an active tennis club in the village, where he was made very welcome and was soon involved in playing in local matches. For all that, his life still felt strangely empty.

One Sunday afternoon when he was feeling particularly lonely, Ben took it into his head to make contact with Grunge. She had said she wanted to visit, and although the place was nowhere near to taking visitors, he relished the thought of showing someone his new home, and the delights of the surrounding area. He couldn't think of anyone better.

Fortunately, she was home watching something uninteresting on television.

'Ben!' she exploded. 'How great to hear from you. How's it going?'

Ben filled her in on how things were developing and then said, 'But it would be best if you come and see for yourself.'

'When?' was the reply. No sign of any reason why she couldn't. No glimmer of an excuse. Just "When?".

'When you like,' replied Ben. 'Can you get time off work?'

'No problem. I'm due some summer holiday, and I haven't made any plans. Guess I could come any time. How do I get there?'

'If you can fly to Nantes, I'll pick you up from there. Unless, of course, you want to drive down. Oh, and bring some old clothes with you. The place is in a bit of a mess with all the building work. And I could do with a hand in the garden!'

'Cheeky sod! Hey, I'll let you know in a couple of days. I'll probably fly.'

The call left Ben excited and he felt comforted by the thought that for a few days, at least, he would have some company at the cottage. It would be a relief to use English as a language, too. His French was improving by the day, and yet he still found it a strain sometimes not to be able to express himself freely in his mother tongue.

Ben met her at the airport three weeks later, on a swelteringly hot and humid day at the end of July. As he scoured the people coming off the plane he hardly recognised her, such was the change in her appearance. Gone was the quirky Grunge look, replaced by a much more sophisticated, cool, fashionable Georgina. She looked striking, dressed in a long white top over azure blue trousers. Ben raced over to greet her receiving a hug and a friendly kiss on the cheek. After waiting for a few minutes for her luggage to appear, he picked up her single bag, and they made their way back to the van.

'What's this?' joked Georgina. 'Never thought of you as a white van man!'

'Necessity,' Ben told her, 'I brought a lot of stuff over with me, and now I use it to pick up building materials, and get rid of rubbish. It's a good old work horse. Sorry it's not a bit better. I was expecting the old Grunge and not a cool chick like this.'

'You're not disappointed are you?' she quizzed.

'Not at all. Surprised that's all. As long as it's the same old you underneath.'

They hardly stopped talking during the fifty kilometre journey to Sainte-Justine. Ben need not have worried. Despite the new external appearance, she was still the same funny, likeable, crazy girl.

When they turned into *La Sanctuaire* her eyes widened.

'Christ! This is lovely!' she enthused.

'Well, it will be when it's finished.' The eyes of all of the builders were fixed on her as she got out from the van. She grinned, and waved to them. There was no embarrassing this girl! 'Come on inside. We'll get you installed and then decide what we want to do. How long are you here for, anyway?'

'Just a week, I'm afraid,' she said. 'I couldn't persuade my boss to let me have more than that.'

'Never mind. We'll just have to make the most of it. But I must warn you, I haven't come across anything like *The Dungeon* over here. Even so, I know you'll enjoy what is here, and I'm certain you'll like the friends I've made.'

The ensuing few days were taken up doing the things holiday makers do. The first day was spent in Angers, a tour of the *château*, lunch on board a boat moored on the river and a good look around the shops in the afternoon. Subsequent days they took trips to the coast, some of the surrounding *châteaux*, and ate at many of the region's restaurants. Ben gave little thought to the progress of the dairy that week, although they both got stuck into the garden during the couple of evenings which they decided to spend at the cottage.

Ben was surprised by Georgina's knowledge of gardening, and took her advice on a number of things.

'I'll have to come back when you start planting stuff,' she said.

Ben hoped she meant it.

'What about you?' he asked one day. 'How's your love life? Anybody special yet?'

'Nah! Not me,' she said. 'I'm just happy having friends I like and that like me. Don't want to get serious with anyone, and I can't see how you can have a sexual relationship unless you want it to go further. So I just hang around with people like you, who I know don't want more than to be friends, full stop.'

For their last evening, they decided to stay at the cottage. The day had been spent visiting Angers and the local markets again. Georgina was really struck by the colourful displays and the smells of the fruit and vegetables, and the quality of the merchandise. Each piece of fruit looking as if it had been hand polished.

'It's nearly all produced locally,' Ben told her. 'This is one of the major benefits of living here. I just love coming here on market days, and going away with bags full of good healthy stuff. I never felt like this in Reading.'

'It certainly is something else,' she admitted.

She wasn't so taken, however, with the cheese stalls. Ben went to his favourite stall where they could sample some of the local cheeses before buying.

'Thank God they taste better than they smell!' Georgina said. 'They certainly do honk a bit.'

Having chosen the ingredients; tuna, anchovies, olives, new potatoes and a selection of green salad leaves they took their purchases back to the cottage, and enjoyed preparing a splendid *niçoise* salad together.

Ben couldn't understand why they got on so well. There was not a hint of romance between them; more like brother and sister. And yet they so enjoyed each other's company, could laugh and joke all day.

It was on the last evening she was there, Ben suddenly blurted out, 'Do you know, it's over six months since Mary and I split up. Do you see anything of her?'

Georgina was not ready for this question, and had to think quickly before answering. She so wanted to tell Ben everything but she had made a promise to Mary. She considered that, regardless of the promise, it may well do more harm than good to be honest about it now.

'I haven't seen her for some time. As far as I know she's OK with her beloved Donald.'

Ben didn't pursue his question, but asked another one.

'So. Be honest, what do you think of this place then?'

'Well, you know me, I won't beat about the bush,' glancing around the interior of the cottage, 'I think it could be really beautiful.'

'Could be?'

'Yes. It's so obvious that a bloke has done all this. It's all so minimalistic.' She pointed around at all the new white paint. 'There's no way a woman has had any input. It needs colour, something to grab attention, something warm. At the moment it looks rather like a cell. A comfortable cell, but still a cell. There. You did ask!'

'Thanks!' he said looking at all his painting work. 'No, really. I always appreciate your candour, and I guess you're right. Pity you can't stay so you can put your mark on it.'

'Yes it is. But I'm sure somebody will sooner or later.'

Peculiar thing to say, Ben thought, but didn't follow it up.

The evening was so beautiful they sat outside, down by the stream, until late, sipping their drinks. Together they watched the evening sky change from gold to red and then the blood coloured sun dipping below the horizon. Ben was able to tell her of the wildlife he had spotted while sitting here during the warm, balmy evenings.

'It's simply amazing. I've seen hares dancing around in the field over the other side of the stream. Lizards, of course; they're really common, but I think they're intriguing to watch. Foxes are regular visitors here too. I've seen them coming right up to my front door sometimes. The first time I saw a fox, it was on my first night here, it scared the shit out of me. It was dark, and I wasn't expecting anything like that. But the most impressive of all the animals I've come across was the Beech Marten. I've only ever seen one. I didn't know what it was when I first saw it, but I'm told that's what it was. A really pretty little thing, with a cute little face, and dark brown fur with a white front – looks like a big white bib. I'll tell you something else,' Ben enthused. 'The sunsets are spectacular. I often come down with a bottle of wine, and just sit here watching the night come in. Honestly, the stars and the moon look ten times brighter than they did in Reading. Not that I often used to look at them then.'

Georgina was amazed by his enthusiasm for nature. Hardly the guy she remembered from Reading.

'Sounds like you're really into all this, then,' she said.

'Yeah, I am. I hope to have my own chickens eventually, and maybe even a goat or two to keep the grass down!'

'Have to watch out for the foxes then, I guess.'

'And the Beech Martens, apparently. They like chickens as well, and more especially their eggs.'

'I really envy you – I think. But it's a bit lonely isn't it?'

'That's about the only drawback. I hope, once visitors start arriving, I'll get over that problem.'

The week was over much too soon when Georgina had to return home. Ben returned to his solitary state thinking how nice it would be to have that kind of company as a permanency. How wonderful it would be to have the situation he had had back in Reading, with Mary back in his life and under his roof again, but here.

Chapter 20

Life for Katie and Dave soon settled into a normal routine. Or as near to normal as Katie's life could ever be.

She was happy to return to her job and was greeted by all the girls who wanted to know everything. They learned little from her regarding the wedding and even less about the holiday.

'Those memories are all mine!' she teased with a grin that said far more than her words.

At the end of her first week back at work, she was summoned to her manager's office. Her first reaction was "Oh Christ, what have I done now?"

Her manager told her they were increasingly impressed with her work, and they were offering her a new challenge in the support department.

'You're so good with customers,' she was told, 'we think you'd be an asset to the customer support team.'

'I don't know anything about computers or computing,' she said, terrified by the mere suggestion of such a move.

'No need to worry about that. We'll give you all the training you need, and anyway, our support team have produced scripts that you can follow for just about any problem a customer may have. You'll sail through.'

'I'm not too sure about that,' she said. 'I really enjoy what I do now. I don't really think I want a change.'

'Will you just give it a go for us? The money is much better than you are getting at the moment, and I think the challenge will be good for you.'

'I'm not too worried about the money,' she said. 'It's much more important, as far as I'm concerned, to enjoy the job. But OK, I'll give it a try.'

'That's great. I'll get things organised in the next week or so. I actually think you'll enjoy it. I hope so. You're becoming a valuable member of the team here.'

And with that, the meeting was over, and Katie went back to her desk in reception, not at all enthralled and wondering what the new job really held for her.

When she got home that evening, she told Dave, and he reiterated what her manager had said.

'It'll be a cinch for you,' he told her. 'You are really good with people on the phone.'

Then he announced he was off on one of his journeys again. He didn't know how long it would be and was not too sure exactly where he was going. Tickets were awaiting him at Gatwick. He admitted that for once, he wasn't really looking forward to the trip at all.

'I'll be dealing with people I've never met before,' he told her. 'I'm told they're a bit volatile and someone has upset them. I'm going out there to pick up the pieces and try to calm everything down. No need to worry, though. I can well look after myself. But will you promise me that if I'm gone for longer than usual you won't worry, and more importantly, I don't want my father to be worried either. He's not as well as he makes out, and the last thing he needs is to fret about me.'

'All sounds rather sinister,' Katie said, looking worried already. 'How long do you think you'll be away? Any idea?' she asked.

'Difficult to say,' Dave told her, putting his arm round her shoulder. 'It shouldn't be much more than a week or two. Might be more, might be less. I really don't know.'

They went to bed early that evening. Once they were cuddled up together in bed, Dave was aware of Katie giggling, her whole body shaking, and then her laughing so much that at one point he thought she was going to choke.

'What's so funny?' he asked her.

'I was just remembering the last day of our holiday, what happened in that field,' she replied, tears of laughter running down her face.

Katie had been determined to find somewhere where they could have sex *al fresco,* something she had not managed to experience before. They had driven miles around country lanes until they found a location which they both thought looked suitable. They had found themselves in a narrow lane so they parked the car and made their way through a wide gate into a field which seemed to be far enough away from roads and footpaths for their needs.

They had crossed the field to the far side, where the field sloped away. Secluded by a hedge, Katie laid a blanket on the ground and after minimal foreplay, stripped off and made love with the sun shining down on them. What they didn't know was that just the other side of the hedge was where a group of fourteen and fifteen year old schoolboys were dropped off after school athletics. When the boys alighted from their bus they were aware of something happening on the other side of the hedge. Drawn by the squeals of delight emanating from Katie as she rode Dave cowboy style, first one and then the whole group went over to the hedge from where they could see everything going on. When the pair reached their noisy climax, there were hearty cheers from the boys.

They had calmly dressed, gathered up their things and walked nonchalantly back to their car where they had collapsed in a heap of laughter. 'Well, that should help them with their biology,' Katie had said.

A week later Dave was off on his travels and, on the same day, Katie started her new job.

141

She found the training difficult, confusing and not too helpful, so she persevered. Within a few days she was carrying out her new tasks, albeit with someone looking over her shoulder.

The manager was pleased with her, and they had not had any bad reports back from customers. However, Katie was aware, by the tone of some of the male callers, that they didn't think a woman could do this job as well as a man. How could a girl know the complexities of computer programs? What concerned her even more was the occasional sly laughter going on behind her from some of the other support guys which she suspected was at her expense.

You're getting paranoid, she told herself. Even so it didn't take long for her to realise this was not going to be the job for her and at the end of the second week she went to see her manager.

'I'm sorry,' she started, 'but I'm not happy about the new post. Is there any chance of going back to what I was doing before, in reception?'

She was surprised when she was told her old job had been taken by the Managing Director's daughter who had just dropped out of university. If she were to read between the lines, she had been moved, not, as she had been told, because of her performance; much more likely because the M.D. wanted a job for his little girl.

'Well, if that's the case I won't be staying. I'll have my resignation on your desk in the morning. I think this stinks.'

She stormed out of the office, went back to her department, grabbed her coat and walked, fuming, out of the building.

She served her notice period stoically, ignoring the comments being made about her. Secretly she was counting the days, the hours to her being free from the place. Her manager did take her aside one day, and assured her that she would get a glowing reference from him, if that was any consolation, to which Katie merely grunted.

A week later a leaving party was arranged for her by some of her female colleagues, and she felt a lot better leaving on a higher note.

It was late that night when she got home and took herself off to bed, having had rather more to drink than she was used to.

When she got up late the following morning she had a curious feeling that something was not as it should be. She looked around her and could see nothing wrong, yet she still felt uneasy and sensed that someone had been in the house. She started noticing that things had been moved and carefully replaced in an attempt to hide the signs of intrusion. Some photographs were facing different ways, ornaments were not in their usual places and when she went to her bedroom, items in the drawers had been disturbed.

Was it Dave? Had he come home yesterday? But why would he be going through her drawers, and moving things? He'd never done anything like that before. And where was he? It was now three weeks since he had left and she still had no idea where he was.

There was no sign of a break-in. Whoever had done this must have had keys, and had tried to cover the fact that they had been there. She stood in the middle of the lounge trying to make sense of what was happening.

The phone rang, and startled her.

'Hello,' she said her voice a bit unsteady.

'Is Dave there?'

'No. He's away.'

'Can you tell me where he is?'

''Fraid not. I don't even know myself. Can I ask who you are?' She was going to ask for the caller's number so that she could call him back if Dave contacted her but the phone went dead. She checked on 1471, only to be told that the caller's number had been withheld.

She went to call Dave using the land line, and then thought that with all this cloak and dagger stuff going on, it would be

143

better to use her mobile, so the call could not be traced back to the house.

She dialled the number. There was no reply, no answering service. It was dead.

She searched Yellow Pages for a locksmith, and found one who could change her locks and make the place a bit more secure that day.

'You really ought to report this to the police,' she was told after she had relayed what had happened. 'If somebody has got keys to your house, and used them without your permission it amounts to burglary. I do advise you to call them and let them have a look around.'

'Yes, perhaps I will,' Katie lied. She knew the last thing Dave would want would be the police being involved.

She felt a bit easier knowing that whoever it was in the house the previous day would find it a lot more difficult to gain entrance again. Nevertheless, she was still worried that she could not even leave a message for Dave, and was becoming increasingly panicky by what was happening.

For the rest of the day she decided to stay indoors. After all, there was a bit of tidying up to do, and it was best that she stayed at home just in case anything else should develop.

Other than two more phone calls from people, different people she thought, trying to get hold of Dave, nothing else transpired that day.

Every day there were phone calls asking for Dave which kept her nerves rattling. Each caller getting increasingly annoyed when she kept repeating that she didn't know his whereabouts. Not one of her many attempts to reach Dave on his mobile was successful. She presumed he was in some remote part of the world where there were little or no signals, and his business was taking longer than he had expected.

After leaving SRX Solutions she had taken on a temporary job as a receptionist for a group of solicitors and enjoyed the variation of tasks she was given. She also made a number of new acquaintances. She was covering holiday leave and the job was over in just a few weeks.

Katie went out for a few drinks one evening in mid-September with some of the girls from the office. They had had a really good time, moving on to a club when the pub closed. Katie found herself unwinding, caught up with the noise, the music and the alcohol and it was the early hours of the morning before she made her way home. She decided to call a cab, and arrived at her front door sometime after two o'clock.

Tomorrow, she told herself in her half-drunken state, I have got to do something about Dave. She remembered Dave saying not to tell his father anything, but she thought she would *have* to tell him, if only to see what he suggested. Perhaps they would have to inform the police?

It was a cloudy night with the moon occasionally poking its pale face through the dark clouds that moved quickly across the sky. The orange street light emitted little useful light. It took her a few moments to open her shoulder bag.

As she fumbled in her handbag for her keys, an arm was fixed around her throat from behind, and a gloved hand placed over her mouth. Her attempts to struggle were in vain. She was no match for the person holding her.

Chapter 21

Dave's flight from London Gatwick to Mother Teresa airport at Riinas had been comfortable enough but when the plane touched down Dave felt extremely nervous – more than the usual adrenaline rush he often went through. He had a strangely uncomfortable feeling about this trip, and was keen to make the return trip just as soon as he could.

He didn't like what he was doing, but was beholden to a group of people who were involved in human trafficking. He knew they could easily get him into serious trouble because of their knowledge of his past. He had tried many times to escape from their hold on him but to no avail. It was like being blackmailed. Always at their beck and call.

'Thank you Mr Westerman' the customs clerk said as he handed back Dave's false passport. 'Are you here on business?'

'Yes,' lied Dave. 'I work for a British travel agency, and I am doing some research on your holiday resorts.'

'Well, I hope you enjoy your trip. How long will you be staying?'

'About a week, I guess.'

He sought out a taxi to take him to Tirana, Albania's capital city and arrived there about twenty minutes later.

Dave saw that, like many other Eastern European cities, Tirana was a mixture of the old and the startlingly new. Tower blocks of shining steel and glass offices and apartments peered down on to sprawling areas where the old, dilapidated tower blocks had been painted in bright, gaudy colours. The city centre portrayed a feeling of opulence. There were huge hotels, ultra-modern museums and office complexes. The streets were busy with cars, a surprising number of top-of-the-range saloons, but a fair proportion of old wrecks of vehicles, clearly highlighting the class divide. But Dave was not here to sight see. His business was rather more portentous.

He had to wait for over two hours for his train to Vloras, a journey of almost 150 kilometres. When the train came into the platform he found a seat in one of the compartments, and did his best to relax. He hated travelling like this, surrounded by people chattering, not being able to understand a word that was being said. He shut his eyes and tried to ignore the noise going on all around him. They seemed to be an excitable crowd. The poverty was there to be seen, to be felt. What were these people, a preponderance of women and children, doing on the train? Where had they come from? Where were they going?

As the train, pulled by an ancient, smelly diesel locomotive, made its punctuated journey through the suburbs of Tirana, many of the passengers alighted from the carriage, and the clamour of conversation subsided.

Once out of the suburbs the train increased its speed. Dave stared out of the window at the rugged mountainous landscape, surprised by the vastness of uninhabited, uninhabitable land. A small township occasionally flashed past as the train raced towards its destination, then more miles of grey, slate-like landscape. Three hours later, he arrived at Vloras, a holiday resort on the Adriatic Coast.

He had been pre-booked into the Hotel Adriatix, and when he eventually found it, he paid for the first two nights of his stay. Making his way to his room, he slumped down onto a remarkably comfortable bed.

He had nothing to do now until the following morning. After a short rest he took the opportunity to take a look at this coastal town and was overwhelmed by its rugged beauty. The mountainous terrain was almost white, like chalk, and the few green shrubs and trees looked as if they were struggling to survive. Many of the hotels and houses were built into the rocky

147

cliffs running down into the Adriatic Sea. Small sandy coves lay at the base of towering cliffs, some of bare grey rock, others covered in a green carpet of grass and shrubs.

Compared to some of the towns he had passed through in the train, Vloras was much wealthier, and it was busy with both locals and tourists frequenting the many bars and restaurants dotted around the bays. Young people gathered in groups, in the smart town centre and on the beaches. Dave thought that he could well be in any European coastal resort. The town was, for the most part, modern, with an enormous Trade Centre. Luxury hotels were to be found around the town, and a diverse selection of restaurants occupied most corners. It was surprisingly lively. Not what he had expected at all.

Dave took his time taking in the sights and sounds. Only on one occasion did he hear English being spoken which was strange given the number of British cars he had seen. For all the similarity to other European cities, he felt strangely alone, unnerved. Fortunately, there was a strong Italian presence here, Italy being only a short distance across the Adriatic Sea. In the early evening he found a small Italian restaurant where he enjoyed a pleasant, if unusual, gnocchi washed down with some local beer.

Later that evening, he made his way back to his hotel. He doubted he would sleep.

His appointment the following morning was with a man he had never met before called Bekim. The meeting was in Auloa Park, within walking distance of the hotel, at 10 o'clock. He knew no more except that he was to collect a substantial amount of US dollars and sufficient details and photographs to enable the forgers to create passports.

Auloa Park was a run-down area that might once have been a park, but was now a scrubby, deserted and cheerless place. Bekim was waiting for him and beckoned him to a long-abandoned building. Bekim was smartly dressed in a blue denim jacket and cream chinos. He wore a smart black beard, and his eyes seemed friendly.

Bekim explained they had to meet in this way as there was an organisation in Vloras who were trying to stamp out this kind of operation, so he had to take every precaution.

He was eager to tell Dave of the dangers of living in the area. Dave was equally eager to get away. The business was transacted swiftly and affably. Dave was handed the money he had come to collect, along with all the necessary details and photographs of the people requiring the passports. He carefully packed everything into the backpack that he was carrying and wished Bekim good luck.

'How long will this take?' Bekim asked as he was about to walk away.

'You should hear something within a couple of weeks, I expect.'

Dave turned and walked down the narrow lane away from the park, pleasantly surprised how easily the meeting had gone. The pathway was of loose gravel and he was acutely aware of the noise his footsteps were making. At one point he stopped walking because he thought he heard other footsteps behind him.

Must have been echoes, he told himself.

A few metres further the pathway became quite steep. Now he was certain he heard something in the thick undergrowth to his left. He definitely hadn't imagined that. Instinctively, he increased his pace.

Rounding a slight bend he was confronted by a group of five men. They appeared to know exactly who he was and why he was there.

The group surrounded him.

Grabbing Dave fiercely by his arm, the spokesman pointed to the oldest man in the group.

'Your people took this man's grand-daughter to England. He paid them a lot of money. They promised him that she would be safe, told him that they would find work for her. But there was no work there,' he told Dave. 'She was made to be a prostitute, and was abused every day. She had no freedom; she was not even allowed to call home. She was a prisoner. Much better if she had stayed here. And now you are here again, making the same arrangements for other people,' he yelled.

Dave held up his free hand in front of him.

'No. Hang on. I'm not involved with that at all. I just arrange passports. That is all.'

Dave thought they must be able to hear his heart beating.

'But that is the start of the process, isn't it? You start things by getting passports for these poor people, and then...' was the angry, accusing reply.

'Maybe,' Dave interrupted, trying not to let his voice falter, 'but I don't have anything to do with the transporting of the people or what happens to them in the UK. My job is done.'

The man turned to his attendant friends, and presumably told them what had been said. Dave was aware of the angry, animated conversation going on and the indignation growing amongst them. He was also conscious of the beads of perspiration running down the side of his face. It seemed an age before the man broke away from the group and came back to him.

Wearing an evil looking smile, his white teeth shining out from his swarthy, unshaven face, the man looked Dave straight in the eyes.

Dave was terrified. He could feel his blood coursing through his veins. Was this the end?

'OK,' the man said quietly, his face now so close that Dave could smell his sour breath. 'We accept what you are saying. You can go,' and gestured for Dave to continue down the hill.

Dave found it difficult to breathe. He took a deep breath in and exhaled slowly, hesitantly walking away from them, down the track towards the exit of the park. Gradually he increased his speed, and was almost running when the first shot caught him in his left shoulder. It stung, but did not stop him from running. The second shot hit his left thigh, and all but paralysed him, now his adrenaline kicked in enabling him to keep moving. He attempted to run but couldn't summon the energy. The third shot entered his body at the base of his skull.

Nothing.

His killers ran to where he had fallen, took everything they could find on his person along with the backpack containing the money he had been given. They were meticulous, checking every pocket, tearing out every label from his clothes and finally kicking his body off the path down into a deep ravine, watching with grins on their faces, clenched fists reaching to the sky.

Dust from the path was kicked over the bloodstains.

Walking back to the park, they laughed in celebration, holding their spoils high in the air.

'It's so easy,' the leader said. 'So bloody easy.'

Chapter 22

Katie was dragged hastily backwards down the three steps that led from her front door, her upper body being held firm by her captors. A few metres down the road she was blindfolded then roughly bundled into a large car and told in no uncertain terms that if she valued her life she would keep quiet. Katie knew she had little choice in the matter and saw no point in yelling. Her heart was pounding in her chest. She sat still, wondering what on earth was going on. She presumed this must have something to do with Dave, but what could they possibly want with her? She couldn't tell them anything. She was petrified. Were these the same people who had been in her house? What were they going to do to her?

Despite her state of terror, she was determined not to show it. She would not scream. She would certainly not cry. That would give all the wrong signals. She remembered a saying that she learned from her foster parents: *Smile – It confuses people!*

The journey in the car was not a long one, and before she had time to think, she was pulled out of the car, her blindfold was removed and she found herself in what she presumed to be a lock up garage. Plain grey breeze block walls, the only light coming from a single bulb swaying on its flex from the ceiling. There were three men, their faces hidden by balaclavas. One appeared to be English and two others, who were of much bigger build and who had trouble speaking more than a few words of broken English. It seemed it was they who were in charge of the operation.

The English guy spoke first.

'Look, all we want to know is where Dave is. It's urgent that we contact him. We can't believe you don't know where he is. You must've been in contact with him?'

'I wish I could help you,' Katie almost whispered, such was her fear. 'I've been trying loads of times to reach him on his mobile to leave a message. There is no reply, no voicemail, no answering service. His phone is dead. I've tried and tried. I just don't know where he is. I haven't a clue.'

'So, he not tell where he going?' It was the smaller of the two foreign ones, not so much asking a question, as stating a fact.

'No. He never tells me where he's going or what he's doing when he goes away. Even so, I have always been able to contact him before if I needed to. He's always secretive about what he does. I don't ask questions.'

'That's a pity. Perhaps you should ask the questions, yes?'

'Maybe I should, but I don't.'

'Well perhaps a night in the dark here on your own might help you to help us, huh? Because one way or another, lady, you are going to help us to find him. Do you understand?' the Englishman said.

'I don't know where he is!' Katie almost shouted at the man. Then the smaller man spoke again.

'Well, perhaps you start thinking. Where he go before? You never seen travel tickets? Visa statements? Bank statements? Of course you have. You are trying to hide these things from us.'

'I'm not,' Katie started to protest, only to receive a sharp slap around her face.

'So far we've been pleasant, now we're getting pissed off with you. If you want to avoid a lot more discomfort we suggest you search your tiny brain to remember something, anything that might give us a clue to where he is,' the Englishman said.

The slap had come from the smaller of the foreigners. The larger third man just stood and watched. Maybe he didn't speak any English at all? thought Katie. Suddenly the larger man called the other two over to a corner, and there was much discussion between them, all in a language Katie didn't recognise - was it Russian? Sounded something like that, but just for a fleeting moment Katie saw a funny side to it.

Why did they bother to go away from her into a corner to talk when they were speaking in a language she was unlikely to understand? she thought, and that single thought seemed to lighten her darkness just a little.

When they came back to her they told her it had been decided that she would not be left here. 'We have much better plans for you.'

Urgent calls were made on their mobile phones, and then the English speaking one came over to her, and took her handbag from her.

'Piss off!' Katie said as she went to put up a fight but the bag was snatched away from her. The contents were tipped out onto a bench to one side of the garage.

From it they took her mobile phone, her purse containing her credit cards, her driving licence, a few notes, but not much else. Everything else they stuffed back into her bag and threw it back to her.

The larger man left the garage, and returned a few minutes later with some food, and offered her a kebab. 'I should take it,' she was advised by the English guy. 'It could be all you get to eat for a while.' Katie was not fond of kebabs, nevertheless took heed of the advice and nibbled at it.

A short while later she was blindfolded again and hastily bundled back into the car, and they went racing off to another unknown destination. This time the journey was longer and there was on-going, excitable conversation between the men, albeit indecipherable by Katie. It felt as if they were travelling on a motorway. Which one and in which direction, she had no idea.

By the excited sound of their voices it seemed as if they had differences of opinion about something. She tried listening to see if she could possibly make some sense of what was being said, but soon gave up.

Her mind was in chaos. How was she ever going to get out of this? They had taken everything she would need to have any chance of escape. Other than a meagre amount of make-up, all she had been left with were a few coins. Perhaps she might be able to get away and make a phone call?

Eventually the car appeared to turn off the motorway, continuing at a slower pace until they turned into what transpired to be a small storage unit, presumably on an industrial estate. She was allowed out of the car, and her blindfold was once again removed. Inside the unit there were three white vans of different sizes, and dozens of packing cases piled up along one side of the building. Two more men were busy unloading one of the vans. They were not disguised in any way. Katie took a good look at them and made mental notes.

'Bit unusual taking paying customers in this direction, eh?' said the Englishman who had been in the car. The reply was also in English, but Katie was too far away from them and unable to take in any detail. She was offered the use of the toilets, given a bottle of *Fanta* and then pushed up into the back of one of the vans towards the front end. She was not blindfolded and was able to see what was going on. To her surprise, a door in the front wall of the van was opened. It was so well camouflaged she had not even noticed it.

Katie was pushed into a seat in this small compartment, and firmly strapped in.

'Don't waste your time trying to yell for help, there's no way anybody will hear you,' she was told. The door was then shut, and she could hear crates being loaded into the back of the van. She was well and truly locked in, and unable to do anything about it.

The only light to her compartment was from a small section of a roof light. When she became accustomed to the light, Katie could see there were five seats across the width of the van, facing backwards, and she was in the centre one. No chance, then, of even getting to the side of the van to bang on the walls.

The only indication she had as to where they were going was by the light coming through the roof light. At first there was a general orange aura from the sodium street lights, then the flashing of whiter lights as they turned on to roads leading out of town. The street lights disappeared altogether as they drove further into countryside. The sensation of speed increased and there were infrequent, sporadic yellow flashes of more sodium lights. She presumed they were travelling on a motorway.

Things were happening so fast that it was all she could do to keep up with it. What did they mean about better plans for her? What were they planning to do with her? It was getting late, and Katie decided that as there was nothing she could do about the situation she must try to relax. She couldn't. She tried to instil all the voices into her brain. She re-visited every stage of the day. Every last detail of her nightmare was analysed. Were there any names? Not that she could recall. She almost screamed at herself that she had not noticed any of the vehicle number plates. Her major worry was what they wanted her for. What were they going to do to her? If she couldn't help them to find Dave, what would happen to her? Her head was a kaleidoscope of sounds, sights and smells. She wanted it to stop, but it wouldn't.

She must have fallen asleep for it was sometime later that she was awakened by a strange sensation. The van's engine was no longer running, and yet she was feeling movement.

'Christ almighty!' she almost yelled to herself. 'I think I'm on a boat. Where the hell are they taking me?'

It was not a long crossing. Must be Dover to Calais, she told herself, not that the information helped a lot. Once again she felt she had to put as many pieces of this jigsaw together, remember as many little clues as she could. She had tried to retain what images she could of her first three captors, though with their balaclavas, it was a vague description. Who was driving the van she did not know, or even whether there was more than one person involved.

The movements stopped. They were disembarking. If she screamed loudly, would anyone hear her in the bedlam of the docks? She doubted it, and it could cause her some nasty repercussions if she tried. As difficult as it was, she decided to remain as calm as she could be under the circumstances, and to see how things progressed, waiting all the time for that one opportunity to slip away.

Not far down the road, the vehicle stopped, and there were movements in the back of the van. Her camouflaged door was opened, and she was untied from her seat.

'Now, don't try anyssing stupid. Zis is just a toilet stop, nussing more. Try anyssing brave and you vill very much regret it,' she was warned. This was a different voice to any of the ones she had heard previously. At least they speak some English, she thought to herself.

She did not reply to the warning. She was man-handled past the crates and boxes in the van, and made to jump down onto the grass where they had parked the van. It was obviously early morning. Everything was still, the sun only now beginning to show itself over the horizon.

Two men held her in a tight grip as she was marched to an area where there were toilets.

She was warned again not to even think of getting away, as she wouldn't get far, and she would be made to regret it if she did.

'No problem,' she heard herself saying, much more calmly than she actually felt, 'I know when I'm beaten.'

She tried to get some clue as to where they were. It was almost certainly France. This much was clear by the antiquity of the toilet. She had heard about these things. Just a hole in the ground, a metal bar to hold onto and almost impossible to deal with in such a lack of light. She squatted down where she thought the hole might be, hoping that her wee was going down the hole and not saturating her clothes. The stench in there was appalling. She wanted to get back into the fresh air as quickly as she could. As she appeared from the toilet block she was grabbed again by her captors. Then it was back to the van, and to her seat. She was relieved that this time she was not tied in so tightly, so she would feel a little more comfortable.

Other than a stop for fuel, they did not stop again until they reached their destination. She had lost track of time although she knew it had taken several hours. She felt stiff and uncomfortable and she now had no clue at all as to her whereabouts.

When they finally arrived she was taken from the van and led out to a narrow street then man-handled across the street and up a short flight of steps. Once inside the building, she had the first real chance to see her captors, two guys, probably in their late twenties, dressed casually in jeans and sweat shirts. They were joined by a third man who spoke really poor English and sounded similar to her initial abductors.

She was told this third man would be looking after her until such time as they found, or at least made contact with Dave.

It must have been an hour later that a fourth man arrived. He was older than the others, and more smartly dressed. His black hair had been styled, his beard neatly trimmed. There was a lot of secretive talking between them. The older man, whilst conversing with the others, was looking all the time at Katie. If only she could understand everything that was being said. It obviously involved her. Minute by minute her nerves became more on edge. She felt sick. She was sweating yet shivering with fright.

Eventually the recently arrived man turned from the other three and came over to where Katie was standing. After looking at her from all angles, he spoke in very good English.

'You could speed things up a lot,' he told her, 'by trying to give us some idea of where we should start looking for your husband. It's him that got you into this mess, so you don't exactly owe him any favours do you?'

'I keep telling you …' she started only to be told to shut up.

'Yeah, yeah, we know all of that. The trouble is we don't believe you. Well now it's up to you, sweetheart. You help us, we'll help you. You see, Dave owes us a lot of money. Now, we know that he collected the money. Then he disappeared. So either you help us, or you will be paying us the money he owes us.'

'I haven't got any money.'

'I know. But you are a very beautiful girl, and you could easily earn enough to pay your husband's debts.'

'What? How could... Oh, my God! You mean...?'

'Yes, that's exactly what I mean...'

He came to face her, reached out and held her head up with his hands under her chin so that she had to look him in the eyes. 'Such a pretty face! So perhaps now you see that we mean business. Nobody cheats us out of money. Nobody plays silly games with us.' He flung her head to one side as he let go of her face.

'I'll be in touch in a few days,' he said to the other men, and with that strode out of the room. 'Take good care of her.'

Katie looked around. The room she was in was too filthy to be put into words. There were used take-away cartons, pizza boxes, and dozens of drink cans littering every surface and much of the floor. A single light, framed in a shade that was once cream, glowed bravely over a table, and there was not one chair that could be used before first discarding a selection of papers and magazines or discarded food containers. The furniture was old and tatty, and there was a foul stench permeating the air, but at least there was a meagre element of comfort here. She was offered coffee and some toast, which she accepted gratefully. The coffee was black and cheap, the toast was burnt, but it was food and drink which she desperately needed.

There was a lot of talking between the three men. It was obvious her new minder was not too happy about the situation. He was a big man, well over six feet tall, wearing a supposed-to-

159

be-white vest and exhibiting a rather overweight, hirsute body. His head was shaven and he sported an unkempt black beard. She got the impression that he had not been told of her arrival, and was far from happy that he had the job of looking after her.

Eventually things calmed down. She was shown to the room where she would be sleeping, and the bathroom. Yet more warnings about the futility of escape were made, and when she finally went to her room, she heard a key turn in the lock. She tried the windows, only to find that they were firmly shuttered, and locked.

The same all-pervading smell was present here as well. It reminded her of dead fish. She tried to put the thought of rats to the back of her mind.

The room contained four bunk beds. Katie chose the only one with covers on it. It was filthy and covered in all manner of stains, but it might just keep her warm.

She lay exhausted on the bed, which was not uncomfortable, but certainly not clean. Within minutes, through sheer fatigue, she fell into a fitful sleep, waking every few hours re-living some part or the other of the past twenty four hours, each time cursing Dave for getting her into this mess.

She determined that night that her first and only strategy must be to get out of this place, and quickly. The alternative was too awful to think about.

Chapter 23

During September the building work at *La Sanctuaire* had gone on apace, and Ben could at last see things developing nicely. New septic tanks had been installed, and the drainage and utilities had all been completed and covered in. It no longer looked like a building site.

Ben was thrilled with the work going on in the dairy and went to look inside every day when the workmen had left. It was more than he could have wished for and certainly more than he could have imagined. He could see the whole concept taking shape day by day.

Taking on board what Georgina had said, he had done his best to instil some colour into the rooms of the cottage. He didn't really understand what she had meant, and even if he did, how did he go about creating it? He bought a few brightly coloured cushions, some large vases and pots, found a couple of prints he liked and hung them on the walls. That was about as far as his creativity took him.

He still sometimes felt lonely but had made great efforts to overcome this by getting more involved in the local tennis club and gym. He frequently visited Madame Delphine for a meal with some of his new friends. Now he knew of Madame Delphine's history, he could see for himself much more of the detail of the place, and how so much effort had been put into the décor to create the risqué atmosphere that filled the restaurant.

With autumn fast approaching, he busied himself in the garden, although he was aware of how little he knew about the subject. There was not much he could do. He had divided the area into plots down either side where he would eventually want to grow his produce. He knew he wanted to grow some soft fruits, and considered salad-type stuff and winter greens should be easy enough to grow, so he allowed areas for them and dug over the soil to prepare for planting when the time came.

His current vision was to develop a pleasant patio area at the far end of the garden, down by the stream. He had started by laying paving stones, installing some white fencing panels around the perimeter and creating an area for a flower bed around the edge inside the fencing. He could envisage many a balmy summer evening down there with a glass or two of wine. He made a mental note to do some research into how he could attract more local wildlife to that part of his garden.

All-in-all, he had plenty to occupy his time as the summer turned slowly to autumn. He had never seen France at this time of the year, and the colours were amazing. The countryside behind *La Sanctuaire* ran gradually down into a wide valley, each field bounded by trees and hedgerows. Each day the colours changed from green, through yellows and oranges to deep reds and maroons.

As he got to know more people in Sainte-Justine, he had been approached by those who wanted to use his expertise in computing, and had even been asked by a *Lycée* in a nearby town to help with English tuition for their older students. He did not accept either offer as he didn't want to take on anything else at that moment. He did, however, get involved in some informal sessions with local people who wanted to improve their English. This entailed visiting other people's homes and he had many a happy evening getting to know his neighbours and learning more about life in France.

His business was taking up more of his time, with the volume of users increasing all the time, although something seemed to be going wrong. There were a growing number of complaints from clients that their web sites were not staying at the top level on some of the search engines. Ben had reported this to his colleagues, and was told they were aware of the problem, and were "working their butts off trying to put it right".

Suddenly the world that had been ticking away so nicely stopped.

He sat and stared at the text on his screen, mesmerised, hardly believing what he was seeing.

Message from Katie the subject line of the email said.

Ben clicked on the subject and saw:

"I receive this message on a piece of paper from lady in street today. It say: *Ben, I need your help. You did say "if I needed you." And I do!! Please help me. I don't even know where I am, but please try to find me and get me out of here! Katie.* I not know any more than that."

Could it be a joke? He immediately dismissed that thought from his mind. No. This was genuine. This was serious. What had the silly girl done now?

He responded to the email immediately, asking who the sender was, and where he was located, and could he describe the girl.

The reply told Ben that the emailer was Polish, his name was Gerek Kowalski, and he spent a lot of his time in an internet café in Frankfurt. That was where he had been handed the note. His description of Katie was accurate enough to be believed.

Ben emailed again to ask if he had seen her since he was given the note, and he replied that he had not. But he would let Ben know if he saw her again.

Asking for more detail, Ben learned that when she handed the note to Gerek outside the café, she had been with a man, who had hold of her by her arm. 'But I not think they were friends,' he added.

Ben felt his life had suddenly been put on hold.

I will come to Frankfurt in a few days and I will meet you there, Ben wrote to Gerek. *I will try to work something out. Are you there every day?*

Gerek confirmed that he worked at the café and was there for a majority of the time most days.

Ben could think of nothing else now. He was in no doubt this was connected in some way with Dave Atkinson. I told her he was trouble, he screamed in his head.

He tried to picture Katie being marched down the road by some burly bloke. The more he thought about it, the more concerned, the more furious, he became. Not so much with her captors, but with her husband. How could Dave allow this to happen? Why was it she was asking for *his* help, when it should be Dave getting her out of this mess? He became increasingly worried about her, scared for her. How much danger was she in?

That evening he managed to book a seat on the TGV to Paris from Angers and a flight from there to Frankfurt.

He had little sleep that night and the following morning he told the workmen he had to go away for a few days, and they were to carry on in his absence, and they would be paid up to date as soon as he returned.

He packed a few clothes and toiletries, and, with his laptop slung over his shoulder, made the now familiar journey to Angers. He boarded the train for the ninety minute high speed journey to Paris and from there a connection to Charles de Gaulle airport. There was the usual wait for about an hour before boarding a flight to Frankfurt. While sitting in the departure lounge and throughout the journey he could not get the picture out of his mind of Katie being trudged down a road in Frankfurt. He was urging the plane to get there quicker.

He was walking into the unknown with no preconceived plans. He had no idea what he was going to discover, or how he was going to find and then liberate Katie, but he had to try. He had promised the girl, this silly, silly girl. Somehow he had to succeed.

It's like being a bloody knight in shining armour, he thought. But I don't know whether I'm cut out for it. We'll just have to wait and see.

Ben arrived at Frankfurt am Main airport in the middle of the afternoon. He took the shuttle bus from the airport into the City, then the U-Bahn to Haupt-Wache and finally made his way to Tongesgasse where the Internet café was situated.

The signs of September were all around. The sky was heavy with cloud and the trees that lined the street were losing some of their golden leaves forming a carpet of colour along the pavements.

His adrenaline was pumping as he went into the café and asked for Gerek Kowalski. He was informed that he was not in today but would be there the following morning. He asked whether anybody knew about the girl that Gerek had seen, but nobody seemed to recall anything.

Ben left the café, walking up and down Tongesgasse, picturing Katie being taken down here. Which way? Where were they going? More importantly, where had they come from?

She's a clever girl, finding a way to get a message to me through an Internet café, he thought.

Ben was frustrated that his detective work could not start straight away. He knew there was nothing more he could do that day. Just a short distance away, he found a Miramar Hotel, and booked in. He told the receptionist he did not know the length of his stay. He agreed he would keep them informed, and would settle up every couple of days.

His room was basic but comfortable. He took a shower then went back out to get a feeling of the surroundings. He wanted to be absolutely sure of the streets in relation to the Internet café, and wandered round and round again, making notes of which side roads linked to others.

Soon he realised that he was getting hungry and started to look for somewhere to eat.

Ben had been to Frankfurt once before, earlier in his life and his thoughts kept returning to that short-lived experience, and the fact that then it had been worth seeking out a decent Italian restaurant at which to enjoy a meal. Now, it seemed, there was much more choice of cuisine. Nevertheless he settled for a small Italian bistro on Tongesgasse taking a window seat, just in case he might catch a glimpse of Katie. But he didn't.

After his meal he returned to his hotel, and checked his emails only to find that there were more complaints about their service than ever. He passed on the information to his associates in England again, and asked whether their new solutions were going well.

He knew that his best strategy was to get a decent night's sleep, as there was nothing else he could do that evening. He was already wishing he was back at his cottage. He didn't feel at home here, nevertheless he had promised Katie that if she needed him he would be there. He must do everything he could to get her out of this mess. He wished he didn't have to wait until the morning before making a start.

After an early breakfast the next morning, he made his way over to the Internet café.

This time Gerek was there. He explained to Ben that he worked behind the café's bar. He was a pleasant young man from Krakow who had worked in Frankfurt for several years. He was a small part of the ever growing Polish population in the city, he told Ben. He had a pale, sullen complexion and his untidy stubble did not make him any the more attractive, but he was friendly and seemed keen from the start to help in any way that he could.

Ben asked him whether he had seen Katie since he sent his message.

'Only one more time,' he replied in his broad Polish accent. 'Two days ago. She was being taken down the road by the same man who hold her arm tight.' He told Ben they came back past the café again just a few minutes later. That was the only other time he had seen her.

'How did she look? Could you see?' Ben asked.

'She was not happy, I think,' Gerek replied.

Ben told him that he was here to try to get her away from this guy, and would probably need some help when he had worked out a plan of action.

'I have good friends here,' Gerek told him. 'We can help for sure. She look like a nice girl. She is your girlfriend, I think?'

Ben told him a little about Katie and himself, and of the fact that she had married a man who was just a load of trouble.

'I don't know what they want with Katie,' he told Gerek. 'I think it must be her husband they want, and have kidnapped her in an effort to find him. All I know is I want to get her away from here as soon as I can.'

He gave Gerek his mobile number, asking him to call him if he saw her again. He would come over immediately, he told Gerek, find out where they went when they came down the road, and try to follow them back to where they were holding Katie.

Two more days passed with no sign of Katie. Ben felt less and less comfortable here and was beginning to think that she had moved on. The atmosphere was so different to that back in France. He was aware of the noise and pollution from diesel and petrol fumes, so different to the pure air that he was used to now.

Then he saw her for the first time.

As was becoming his habit, he was in the café having a coffee when he happened to look out of the window onto the street, and there she was just a few yards from him walking past the café. Hardly the girl he knew back in England. This girl was walking with her head down, being manhandled by an unpleasant looking individual about a foot taller than her. She looked totally unkempt, her hair was a mess, her clothes looked awful and she gave the overall picture of a street dweller.

It made him all the more determined to get her out of here. He left his coffee on the table, and followed her at a distance down the road. He would have liked to have run down the street, grabbed her away from her captor and run off with her, but he could not take that risk. It could all too easily go wrong.

After a short distance they crossed over the road. Ben stepped back into the nearest shop doorway. He watched as they went into a chemist and, after a few minutes, emerged again. They retraced their steps back past the café, turning into a side street some 250 yards further up Tongesgasse. Ben followed at a distance, watching as they stopped outside a greengrocery shop. Her captor pushed her in front of him up a few steps to the left of the shop, unlocked a door, and they both disappeared inside.

Ben stood on the street corner, deep in thought, wondering how he was going to reach her. He noticed that, although she was always held in a strong grip, she was not restricted in any other way, so there was just a chance that he would be able to pull her away from the man. It would have to be organised, and he would have to make plans as to how and where such a strike could be engineered. All the more difficult because he had no idea when she would appear again.

There was no further sign of her for two more days. Ben was beginning to worry again. Had he missed his opportunity? Had she moved on? He was considering contacting the police. But what would he tell them? What facts could he produce? Would he be able to convince the police that she was being held against her will?

The following day his luck changed. He was having his breakfast when he got a call on his mobile.

'She's here!' It was Gerek. 'She's in the café with the man.'

'I'm on my way!' Ben said, leaving his breakfast on the table, and running all the way to the café. He didn't want Katie to see him, so he walked past the café so that he could see where she was. He could see that she was sitting with her back to the entrance of the café, facing a computer screen with her abductor sitting in such a way as to prevent her from getting past him.

Ben wandered into the café, took a seat where he could keep an eye on Katie without being seen by her, and beckoned Gerek over.

'Is there any way we can distract him?' Ben enquired.

'I will try to find a way.' Gerek returned to the bar, then as soon as he arrived there, both Katie and her attendant got up from their seats, and walked out of the building.

Ben so wanted to reach out and touch her, but thought better of it. It was best if she was not aware that he was there. If they were to be successful, they must have the element of surprise on their side. Nevertheless, he felt disappointed to have been that close once again and unable to help her.

Once they were gone, he went to the bar.

'Sorry,' said Gerek. 'They left before I do anything. They will come again, I think. He said his computer was broken. That is why he comes here.'

'So can we think of a way of getting him away from the girl if they come in again?'

'Yes, I think of something.'

Gerek told Ben of his idea which, whilst being really simple, could still easily go wrong. Ben suggested that there should be a plan B just in case the first idea did not work.

Back in his hotel he spent the rest of the day considering the idea Gerek had come up with. He had to get everything right. He worked on the details of how he would get her away from her kidnapper and where they would go. He constantly reminded himself that their plans had to work. There would be no second chance. They had to get it right first time.

His head was spinning and the adrenalin was pumping as he put the final details to the plan. Eventually he took himself to bed and tried to sleep.

Chapter 24

'Ben. Where the fuck are you?' Mary was in the delivery ward of Wallingford Community hospital. 'Why aren't you here with me, you bastard?'

The nurse asked her to try to be a bit quieter. 'You'll wake everyone,' she was told.

'There's only one person I want to wake at the moment,' she shouted back at the nurse, 'and I don't even know where he is. Ben, where the hell are you? I need you, I need you here, and I need you now!'

Things had not been going well for Mary since that awful night when she had been forced to tell Donald the truth. For his part, he had kept his promise. They had continued together, although they both knew it was a sham. He showed no interest in her preparations for the birth. Whilst she enjoyed it, she was on her own in choosing clothes, pram, nursery toys and all the other paraphernalia. He had shown no feeling regarding the difficulty she had towards the end in carrying the child. She had gone on her own to pre-natal classes, where most of the other mums-to-be had their partners with them. She was alone for every visit to the medical centre to see her midwife. She so envied the other girls who always seemed to have their men with them.

She felt that it would be so much more enjoyable, exciting even, if she could share the experience with someone else, but she had to come to terms with the fact that she had to do this on her own. The months had dragged on, and she felt ugly and ungainly with the load she was carrying. She tried to make things as good as she could, enjoyed searching through the books of names, and had finally chosen the names she wanted for her little boy. She knew she was carrying a boy because the nurse had told her during one of the scans, and she was pleased about that.

Mary could still not understand why Donald had not sent her packing, as it was obvious that her baby was anathema to him and their relationship was becoming increasingly fragile. She sometimes thought that it would have been better if he had told her to leave. But he had made it clear on a number of occasions that he wanted her to stay. So, for the sake of her baby having a sound home to start his life in, she had stayed.

Donald had suggested that she use another bedroom where she could sleep with the baby. He did not want to be kept awake all night, he had told her. Mary grabbed the opportunity, and in what spare time she had, created a welcoming nursery room. She had enjoyed selecting the pale blue and white wallpaper with rabbits, kittens and bluebirds on it. She managed to find lampshades in the same shade of blue and matching covers for cradle and cot completed the picture. She had searched for a long time before she found the cradle that she wanted.

It was a light, airy room, looking out over the gardens to the rear of the house and was well separated from the master bedroom. She was sure her baby would be happy here and it would be a private place where she and her little boy could share precious times together.

Will he look like Ben? she had wondered on many occasions. She was undecided whether she hoped he would or not. Would she want to be reminded of his father every time she looked at him? Or was Grunge right that she should just be pleased to have a bit of Ben remaining in her life? She was totally undecided as to what she wanted or indeed how she felt. Could she stay with Donald if he had no interest in the child at all? All she could do was to wait and see. Perhaps she would be pleasantly surprised by his reactions once the baby was born.

Today she was about to put this all to the test. Donald had done well in attempting to keep her calm during the early contractions at the house, showing no sign of panic himself. He had spoken with the midwife on the phone, and had taken her instructions on board as to when he should call for an ambulance. He handled all the practicalities as he would organise a business function, timed down to the last minute. He had ensured that her bag was packed and ready in the hallway and eventually, when the time came, the ambulance was called and Donald followed behind in his car.

Now here she was in the labour ward. She had been in labour for almost twelve hours now and she was exhausted. There was no way she could relax. The pain was almost unbearable, and each increasingly frequent contraction only concentrated the pain more. Donald was with her, in that he was in the hospital, but he was not by her side. His excuse was that he was useless in hospitals, and that he would probably make things worse for her rather than better. The only person she wanted there now was Ben.

At 3:55 am on October 2nd, while Ben was searching for Katie in Germany, Alex Benjamin was born, weighing in at seven pounds and four ounces. She had taken what Grunge had said to her about this little person being a part of Ben, and had decided to give him his father's name. When the time was right she would tell him about his Dad.

Mary was totally spent, but instinctively found the strength to take her baby in her arms, and hold him as tight as she dared. He was so small, so beautiful, so much like Ben with lots of hair and his father's grey-blue eyes.

All the pain seemed to dissipate as she gazed upon this little miracle.

'Oh, boy,' she said to him, 'you are going to be loved so much! Your daddy is not here, so I will have to give you twice as much love to try to make up for that. You'll see, we will be such good friends.' Tears were running down her face. Tears of joy, of love, of sheer relief.

The nurse came and took little Alex away from her so that she could get some rest. Still Donald showed no interest. He asked the nurse to wish Mary a good night's rest, and that he would come in to see her sometime the following day. When the nurse returned to the ward where she had been moved, Mary was fast asleep.

She only slept for a few hours, and then, on impulse, went to find her son. She found him in a room with all the other new born babies, and she tiptoed over to the cot where he lay in a peaceful sleep. He was indeed a beautiful little fellow, even more so now that he had been cleaned up. She was tempted to pick him up for another cuddle when a nurse came in the room, and advised her that she should let him rest.

'In fact,' she said, 'you should be resting as well. There will be plenty of nights to come when you would welcome a chance to sleep in peace. So my advice is to get back to bed. You can have him to yourself tomorrow.'

'OK' Mary replied. 'I'll just stay here a few more minutes if that's OK.'

With that the nurse disappeared, and Mary just stood and looked at little Alex Benjamin. Before she left, she leaned over the cot and touched his tiny hand. To her surprise and delight he grasped her finger in his hand, and held it tight for just a few seconds.

'Oh, Alex!' she whispered. 'Your daddy would love you. Perhaps one day you'll meet him. That would be good wouldn't it?'

She looked over her shoulder to make sure the nurse had gone, only to see her little old lady standing there. They just gazed at each other each with tears in their eyes.

'Do *you* think he will ever see his daddy?' Mary asked.

'I wouldn't be surprised,' was the reply. 'Just have patience. Keep on hoping. If that's what you really want it will almost certainly happen.'

'Oh, I do. I know I do,' Mary said.

When she looked round a few seconds later, there was nobody there.

Reluctantly, she made her way back to the ward, climbed into her bed, and slept soundly until she was woken early the following morning, when Alex was wheeled in to be beside her, and breakfast was brought to her.

Chapter 25

Katie was awake early the following morning in her dark, dismal room, trying to piece together everything that had happened the previous day. The more she recalled, the more nervous she became. Her stomach contracted into knots and she began to feel sick. She dreaded what today would bring.

She listened for sounds. At first she could hear nothing. Then she recognised the familiar sound of the tapping of a keyboard in the adjoining room.

She got out of bed, intending to go to the bathroom, and then remembered that she was locked in so she rapped on the door, and waited.

The door was opened.

'I need to use the bathroom,' she said.

'Bathroom? Oh, yes. Come.'

Her minder's face showed nothing. His dark eyes, set well into his face were impassive. As he spoke to her there were suggestions of a leer on his mouth. He took her by her arm and roughly led her along the landing, opened the bathroom door, and she walked in. 'You shout when you finished, yes?'

'Yes,' she replied.

She looked at herself in the mirror.

What a sight! Her face still showed a slight bruise from the slap she had received. Her hair was a mess. She looked and felt dirty.

She realised immediately that this is where the stench was coming from. The bathroom was vile. The toilet was stained dark brown and stank, and the floor held grime that must have been months old. The smell of stale urine made her eyes water.

She ran some water into the filthy washbasin in an attempt to clean out some of the mess and splashed water over her face. There was a remnant of a bar of soap which had no signs of being used recently, encased in a brown shell. Managing to break most of the crust off, she used what remained to wash herself as best she could. There was a bath, but the state it was in did not induce her to use it. Perhaps she would attempt to clean it one day soon. They had left what make-up she had in her handbag, and she used what was there frugally. At least it made her feel a bit more human. Her hair, she decided, would have to wait for another day.

Looking at her reflection again in the mirror she told herself that she must not show fear, however scared she might be. 'There *will* be a way out of this,' she said to her reflected image. 'It's just a matter of waiting. At the moment, girl, they seem to need you, so it's unlikely that they will do you any harm.'

Not totally convinced by her argument, she knocked on the door and was led into the main room, which acted as a dining room and lounge. In keeping with the rest of the place, it had seen neither a duster nor cleaner for a long, long time.

Her captor pointed to a chair at a corner of the table.

She cleared a pile of men's magazines from the chair and sat down. After a long silence she decided to take the initiative and attempted to start a conversation.

'Look, as we have to be together,' she said, 'I'm Katie. Can I ask what your name is?' There was no response. She tried again. 'I do need some clothes. I can't wear these things all the time. Is there any chance of getting some other clothes?' No reply.

'What happens about food? I might be able to help with the cooking.'

'I get food. I cook,' was the reply spat at her. Katie thought Oh, I'm really looking forward to that! Not!

'OK. Is it all right if I do a bit of cleaning, then?' she persisted.

'You want to clean? You clean.'

'Is there any food in the house? I'm so hungry.'

'You look in kitchen. You see.'

Katie considered that was as far as she was going to get in this session and went to the kitchen. In the fridge she found the remains of a loaf of bread showing signs of mould on the edges, some coffee, and a half pot of jam. She did the best she could for herself and at the same time took a cup of coffee to her captor.

He looked up and nodded his appreciation, but no more.

After eating, Katie set about searching the kitchen and bathroom for anything resembling cleaning equipment. There was a vacuum cleaner which would have been welcome in any museum, a few cloths that were dirtier than the surfaces she wanted to clean, and little else.

She noticed that there were more rooms along the corridor from the bathroom, and looked into the first one. It, too, was fitted out with bunk beds.

She managed to wash out the cloths she had found. Whilst she could not get them anywhere near clean, at least they were usable. The thought of food being prepared in such a filthy place was utterly horrifying so she started work on the kitchen and in an effort to make the most of a worrying situation, she kept herself busy during the ensuing few days trying to clean the most important areas of the house with what little equipment she had at her disposal. While she was working her smart, devious, female mind was taking stock of everything that was going on. All the time she was making mental notes, watching her captor's habits, his timetable, his every move.

It was her optimism that kept her going. I've been in some pretty nasty situations before, and I've always come through them, she told herself. One morning while she was clearing away some cups from the table in the living area she slipped a pen into her pocket. Later, when she was on her own, she scrawled a note on a scrap of paper which she found. She put Ben's website address on the top of the page and wrote: URGENT. *Please send this message to the above website for me: 'Ben, I need your help. You did say if I needed you. And I do! Please help me. I don't even know where I am, but please try to find me and get me out of here, Katie'*, and hid it in her handbag waiting for a chance to use it.

It was essential now that she find a way, an excuse, to get out of the house. How to do that she had no idea. She would bide her time, keep nagging her abductor, and try to please him in a few little ways, just to relieve the tension between them. She kept herself occupied by working, cleaning wherever and whatever she could, and kept asking for different items to be replaced. The response was minimal. It was three days later that he capitulated. He told her that he had to get some food in, so she could come with him to the supermarket. There was the usual warning that any attempt to escape from him would result in severe punishment.

She happily agreed. At last she left the confines of the flat above the greengrocery shop, walking down the small side street into a much busier road. From the signs, she could now confirm that she was in Germany, but little else. They walked briskly, and she was held tightly by the arm. Upon reaching the supermarket, she was instructed to push the trolley. 'Nothing else. You keep hands on trolley. You understand?' She did exactly as she was told, requesting certain things from the shelves as they made their way round the store.

The bill was paid for in cash, and they made their way back as rapidly as they had come, arriving back at the shop where she was ushered into the flat above.

Katie wondered whether there was a chance that the people in the vegetable shop might help her if she gave them her note. She made a note to take her little scrap of paper with her next time she went out. She presumed now they had been out once, and she had shown she could be trusted, they would almost certainly go out again.

She continued asking for clothes, as she was still wearing the same things that she arrived in, managing to wash the essentials overnight. She felt that the situation was becoming a little more relaxed, and they did venture out a few more times. Each time she was told not to take her bag with her.

Upon the onset of her period, she explained, with considerable difficulty and a little embarrassment, to her abductor that she needed to go to a chemist to get her tampons. She knew from past experience that men were always uncomfortable about such things, and, sure enough, he agreed that he would take her to a nearby chemist that day.

This time they turned left when they came to the main road, and walked some distance down the road. This was the day that Katie managed to pass her little scrap of paper, which she had tucked into her pocket before leaving, to a guy standing outside a café. She mouthed the word "Please?" to the man as she walked past him pushing her note into his hand. She saw from the corner of her eye that he had unfolded the paper.

They walked on to the chemist where she made her purchase, and paid for it with the cash that her captor had given her. Hurriedly, they walked back to the flat. As she walked past the café, the man had gone, but to her delight she realised that it was no ordinary café. It was an Internet café, which really brightened her day. Now, she thought, there might be a chance to call Ben's bluff, and see if he meant what he had said.

Time went by. She desperately wanted to get back to the Internet café, just to see if she could find out whether her message had been sent. She continued to work on her abductor, and eventually discovered that his name was Stefan and that he was Romanian. More than that she could not find out.

Her luck changed a little when he became ill with a flu-like cold, and once again they had to go to the chemist, this time for his well-being, not hers. As they passed by the café, she saw the

179

man she had given the note to inside the café looking out onto the street, but there was no reaction from him.

Unfortunately as far as Katie was concerned, Stefan recovered quickly, and the boring daily routines continued. Katie had cleaned just about everything she could, and although the place smelled much better, she was still having to manage with the few clothes she had arrived in plus a T-shirt that Stefan had found for her. She had kept nagging him that she must have more clothes. He took no notice but one day produced a large, far from clean sweatshirt.

'It not mine,' he told her. 'It left here by somebody else.'

It was about six sizes bigger than she wore, but at least it meant that she could wash her other top every couple of days or so.

She began to watch every move he made, logging the things he did on a regular basis, the times he did them, everything she could make a note of, she did.

It should have dawned on me earlier, she said to herself lying in bed one night. There are two things he relies on here. One is his mobile phone, and the other is his laptop! I can't do much about his phone, so perhaps I can put his computer out of commission.

She planned it all meticulously. She would move a couple of chairs around into different positions when she cleaned the room so that when she brought in his coffee, she could pretend to trip over one of them, and spill his drink all over his laptop. She knew what damage that could do because she had done the same thing to a computer at one of her temporary jobs and was subsequently asked to leave.

'Coffee?' she asked about the normal time in the morning.

Stefan nodded, busy at his keyboard.

The cup had to be full and hot, and to make it look more like an accident, Katie brought her own cup in at the same time. The laptop was open on the table, and was switched on. Perfect, she thought.

Approaching the table slowly, Katie managed to get her foot caught on one of the chairs she had repositioned, and went flying toward and onto the table, the coffee from both cups going everywhere, a majority of it over the keyboard of the laptop, and a substantial amount of it down her front.

The language that emitted from Stefan's mouth was unknown to Katie, but she guessed he was not saying "what a pity!" He turned on her vehemently, grabbing her by the wrist, and a torrent of abuse was directed towards her.

'Look, I'm sorry, OK? I have burned myself as well. It's only a computer!'

'Only? Only?' he ranted. 'You may have finished it! See! It not working now. You stupid girl. It not working, see?' He tried everything on the keyboard. All he got was a bell-like sound at each key stroke.

'I'll get a cloth,' Katie said and went running off to the kitchen thinking '*Yes!!*' but not allowing herself to say it out loud. She returned with a cloth, and between them they tried to dry up the mess, but nothing made it any better. The machine had passed away.

Katie tried her best to look upset at what she had done. 'I'll get you another coffee,' she said.

'No! No! No more coffee. If I want coffee, I get coffee, yes?'

'Sure, OK. Look, I am sorry. Perhaps it will work again when it has dried out?'

'Perhaps. We see,' said Stefan.

He tried several times during the rest of the day, but could not resurrect the machine. The next morning gave the same result. Perhaps not so many bell noises but still nothing on the screen. She had done a good job.

'Stefan,' she said later in the morning, round about the time he normally used his laptop, 'there's an Internet place just up the road. Maybe they could help you repair it, or maybe you can use one of their computers.'

181

'Where is this place? I don't see Internet place.'

'It looks like a café from outside, but it says Internet something as well,' she told him.

'OK. We go and look.'

Wearing her oversized sweat shirt in an attempt to keep warm in the chill autumnal air, she accompanied him to the café, and he sat her in a corner where it would be impossible for her to get out without him seeing. She had no intention of running away. She had no money other than a few English coins, no credit cards, not even a passport. She couldn't do this on her own. She tried to catch the eye of the man who had taken her note, just to see if he would let her know that her message had been sent.

Stefan was taken to one of the many computers that were there, dragging Katie along with him. He turned the screen away from her while he tapped away on the keyboard, no doubt telling somebody on the receiving end that this stupid girl had killed his laptop. She did not want to know, she had no interest in what or to whom he was writing.

Eventually, he finished his tapping, and called one of the members of staff over. He tried to explain, in broken English, what had happened, and enquired whether they did repairs.

Katie did not hear the reply. It was in German anyway. However, she did catch the attention of Gerek. She just looked at him with an enquiring look on her face, and she was sure that he nodded, just slightly, to confirm her unspoken question.

That was good enough. Another splendid day's work, she thought.

As they walked out of the café, she noticed a familiar smell, a men's perfume. Feint, but it was there. She remembered that Ben had worn something similar last time she saw him. She felt strangely reassured.

Satisfied that at least something, however tenuous it might be, was happening, she vowed that she must frequent the café as often as possible.

Chapter 26

Ben met with Gerek and two of his friends that evening, and they went over their plans in great detail.

There were two plans, A and B.

Ben made it absolutely clear that they would only have this one chance. They had to get it right first time. If they messed it up, Katie would be in a lot of danger. They parted company, each of them well versed in the exact details of the plans.

They didn't have to wait long.

Just two days later the call arrived on Ben's mobile.

'They are here again!'

'I'm on my way.' Ben threw on a jacket and raced the short distance to the café.

Once there he ambled in and sat at the same table as previously. He could watch Katie without being seen by her.

He hardly recognised her. She had on an enormous sweat shirt, which hung off her shoulders like a sack.

Stefan used the computer as usual, and went to pay using cash. He handed over a fifty Euro note, took the change, and was walking back to his seat to collect Katie, when he was stopped in his tracks.

He was taken back to the counter and was told the note that he had given them was counterfeit. Stefan remonstrated with them that it couldn't be a fake, as he had obtained it from a bank ATM.

The café manager came out from his office behind the counter and addressed Stefan in perfect English. 'I'm sorry, sir. I am not interested in where you got it from. All I know is that it is a forged note, and that we have been asked by the police to report to them whenever we receive one.'

'How do you know it is a fake?' Stefan asked, suddenly going pale.

'We have a machine,' he was told. 'Look, see for yourself.'

The note was placed in a small reader, and sure enough, as soon as the note in question was fed into the machine, a loud beeping sound was heard, a red light flashed and the note was spat out.

'I don't understand,' said Stefan, beginning to panic. 'I got that note from the bank. How could it be a fake?'

'You will have to explain that to the police, sir.'

'The police? Look. Give me that note back. I have another one here.'

'I'm sorry, sir. We have to report each case to the police. My colleague is calling them as we speak. I'm sure if you tell them what you have told us, the matter can be resolved without a problem.'

Stefan tried to run away from the counter, but was apprehended by a burly individual, who, it turned out, was just a customer.

'That was a bit silly, sir,' Stefan was told. 'I think it would be best if you came into the office so that you do not disturb my customers any more.' And without further ado, he was bundled off into the office behind the counter.

Katie sat and watched, intrigued by what was happening. She decided to sit tight and wait.

There was no panic as Gerek casually walked over to her.

'Katie, come with me. Ben is here for you. Don't rush, just walk out casually.'

Katie slowly got up from her seat and walked toward the door with Gerek. She was joined by Ben as she walked past his seat, and they calmly made their way out into the street. It was only then that they looked at each other.

'You're a mess!' Ben said to her laughingly. 'Have you any idea what's going on?'

Katie merely shook her head. Ben put his arm around her, and they walked back to the Miramar Hotel, and up to his room. Katie thought how lovely it was to have a warm, friendly arm round her again and pushed into his body.

Plan A had been a great success. The swapping of Stefan's genuine note with a fake was seamless. Stefan had told Ben they had a collection of counterfeit notes behind the counter, so whatever Stefan had offered them would have had the same results. He had been well and truly stitched up. The police, of course, were never called. Nevertheless Stefan was held in the office for almost half an hour.

Plan B was not needed.

Later, when Stefan was released from the café, having received a stern warning from the manager not to try anything like that again, he was running back to the flat, when he was tripped up by a man he had never seen before and landed rather badly on his hands and knees. Before he could recover, he received an unwelcome kick between his legs, which made him cry out in pain and writhe in agony on the pavement. That was plan B!

Back at the hotel Katie collapsed into an arm chair, slumped with her head in her hands and sobbed loudly. It sounded to Ben like a wild animal in distress. It was a horrifying sound.

Katie had built up so much tension during the days of her incarceration that things were still flying round in her head. Noises, such noises! Like being in the midst of dozens, if not hundreds of motor bike riders racing past her, round her. She wanted to shout out for them to stop but she couldn't, was not allowed to. The nightmare was intolerable. Wherever she looked there were locks to stop her from escaping. Bars on the windows, blackness, too much to handle, too much to bear.

Chapter 27

Ben knew he was way out of his comfort zone.

He had never been able to cope with women's tears and emotions, and this was rather more than he had ever had to deal with before. He decided to let her do what she had to do to relieve the pressure she was under. Even so he wanted to do one more thing to tidy up the loose ends from the day's events. He had to talk to her but it would have to wait for now.

It was more than an hour before Katie's trauma subsided enough for him to try to pacify her.

'Katie, sweetheart,' he said quietly, 'I know you won't want to talk about this yet, but there's one thing I need to know. Do you know who the man was who was holding you?'

With tears still streaming down her face she told Ben the only thing she knew was that his name was Stefan and he was from Romania. 'There are others as well - the ones who actually captured me,' she told him.

'OK. That will do. I only want to know about this man for now. Look, I've got to go out for a few minutes, just to tie this up. I'll lock the door when I go out, and I am the only one with a key. So you're safe here. Do what you want. Have a bath or a shower, or just rest on the bed. I will be back in just a few minutes. OK? Just one more thing, though. Is there any way in which we can prove you have been in that place?'

'Sure. My handbag is in the bedroom that I used. First door on the left along the hallway.' and she gave Ben a brief description of it.

Once Ben had left, Katie tried to get to grips with the situation. She was safe now, she told herself. She was still locked in, but this time it was for her own safety. She reminded herself again of some of the scrapes she had been through in the past, and even raised a smile at some of the recollections. She decided to treat herself to a hot bath, and went into the bathroom. She stood and stared. It was pristine, spotlessly clean, and for a few minutes she picked up all the freebie shampoos and shower gels, the soap, the towels. Just holding them made her accept she was back in the real world again. She undressed, showered and washed her hair, only then slipping into the perfumed bath water, and luxuriated there for some time.

Ben went out of the hotel to a telephone call box, and dialled the police emergency number. Fortunately for him the woman who answered could speak English.

'I want to report a crime,' he said. He told them of Katie's kidnap, and said he knew little about the man, but suggested that they get someone round to the flat above the greengrocery shop as soon as possible.

'I think, if you act fast, you will find that he is part of a larger gang, and if you keep a watch on the property for a few days, you may even get more of the people involved.'

He was asked to identify himself. He declined, saying that the girl was now with him, and in safe hands. However he felt that if they did not apprehend the Romanian he was sure Katie would remain in great danger. He promised that once the police had the man in custody they would both be willing to talk more. He also advised them that Katie was in a terrible state of shock, and would not be in a fit state to talk to the police at the moment. He gave them his mobile number and said he would let them know where they were staying when Katie was ready to talk to them. Once the man was arrested they could visit them. He was not sure whether he had done enough, but he put the phone down and just hoped they would treat the matter seriously.

He made his way back to the hotel, and Katie.

She was still slumped in the chair now adorned in one of the hotel's robes. She looked more relaxed than when he had left her, but still showed signs of the stress she had been through. She was obviously tired. Her eyes were paler and seemed to be set further into her face, not the penetrating blue they normally were. Nothing could hide the signs of her crying. She was going to need a lot of support if she was to get through this, and he was going to have to supply it.

Ben brought her coffee which she took from him, looking up with her ashen face, and attempting a smile.

'Thank you,' she whispered.

'It's only coffee. Instant at that,' he said.

'No. Thanks for everything. I think you might have saved my life.'

'Yes, well, always the hero, that's me.'

As they were exchanging these few words, Ben heard sirens not far away.

Could they be that efficient? He went to the window but could not see over the buildings on the opposite side of the road to be able to observe the streets further away. All he could do was to hope.

When he turned back, Katie was asleep. She looked far from comfortable. He waited a few minutes then picked her up in his arms and gently carried her to the bedroom and managed to get her into the bed without waking her.

He returned to the lounge and sat contemplating what had happened, how lucky they had been that everything worked out exactly as they had planned. He made himself a coffee and just sat.

It was early evening when his mobile burst into life. It was the police. They had apparently arrested a man, and would now like to talk to Katie to obtain more information to help them with the case. Ben crept into the bedroom, and found Katie awake. He asked her if she felt up to dealing with the police this evening.

'Yes, let's get it over with,' she said.

When the police arrived half an hour later Katie was able to give them a lot more information as well as descriptions of some of the other men involved in her abduction. The officers, a man and a woman, were calm and patient. They stayed with her for nearly an hour. Everything was written down, read back to her and Katie signed the statement as true. As they were leaving, Ben told them that he wanted to take her to his cottage in France, saying that he could be contacted by mobile or email, and if it was necessary, they would be willing to return to Frankfurt to give evidence or further information at a later date.

Once the police had gone, they both wanted nothing more than to get to bed.

The room had two single beds. Ben hoped he would be able to get a good night's sleep. He didn't. Every hour or so Katie would be fighting the air, waving her hands around. 'No! No! Go away! Oh, my God! Get off me! Go away! Get me out of here!' and each time Ben calmed her down by running his fingers through her hair, or just dusting his hands over her forehead. Her nightmares went on all night.

I don't know how to deal with this, he admitted to himself as he lay in bed. She needs professional help – perhaps even counselling and some form of medication. I am so out of my depth here. The only thing to do is to get her out of here and back to St Justine just as soon as I can. Perhaps I can find somebody there who can help her. I'll see how she is in the morning.

The night had been desperately long, but at last dawn broke, projecting its early morning light into the bedroom. Katie had been much quieter during the last few hours. He crept out of bed, went into the lounge, and while he got himself a drink, he turned on a news channel on the television.

Not understanding German, he could not make out what was being said, but it looked as if they were reporting the arrest

189

of an illegal immigrant. He wanted to wake Katie so that she could see what was going on but he couldn't wake her yet. He would tell her when she decided to get up.

An hour or so later, a dishevelled Katie came into the room, wan and bleary eyed. She sauntered over to where he was sitting, bent over and kissed him lightly on his forehead. Then she sat down next to him.

'How are you feeling this morning?' he asked her.

'I'm alive, aren't I? That's good enough for now.' she said, trying to smile. 'Ben, I've got no clothes and no money. All I've got is what I'm wearing. I really do need to get some clothes.'

'Well, I've never done anything like this before, but if you give me your measurements and so on, and tell me what you need, I'll get out there and find you something to be going on with. How's that sound? I really don't want you going out yourself at the moment.'

'I don't *want* to go out,' she replied. 'That's the last thing I want to do right now. I don't know how I will be able to pay you back. They took my credit cards as well. Oh, and Ben, can you get me some make-up? I think I'll feel better with some lippy.'

'Look, I'll pop out and see what I can do for you. I'll bring something for our breakfast as well. I don't want you to be seen anywhere for a while. And don't bother about the money. That's the last thing you need to worry about.'

Katie gave him her measurements, and he set off to find what she had listed. He had never been too comfortable in ladies' underwear departments, and this was no exception. It was made all the more confusing due to the European sizes being totally different to the UK sizes he had been given. Nevertheless he managed to find bras and panties in the sizes she had given him. Then he went looking for simple T-shirts and trousers which he was more comfortable doing. Choosing make-up for her, however, was even more confusing. He tried to remember the lipstick colour she wore, and just had to guess about foundation.

With a sigh of relief he left the store and picked up some essential food stuff on the way back to the hotel.

Most of what he had bought was OK, but when Katie tried on the trousers, she said 'Does my bum look big in these?' Ben looked up, and immediately understood what she meant. She would need something to hold them up. A belt or braces – or maybe both.

'It must be something to do with European sizes, or maybe you've lost more weight than you thought,' he joked. 'Anyway, your bum looks good in anything.'

'Or nothing?' she said and laughed for the first time. 'Hey, it's better than what I came here in. Don't worry, I'll make them fit somehow. Is it OK if I have another bath? It's such a luxury.'

Ben got some breakfast together while she bathed. When she reappeared, she looked so much better. She had used the make-up that Ben had bought, her hair was washed and dried, and she was wearing her new outfit. Somehow she had made the trousers look acceptable.

'Come and have some breakfast,' Ben invited. 'I must talk to you.'

Chapter 28

When Dave did not check out on the third day of his stay at Hotel Adriatix, the cleaners reported to the manager that Mr Westerman's luggage was still in his room. They were told to clear the room. The pair of Nike trainers, some underwear that had been left in a drawer, the trousers and two shirts that remained on hangers in the wardrobe were all put into a black plastic bag. The bag and his suitcase were taken to the manager and were labelled "To be collected".

It was two weeks later, when the luggage still had not been picked up, that the manager decided that he should take some action.

'I think I need to report a missing person,' he told the duty policeman at the local police station.

'You *think*?'

'Well, yes. All I know is that a man who was staying here never checked out and his luggage is still here.'

'His name?'

He looked on the hotel register.

'Nigel Westerman. He was English.'

'Address?'

Again he passed on the details from the register.

'Car Registration?'

'He wasn't driving.'

After a few more questions he felt he had done his duty and returned the case and plastic bag to its place in his office, changing the label to read: "Unclaimed".

Things do not move at a great pace in Vloras. It was some time before the matter was forwarded to the British Embassy in Tirana as an International missing persons enquiry.

The Embassy staff passed on the information to Interpol and to South Wales Police who covered the area of the address in Cardiff given by the hotel.

When the police checked the address they found that it no longer existed. The house had been demolished two years previously to make way for new developments in the city.

The enquiry then went back to Albania, and a visit from the police resulted in Dave's passport being found in his case. Details were sent back to South Wales Police who checked with the Passport Office in Newport who, in turn, informed them that the passport was a professional fake. There was no record of a Nigel Westerman having a passport with that reference. Likewise, the details of next of kin from the passport were found to be fictional.

The information was sent back to Interpol.

Dave's father had only heard from his son and Katie once since they brought back the Jaguar at the end of April. That was on his birthday in July, It was now nearing the end of October. He wasn't all that surprised. It was not unusual for him not to see his son for weeks or months at a time. He thought he would make an effort to get together with them. If for no other reason, it would be nice to see Katie again.

He tried phoning the house but there was never any reply. His son's mobile seemed to be dead. That could be put down to him buying a later model, he supposed. Dave always had to have the latest technology. There was nothing left but to visit the house.

There was no sign of life there either and on peering through the letterbox, he could see a mountain of junk mail on the floor. They had obviously been away for some time.

He was now in a dilemma. Were they just off seeing the world? Or was there something horribly wrong. He knew his son was not the greatest communicator in the world, but even he would have let his father know if he was going away for this length of time, wouldn't he? Should he contact the police? He was only too aware that his son had on more than one occasion sailed close to the wind as far as the police were concerned. He would not be too popular if he brought them into contact with each other again. What to do?

Procrastination, that's the best policy here, he told himself. I'll deal with it tomorrow.

It was, in fact, a week later that he visited the house again. He peered into the windows, and this time tried the back gate, gaining no more information.

'They've not been here for weeks,' a voice told him. It was the next door neighbour.

'Any idea where they've gone?'

'Not a clue. They just seemed to disappear.'

'How long ago?'

'Well he left before she did. Let's see. It would have been early September, I think. First he went off, and then a couple of weeks or so later, she went, too.'

'Neither of them told you they were going?'

'No, but they wouldn't have. We don't really know them. Just say hello when we see them. That's all. Who are you then?'

'I'm Dave's father.'

'Bit worrying then. For you, I mean?'

'Yeah. It is. I think I'll have to let the police know. Thanks for all your help.'

'No problem. That's what neighbours are for, ain't it?'

Dave's father went straight down to the Thames Valley Police Station in Castle Street and reported his son and daughter-in-law's disappearance. The only recent photograph was one of the wedding. He was told there was little to go on, but that they would put the word out.

'Could they have gone abroad' the desk sergeant asked.

'Possibly. I just don't know.' he answered.

'Well we'll put it out to Interpol just in case. You never know, that might produce something. Anyway, we'll do our very best. We'll get in touch as soon as we know anything.'

'Thanks'

Dave's father went back home more concerned than he was when he started out that morning. He told himself there was nothing else he could do right now.

Chapter 29

Katie was much more composed the next morning. She told Ben more of what she could remember and in rather more detail than she had told the police about the abduction - the compartment in the van, the ferry crossing, the characters involved and the way she had been treated by them.

'I think the best thing we can do is to get out of here as soon as we can today. So I'll book some flights. We'll fly to Paris and then ...' Katie stopped him in his tracks.

'We can't fly anywhere.' she said.

'Why ever not?' Ben asked.

'Because I haven't got a passport!'

'Then we'll go to the embassy. I'm sure they'll be able to give us papers to get us out.'

'No, Ben. You don't understand. I've never had a passport. I've never been abroad before. And what's this about Paris? I'm not on holiday!'

'I live in France now,' he told her. 'There's no way I'm taking you back to England. Or not yet anyway. It's too dangerous. So you'll have to come home with me for the time being until we can work out the best thing to do. All I want to do is to get you away from Frankfurt.'

'Oh, is that where we are, Frankfurt? I'd realised we were in Germany, but I didn't know any more than that. I didn't know you were living in France, either. When did this happen?' she asked.

'Doesn't matter at the moment. OK, if you don't have a passport, I'll have to hire a car. Driving a car with German plates, we'll be able to go straight through the border. No questions asked. Just how we get the car back, I don't know, but we can try.'

Ben turned on his laptop, noticed that there were more emails than ever that needed his attention, but for now he concentrated on car hire firms. He found, to his relief, that the world's number one car hire company, according to the advertisement, could supply a car in Frankfurt that he could leave in Paris.

'Katie,' he asked 'Do you mind staying here on your own again while I go and get a car for us?'

She nodded her approval, adding: 'Be as quick as you can. I've had enough of being locked in to last me a lifetime.'

For the service he wanted, Ben had to get to Frankfurt am Main airport, so it was going to take some time, but he was determined to get it all sorted out as quickly as he could.

Before he set off, he walked over to the Internet café to thank Gerek and his friends for their help. They said they were only too happy to have helped, and confirmed that Stefan had been arrested, and that the police had confiscated his laptop.

Back outside he decided to take a cab. That way he could be taken directly to the car hire office at the airport. The forms were filled in quickly and easily, and within half an hour Ben drove away in the hire car with the necessary papers to be able to drop it at Charles de Gaulle airport in Paris the following day.

He found his way back to his hotel without too much trouble, left the car in the car park and went up to his room. Katie looked just a bit more relaxed than when he had left, then he saw her visibly tense up again when he said they were ready to leave.

'I tell you what,' he said to her. 'I'll go and check out and pay, and then I will make some excuse to come back up for you. That way, I can take you straight out to the car. Is that OK?' Katie nodded nervously.

A few minutes later they were in the car, and making their way out of Frankfurt.

It was going to be a long journey. He had decided to stop over for the night round about Metz, and then drive on to Paris the following day. Once they were out of the city, Ben glanced at Katie.

'Happier now?' he asked.

'Much happier,' she assured him.

Before long Katie was fast asleep leaning back in her seat, snoring quietly. She only woke up half an hour before they reached their overnight stop.

They managed to get a room each at the Novotel in Metz, and ate well in the restaurant before making their way to their rooms.

'Would you mind if I share your room?' asked Katie. 'I'm not suggesting anything. I just don't really want to be in a room on my own yet.'

'No problem,' Ben replied. 'There are twin beds in there. So come on in.'

They both slept like babies, and got up early the next morning to complete their journey, crossing the German-French border without being stopped. Ben drove fast. There was no looking at scenery on this journey. The car was left at Charles de Gaulle airport, and then they made their way back by Metro into Paris city centre to get a train back to Angers.

They ate at a pavement café close to the railway station and later caught the TGV.

By the time they got back to Angers, picked up Ben's van and drove back to the cottage, it was late in the evening. They were both tired yet elated that they had managed to get away from Frankfurt without problems. Ben warned her that it was extremely dark and quiet at the cottage. 'It's taken me a while to get used to it,' he told her. 'And you might hear a few strange noises outside at night. It's just the wildlife. Nothing to worry about.'

Inside the cottage, Katie looked around, bowled over by Ben's new home.

'It's beautiful!' she said.

'You just wait until tomorrow when you can see the surrounding countryside. That's the beautiful part of it. It's a wonderful place to live. It really is.'

It was late in the morning when they both awoke the next day. Ben took her into the garden.

'Oh, Ben. How did you find this?' she asked.

'Long story. I'll tell you it all sometime. It's all down to some lovely friends I've made here,' he said.

'Has Mary seen it?'

The question rather shocked Ben. 'Mary?' he said. 'No.'

'Have you not told her, then?'

'Why would I? She's got her own new life with, er, whatever his name is, er, Donald. She's not part of my life any more.' Adding to himself, more's the pity.

'Did you know she's pregnant? I saw her in Reading a while ago, not to speak to, but she was obviously pregnant.'

'Well, they didn't waste any time did they?' he said somewhat disdainfully and quickly changed the subject.

That little snippet of information stabbed like a knife into Ben's heart. It felt like the final episode to his relationship with Mary. There was no hope now, ever, of being any part of her life. She had played her trump card and he was entirely on his own. The vague hope at the back of his mind that perhaps, one day, they might get back together was now permanently erased.

'Let's go up into the village and get some bread,' he suggested.

Katie still continued having her nightmares, but they seemed, over a period of time, to become less frequent and less forceful. She also disappeared under clouds of depression now and again, at which times Ben just left her alone to deal with her mood, and usually she came out from her doldrums fairly quickly. Ben was amazed just how well she seemed to be dealing with her memories, her traumas.

They did not talk at any length about future plans for her. For the time being she was content to take each day, each week, as it came.

Ben tried on a few occasions to bring up the subject of Dave but Katie did not want to deal with that just yet. Each time she changed the subject or walked away.

Chapter 30

Mary stayed in hospital rather longer than was usual. Her doctor and midwife were rather concerned about signs of jaundice in Alex and, as a result of blood tests, had placed him in a special cot with a blue light directed on him.

Mary's euphoria had been and gone. Her whole world was grey. A great dark claustrophobic cloud was engulfing her. She showed much less interest in Alex, and had to be coaxed regularly to persevere with her attempts at breast-feeding.

'If you don't make more effort to feed him,' she was told, 'the jaundice will get worse.'

Yet Alex didn't seem interested in taking her milk however much she tried. Her breasts became more swollen by the day, and the pain from the excess milk just added to her feelings of failure.

If today was bad, tomorrow was certain to be even more intolerable, she thought. To her each day became more of a nightmare than the one before.

She blamed herself, of course. She had been a fool, an absolute fool, to get herself into this predicament. She had spoilt two men's lives. Poor Donald just could not - or was it, she thought, *would* not - bring himself to accept the situation she had put him in. And then there was poor Ben. She had just walked away from him. It was his son she was now trying to deal with, but he didn't even know that Alex Benjamin existed.

While she was here, at least, she did not have to deal with the major problem that awaited her at home. She couldn't imagine what it would be like to be back with Donald. She would have to cope, not only with the matter of attending to all the needs of Alex but, no doubt, would still be expected to carry on as before. There was no way she could do it all. No way she would be able to cope.

What a bloody mess.

Some well-meaning people who thought they might be able to assist came to visit her. Maybe they could have helped if Mary had been honest with them about her circumstances. They thought this was just a severe case of baby blues, and Mary was not willing to divulge to them anything of her private life. "Busy-bodies", she called them.

After four days, when the jaundice had subsided, she left hospital with Alex and her blues.

As soon as she arrived home, Donald announced, in a rather matter of fact way, that he thought it would be best for her to sleep in the nursery with "the baby". 'I expect you would want to be with him during the night?' he said, making it seem to be a question, at the same time making it perfectly clear that was the way it was going to be.

That suited Mary. As things stood, the more time they could spend apart, the better she would like it.

There were a few cards waiting for her when she arrived home. The girls at her salon had sent a lovely card with some flowers, and there was one from Grunge now calling herself Georgina. How the hell did she know about Alex? Mary asked herself. I don't remember telling the girls at Ray's he had arrived. Still, that's nice.

Somehow, a connection back to her happier days felt good. She made a note to get in touch with Grunge again. If anyone could sort out her mental state right now it was her.

For now she was much too busy to make such a move. Much as she had thought, she was expected to do all the things around the house that she did before, keep an eye on the salon, and deal with the seemingly incessant demands of Alex. Every day was the same. Every night she went to bed totally exhausted to endure another disturbed sleep. Increasingly, she was being told by Donald of things she had not done, things that would have been better done another way. It was getting to the point where she felt that she could do nothing right in his eyes.

Every day was the same. She had lost all her old confidence, and seemed to be on auto-pilot. She seldom went to the salon; never ventured out unless it was absolutely necessary. The weeks came and went and she could see nothing on the horizon to lift her spirit. She contemplated walking out on Donald, but she knew she needed self-assurance to do that, something she didn't have at the moment. Anyway, she told herself, where would I go? I don't know anyone who would be able to help me.

She could now understand how her father had felt, putting up with the constant criticism and never-ending nagging from her mother. She could remember so clearly the day, so many years ago, that he had decided to leave. He had taken her into the garden, out of ear shot, to tell her how much he loved her but that his life at home was becoming intolerable.

Her mother had accused him of having an affair with a girl who worked at his office. He admitted to Mary that he liked the girl, but there had been nothing more than that. His wife had convinced herself and nothing would make her believe otherwise.

The girl in question had left some time previously, but they had stayed in contact by email, and she had said that if he ever decided to leave his wife he would be welcome in Manchester to be near her, for support if nothing else.

'Mary,' he had said with tears in his eyes. 'I have got to get away from your mother. She is sucking the very life out of me, and if I stay I will either end my life – or hers.'

That evening, he had packed his bags and left.

Nobody seemed to know what exactly had happened on his journey to Manchester, only that his car had been involved in a multiple pile-up on the motorway. He was dead on arrival at the hospital. Mary had always blamed her mother for his death, had left home soon afterwards and had not spoken to her mother since.

Now Mary could see that Donald wanted absolutely nothing to do with "the child". He had told her it was no part of him in any way.

'Had it been my child, maybe I could have dealt with it. It isn't. It's the fruit of someone else's loins not mine,' He said.

Mary knew that, to Donald, the child was seen as an intruder; something that had ruined any chance of he and Mary having any kind of life together. What she couldn't understand is why he was so adamant that she should stay.

Chapter 31

Ben leaned back on the wooden gate which led into the circular gravelled driveway to the cottages reflecting on just how lucky he was.

November had arrived. The air was crisp and clear with a few wispy white clouds in the sky, not exactly a warm day, but comfortable enough to be wearing just a T-shirt and light, rather battered, trousers which showed the evidence of the hard work that he had indulged in during the long hot summer. It was late in the afternoon, and the sun was washing everything in an attractive golden light before retiring for the night. The two cottages which he had bought less than eight months earlier stood facing each other to the far side of the cosy, enclosed front garden. He was delighted at the transformation since he had first seen them. The white walls reflected the fading light. The shutters and front door, now painted pale green, set off the tiny windows. Guttering had been replaced, and the roof had been repaired where necessary using matching tiles from the outbuildings. The small garden in the middle of the entrance containing the old Parisian street lamp, was planted with shrubs, encircled by white painted rocks and surrounded by a circular path of cream and brown gravel. The overall effect was enchanting.

Jean-Pierre, from whom he had bought the cottages, would regularly appear at Ben's cottage with eggs or home-made goat's cheese sent by his mother but would never stay to chat. I have to get back, he would say. Mother is expecting me.

Ben had been well received. Whenever he walked through the village to the *Tabac* or *Boulangerie* he would be greeted by someone or other with a bright, *"Bon jour, Monsieur Ben"*

The small local *Tabac* was a great meeting place where individual opinions were regularly vented with raised voices and much gesturing. At first Ben had not been too sure about being drawn into the discussions, especially if the UK or the European Union were in any way part of the subject matter.

The first holiday visitors to the cottage were due to arrive in a few months. The thought of playing host to some fellow Brits was exciting, albeit somewhat daunting. The French builders had excelled themselves, and had finished earlier than had been expected, which was a great surprise as he had been warned to expect many delays. Ben was determined to ensure that his visitors would enjoy their stay and want to return. Not naturally gregarious by nature, being host to people he had never met before would offer another challenge. If all went well it would be the beginning of another, very different chapter in his life.

He knew he would enjoy showing off the area in which he now lived. There were the various châteaux along the Loire valley, each with its own history and unique appeal, just asking to be explored. Similarly, there were the many tiny villages waiting to be discovered, the individual atmosphere of each one so distinctive. Some of the local villages were so appealing that Ben knew that back in England they would be tourist attractions. Here in France they were considered as nothing special by their residents. And then there was, of course, the beautiful nearby city of Angers with its magnificent Château, cathedral and river. To the west was the equally attractive city of Nantes with its overwhelming feeling of history. To the east, Saumur, a busy, tourist-friendly town, a favourite of many a traveller.

He was already preparing plans for next year when he wanted to introduce a "Joan of Arc Trail" tracing her steps along the River Loire from her birth place to her final battle and her death. He had a lot of catching up to do on his history, but he had always had a fascination for Joan, and would enjoy enticing others to join him in his interest.

This particular afternoon, as he leaned on the gate, he knew he should be completely satisfied with the way his life was going. His business, whilst appearing to have a few more problems of late, was doing better than he could have dared hope for. He had managed to procure a property that was as close to his dreams as it could have been. And just today he had brought home his car with French number plates.

This, he told himself, is about as French as I will ever be!

He turned again to look inwards at the two cottages gleaming in the evening sunshine and was pleased at what he saw, proud of his achievements in just a few months. Yet there was something niggling away at him. Some intangible thing that was missing. He had everything he thought he wanted, and yet...

Ben stopped wallowing in today's euphoria and watched as Jean-Pierre's ancient tractor made its way up to the farm and disappeared.

He made his way past the cottages into the garden behind them. There was Katie, eagerly digging away, clearing the more stubborn weeds that still remained.

Slowly but surely she was beginning to get her life back. Still wary of strangers, she was making every effort to live a normal life. She was happiest when she was doing something useful, as she put it.

When she had first arrived, it had been difficult to get her to even walk down into the village. The big breakthrough came when he had persuaded her to go with him to Angers, where she could do some serious shopping for herself, a bit of retail therapy.

'I haven't got any money!' she stated forcefully. 'You know I can't go shopping.'

'Look,' he told her, 'we can settle up some time in the future. For now, you need some decent clothes to wear, to feel good in, to look good in. Money is not a problem, so don't worry about it.'

The afternoon in Angers was a great success. She momentarily seemed to forget about her troubles and really enjoyed looking in the shops, buying things here and there. Nonetheless, she was careful never to be too far away from Ben, and walked close to him as they went from one store to another. Ben could sense her tension, but said nothing. He was content to have her company; happy to act as her guide, her interpreter when needed.

When they got back to the cottage that afternoon, she enjoyed trying on her purchases and parading her new clothes for Ben. This was a bit more like the Katie he knew, her sense of excitement was beginning to return. There was no doubt that she still had a long way to go, but things were progressing day by day now.

Chapter 32

It had been raining all morning in Vloras, but had eased off by lunchtime.

Jeton and his much younger sister, Lule, had taken the opportunity to take their mountain bikes to Auloa Park where the rough terrain meant they could put their new bikes through their paces. The ground was still wet from the morning's downpour, which made things more exciting. They were well protected with the best in cycle clothing so the occasional spill did not do any harm, merely increased the excitement.

They stayed longer than they should, and knew they would be in trouble when they got home, but they were having fun. As the sky started to get darker, they made their way out of the park and down the steep track to the town. Full of adrenaline, they rode furiously down the hill, Lule being chased by her brother.

When she hit a loose boulder at full speed, Lule was thrown from her bike and just managed to hold on to a thin branch of a tree growing out from the edge of the trail. Her bike bumped and somersaulted down the deep ravine that edged the track. Jeton skidded his bike to a halt, dismounted and went over to where his sister hung precariously over the edge of the gorge. She was screaming for help and holding on to the tree for her life.

Jeton crawled over to the edge of the track and grabbed his sister's arms as best he could.

'Just hold on to my arms,' he yelled at her, 'and stop struggling. If you don't keep still, I won't be able to pull you up.'

Lule said nothing. She was crying now, terrified.

'And don't keep looking down,' Jeton told her. 'Just look at me and do exactly as I say. I can get you out of here.'

His sister nodded her agreement.

'Now, grab my left hand with your right hand – now!'

He could now hold her firmly while she let go with her other hand.

'Now, do the same with the other hand.'

'I can't. I'll fall.'

'No you won't. I've got you with my arm. OK? - now!'

The girl grimaced as she let go of the tree and grabbed Jeton's arm. The boy mustered all the strength he could find, and at the same time as creeping backwards on to the track, dragged his sister up to and over the edge.

'You're hurting me,' she cried.

'I know, but you're up now, aren't you? Stop complaining.'

Slowly Lule stood up and studied her bruised legs, arms and face.

'Oh, no,' she shouted. 'My bike. It's right down there. I can't even see it. Dad will be furious.'

'Well, let's get you home and patched up. We'll face up to the bike problem afterwards.'

Jeton sat his sister on his bike and slowly and carefully wheeled the bike down the track. It was dark before they finally arrived home. They were greeted, as they had expected by their irate father.

'Where on earth have you been?' he yelled as soon as they walked into their house.

Mother came to add her opinion, but as soon as she saw the state of her daughter, she only had thoughts of her condition, taking her to the bathroom and cleaning up her many wounds. Lule told her what had happened, and reported to both parents that her lovely mountain bike was somewhere at the bottom of the ravine.

'Well, there's nothing we can do about that tonight,' her father said. 'I'll drive up there tomorrow morning. I'll take some rope, and with Jeton's help, I'll try to climb down and get it back.'

The following morning, true to his word, Jeton's father went with him back up the track to where the accident had happened. Parking the car, he took out a coil of rope, tied one end securely to the rear end of the car, and with trepidation, inched his way down to where he could just see the bike.

As he was securing the bike to the rope, he looked to his left to see two black shoes poking through the undergrowth. He parted the leafy mass to reveal that the shoes were attached to a body, a badly decomposed body. He nearly vomited.

'Jeton,' he shouted up to his son, 'pull up the rope. The bike is attached. I will hang on down here. Throw the rope back down when you've got the bike.'

Jeton pulled for all he was worth, the bike tearing its way through bushes and trees until it was by his side.

'The rope's coming back down, Dad,' he called.

'That's nowhere near me, Jeton. Pull it up and try again.'

Jeton did as he was told.

'Perfect,' he heard his Dad shout.

Now he had to try to help his father climb back up the ravine. Slowly, painstakingly slowly, he inched his Dad up to the edge of the track and slumped down onto the road.

His father went straight to the car and reached for his mobile phone and dialled the police emergency number.

'I've just found a body,' he said.

The police arrived fifteen minutes later, and using much more sophisticated equipment brought the remains of the body back to the track.

'It'll be difficult to trace this one,' one man said. 'It must have been down there for weeks, if not months. This'll be a DNA job.' The body was packed into a black plastic body bag and loaded into the back of the police van.

Jeton and his father made their way home sombrely.

'I wonder who that was,' Jeton said.

'God knows, Jeton,' his father replied. 'Just another body, I guess.'

Chapter 33

One evening in December Ben took a call from François.

'Ben, is it possible for Michelina and I to come over to see you?' he asked. When Ben asked the reason for the visit, François said only that he would be more forthcoming when they met.

Katie was there when he arrived with Michelina. Neither of them had met Katie before so Ben simply introduced her as a friend. François raised his eyebrows in appreciation, offering a knowing smile in Ben's direction.

'Ben, I'll come straight to the point,' he said. 'You know we were talking about Madame Delphine a while ago. Well, it's her sixtieth birthday in a few weeks' time, and I'm sure you would like to do something towards her celebrations?'

'Sixty? I don't believe you!' said Ben.

'It's true. She's amazing isn't she? Well, anyway, we want to do something special for her, and knowing how she has taken to you, we thought you'd like to be involved.'

'*Absolument*,' Ben replied, and then explained briefly to Katie about Madame Delphine, and how she had helped him so much to settle here. 'What have you got in mind?'

'We'd like to have a *soirée* of some sort. I've managed to track down some of her old colleagues from the *Folies* who say they would love to be part of the occasion, and there are a few local people, too, who would want to be there. We're wondering, now that most of the building work is done here, whether you would like to be the host of such an event? We don't want her to know in advance that it is her party, so perhaps we could call it your "house warming", isn't that what you say in England?'

'Me?' said Ben with some incredulity. 'I'd be really honoured. How soon would it be? There's still a lot to do before I would feel happy about people coming here for something like that.'

'Don't worry, there's no rush. It will be the latter end of February. Could you manage that?'

'You bet! I wouldn't miss it for the world. What about catering and so on?'

'That's all under control. My friendly chef just down the road is going to deal with that, and I also have a good friend who is happy to supply some good wines for us. All you have to do, Ben, is supply the venue.'

Ben was so excited about the prospect of being able to do something to show his thanks for the welcome and all the help Madame Delphine had offered him when he first arrived, that he could hardly contain himself. Katie couldn't understand what was making him so excited until Ben explained to her the importance of Madame Delphine's birthday hoping that she would share in his eagerness. She didn't. She told Ben that the thought of all these people coming here was scary as far as she was concerned.

As the evening went on, more details were agreed and more wine was consumed.

When, eventually, François and Michelina bade them both farewell with the usual kisses on the cheeks, Ben was able to tell Katie more about this remarkable lady.

'Being here is all down to Madame Delphine. At one point I'd almost given up ever finding somewhere I really liked,' he told her.

'I'm very nervous about this, Ben,' Katie said. 'All these people coming here, all speaking French. I won't know any of them, I won't be able to understand anything they say and I've heard how unfriendly the French can be.'

'I don't think you need worry. I'm sure that you'll find most of them really friendly. A lot of them will be able to speak some

English, and, in any case, it's weeks away yet and I'll be here with you.' And then, after a few thoughts he continued, 'Anyway, if you're still here, I'll need you to help me. I tell you what we'll do. So far François has only mentioned the food being prepared by his friend. I suggest you and I also put on a little spread of English food. Things that the locals won't have tried before.'

'Can you get real English food round here, then?' Katie asked.

'What I can't cook myself I get from an Internet company. You can order just about anything English and have it delivered. I mainly use them when I begin to long for real sausages, bacon or good old Cheddar cheese. What do you think? Shall we give it a go?'

Katie agreed and began to see that she could be "doing something useful" again.

They both began to work even harder on the finishing touches to the cottages and working in the garden.

The builders had done a magnificent job on the old dairy. Now as you entered the front door, you were in a sizeable dining area with the new kitchen to the left. To the right there were three steps reaching across the whole width of the room, leading down to the new lounge area which in turn led to two bedrooms and a small shower room. Above the lounge was a minstrel gallery behind which were two additional bedrooms, one of which was *en-suite*.

Ben had told them he did not want the interior to look new, so all the woodwork had been roughly carved to look old, and then painted almost black to suggest age. The walls had been stripped back to the original stone. The original flag-stone flooring had been taken up from the dairy and lovingly re-laid. The only modern feature in the cottage was the lighting. Halogen spotlights in the lounge and dining areas were used to highlight the stone wall features, and alcoves. Ben was absolutely delighted with the overall effect. It was so much better than he had expected. Although he had paid out considerably more than he had originally budgeted for, the resulting image of antiquity made it all worthwhile.

He was already getting excited about showing off his new property to Madame Delphine, who so far had not been to visit.

He gave thought to the practicalities. As things were at the moment, car parking would be a bit of a problem so he and Katie busied themselves during the weeks that followed in clearing enough space in the garden areas to be able to park a few more cars.

They had not heard any more from the police in Germany since they returned to France. Ben had regularly brought up the subject of Dave but Katie did not want to deal with it. They still had no idea where he was or what he was up to.

Earlier this month, however, Katie finally agreed that they should take some action. Ben phoned Thames Valley Police and told them of Dave's disappearance.

'Who is this?' the Inspector asked.

'My name is Ben Coverdale,' he told him. 'I'm phoning on behalf of Dave Atkinson's wife. I want to report a missing person.'

Ben gave the Inspector Dave's details.

'Hold on. You said you were speaking for his wife? We already have both Mr. Atkinson and Mrs. Atkinson registered as missing persons. Are you saying you know where Mrs. Atkinson is?'

'Yes, she's with me. I live in France, and she is living here with me.'

Ben then went on to tell of the events leading up to this call including her abduction and incarceration in Germany.

'You should have called us a long time ago, sir,' the Inspector told him, and again Ben tried to explain how things had been for Katie. He could tell that explanations were not being received well.

'Is Mrs Atkinson coming back to the UK soon? We must speak with her.'

'I don't think she will be coming back for a while,' Ben told the Inspector. 'She is still in a state of shock, and wary of venturing out. I guess eventually she will return, but not yet.'

'Well one way or another we have got to interview Mrs Atkinson. I will get in touch with you again when we can arrange something.'

When Ben came off the phone, Katie said, 'For all we know, it might all be a big mistake. He might be completely innocent of anything.' After a pause she added sombrely 'For all I know, he could be dead.'

Chapter 34

Christmas and New Year had been non-events. Mary had bought countless presents for Alex, mainly on the Internet, yet there was nobody to share the delights with. She took copious photographs of him with his presents from Santa Claus. The only benefit to come from it was she began to feel much closer to Alex. That seemed to help her to climb, slowly, out of her depression. She enjoyed more cuddles and special times with him. Maybe, she told herself, between us we can start to see some light at the end of the tunnel.

Two weeks into the New Year, Mary awoke one morning in a completely different frame of mind.

'Today,' she told herself out loud, 'you are going to make a start at getting things sorted out. Today you are going to do something practical. Today you are going to get a future back for yourself!'

She shut her eyes, trying to convince herself, when she saw the now familiar face of her little old lady with her curly silver hair smiling at her.

'Will you help me?' she asked of the vision. 'I really don't know where to start.'

'I think, maybe, you do, child.' Mary followed her eyes. She was looking at the card on the bedside table.

Mary got up and picked up the card that Grunge had sent her. Alex was still sleeping, so she crept out of the room and downstairs to where Donald was already having his breakfast.

''Morning,' she greeted him.

He looked up, somewhat taken aback by the cheerfulness in her voice, and smiled.

'How are you today?' he enquired.

'I feel a bit more human than usual today.'

'That's really good news. I wondered whether, if you like, we could go to ....'

She stopped him in his tracks. 'No, Donald. I'm going out on my own today - well, with Alex, of course. I want to go to see an old friend of mine. I think she would love to see Alex. She's mad about babies.'

Donald said that was OK by him. What he had in mind could wait for another day.

After feeding and dressing Alex, Mary loaded her car with all the necessary equipment for the day, called in at her salon to let them know she wouldn't be in and then drove to Reading. Parking the car, she walked chirpily along to Ray's salon.

'She's not here any more,' Penny told her when Mary asked after Grunge. 'She left us some time ago, and has got a job as a rep for a hairdressing supplies company. Seems she's doing remarkably well. She calls in here now and then trying to get some business, but you know Ray, he doesn't like people leaving him, and he won't ever buy anything from her, even if he knows he needs it. Sad, isn't it?'

'Oh, I was hoping to meet her today. I got a card from her when Alex was born, and I wanted to thank her, and show him off. Have you got her number?'

'Yes, I'll get it for you. Let's have a look at your baby first, though.'

Penny swooned over Alex. He was a bonny baby, and always reacted to people well. Colette came and joined in, and then, to Mary's delight, Ray came out from his office.

'Hey, he's a lovely little bundle,' he said. 'Not looking for a job are you? Perhaps the girls have told you, but Grunge - oh, sorry, it's Georgina now - just upped and left me some weeks ago, and now thinks she's a sales rep.'

'Ray, there's nothing I would like better, believe me, but I've got a salon of my own in Wallingford, and like it or not, I'm stuck with it, I'm afraid.'

'Stuck with it? That doesn't sound too promising. Perhaps you *should* consider my offer?'

'I promise to think about it,' Mary said, 'but I don't think it's on the cards at the moment.'

'Well, you know you would be welcome back any time you like. I really miss you,' he said, and then disappeared into the back room.

Penny brought back Grunge's telephone number.

'Her mobile's on there too,' she said, giving the business card to Mary.

'Thanks, do you mind if I try her now?'

Mary dialled the mobile number.

'Hello, this is Georgina. How can I help?' came the answer.

'Hi Grunge - sorry, Georgina. It's Mary. I'm at Ray's salon. I didn't realise you'd left, just thought I'd bring Alex to see you.'

'Alex? Who's Alex? Another new fella?'

'He's new all right. He's my baby,' Mary told her.

'Oh, of course. I didn't know his name. I just knew you'd had a baby.'

They chatted at length, until eventually they agreed to meet later that afternoon at a coffee house in Friar Street.

'Can't wait to catch up, Mary. I'll have to go now. I'm with a client,' Georgina told her.

Mary put her head round Ray's door before she left, to say goodbye.

'I meant what I said,' he told her.

'And I will give it some thought, too,' she said. 'Ray, Alex needs feeding, is it OK if I use the staff room?'

'Of course. Get one of the girls to warm up the bottle for you.'

'Well, no,' Mary said nervously, 'I'm breast-feeding him. Is that OK?'

'Of course it is. Take your time, make yourself at home!'

'Thanks, Ray.'

She was really enjoying her day, and this time the feeding was enjoyable, not just for her son, but for her as well. 'Perhaps,' she shared with Alex, 'just perhaps, things might work out after all.'

When, later the two girls met as planned, Georgina's first words were: 'Let's have a look at him then.'

Mary took Alex from his pram, and handed him to her friend.

'He's absolutely beautiful. Can't see who he takes after though. Mind you, I've never been much good at that. Some people seem able to see one or other of the parents in babies. I think, to be honest, they are saying what they think the mother or father wants to hear. Doesn't matter, anyway, he's beautiful in his own right. Good for him.'

She told Mary that she had found out about her baby when she called at her salon in Wallingford the day after he was born. If it had not been for that, she would not have known. 'You do keep yourself to yourself nowadays, don't you?' she said.

'Mmm. Not my idea. It seems as if Donald just wants to keep me for himself. I almost have to ask his permission before I go out.'

There followed a lot of baby talk, which Georgina entered into, regardless of the fact that she had not yet had the experience of parenthood, and rather doubted she ever would. And then, inevitably, the subject of Ben was raised.

'Does he know yet?' asked Georgina.

'How can he? I don't even know where he is. I had a spell of feeling guilty back along, and tried to track him down then, but nobody seemed to know what he was up to. I was told he had gone abroad, and I guessed if he had gone anywhere it would probably have been France. Then I decided I might do more harm than good if I were to tell him. After all, he had probably started a new life for himself, whatever and wherever that was, and perhaps it would be best if he didn't know.'

'And now?'

'And now, I still don't know. Do you know where he is?'

'Oh, yes. You're right about France. He's bought these two lovely cottages, and when I saw him a few months ago he was busy doing them up, or at least the builders were. He seemed pretty pleased with himself.'

'You saw him? Did he, by any chance, mention me?'

'Not in so many words, Mary. However, I think I'm rather good at being able to see inside people. On the surface, he seemed happy, yet I could sense that he knew there was something missing from his life. Or more accurately, someone. I think now might be a good time to tell him about Alex.'

'You've got his phone number then?'

'Yes, I have, but I'm not going to give it to you. I've got a much better idea. I'll take you to see him. I think this has got to be a face-to-face thing, don't you? You can't tell him on the phone or text him. That would really be awful.'

'I don't think I can do that. I mean ...'

'That's rubbish! You know I'm right. You must tell him now, or you may never have the opportunity again.'

'But what if ...'

'Doesn't matter "what if", Mary. From what you've told me, you're less than happy with the present set of circumstances. From what he's *not* told me, I think he misses you. That seems a pretty hopeful scenario to me, and let's face it, even if he tells you to piss off, things won't be any worse than they are now, will they?'

Mary went to speak again, but Georgina kept on going. 'Look, I'll call him when I get in tonight, and see if I can arrange to go over to see him again. He said I would be welcome any time. And I'll just say I'll be bringing a friend. He'll never guess in a month of Sundays it'll be you. I just can't wait to see his face! I'll call you tomorrow, and let you know when. It'll only be

221

for a long weekend. I can't afford too much time off with this new job. I'm trying to impress the bosses. Go on, say yes, say you'll come. It'll be a break for you, and it should be fun as well.'

'Seems like you've got it all organised already. I can't really refuse can I?'

'Good girl. I can almost guarantee you won't regret this. You'll have to get a passport for Alex, though. That'll take a while, so I won't arrange anything for a few weeks.'

They left the coffee shop soon after, and Mary's pulse was racing as she drove home with Alex Benjamin. 'Thanks,' she whispered to her little old lady, hoping she would hear.

As soon as Georgina got home she phoned Ben asking if it would be all right if she came to see him again.

'I enjoyed it so much last time,' she said, 'I'd love to come again to see what you've done with the cottages.'

'Have you got a date in mind?' asked Ben.

Georgina told him of her suggested dates.

'I tell you what,' Ben said. 'If you can make it the third weekend in February, I could really do with some help here.' And he told her of the plans for Madame Delphine's birthday celebrations. Georgina gave it some thought, as she wasn't sure that this was the scenario that best suited her plans, but then thought that maybe it could work out well, so agreed, and said: 'Is it OK if I bring a friend with me?'

'The more the merrier, Georgina,' Ben said. 'Let me know what time you're arriving and I'll pick you up from the airport.'

'Oh, that won't be necessary. I'm being brave enough to drive down this time. Have a better look at France. I'll let you know what time I'll be arriving when I've booked the ferry. I'm really looking forward to seeing you again.'

Ben was going to mention that Katie was here, but thought better of it. I'll leave it as a surprise for when she arrives, he decided. He also wondered why he hadn't asked who the friend was. Had she found herself a man at last?

Chapter 35

Mary was still aware of her heart-beat as she manoeuvred her car into the drive at Donald's house.

What she would like to have done was to burst in the house and tell Donald exactly what she was feeling, to share her excitement at the thought of at last being able to meet with Ben, and to show him his son. But of course she couldn't.

Every time she started to get excited at the prospect of seeing Ben again, she had to balance it against reality. What if Ben just didn't want to know about her or Alex? What if he already had some kind of relationship with a beautiful French girl? Georgina had said that she believed that he was missing her, but how could she really know? Ben was never one for showing his emotions. And anyway, that was a few months ago.

Still, she had said she would go, and go she would. If it didn't work out? Well, that was something she would have to face up to later. For now she must keep calm, and make her trip sound like something much more mundane, just a bit of a treat for herself.

'How was your day?' asked Donald as she walked into the lounge.

'Brilliant,' she replied. 'My friend has asked me to go with her to France for a few days. That's all right by you isn't it?' She watched his face. She often felt that she could tell more from his facial expressions than the words that came from his mouth. This time, she thought, it seemed a genuine reply. Rather uninterested, but without any noticeable disagreement.

'That's fine by me,' he said. 'Who will look after the baby?' At this point there seemed a moment of panic on his face, which made Mary smile to herself inwardly.

'Oh, he's going with me. I've got to get a passport for him, though.'

'When will this be, then?' Donald asked, looking more composed again.

'Not sure yet. About four weeks I think. My friend's going to let me know.'

'And where will you be staying?'

'I'm not absolutely sure,' Mary said, thinking how strange it was that she didn't actually know the answer to that question. As far as she could remember, Georgina had not actually mentioned the location. That Georgina is a foxy lady. She hadn't, in fact, told her much at all!

Mary was relieved that there were no more questions, and that it had been received so well, and in the days following she busied herself with getting the passport application dealt with. Getting a photograph of Alex turned out to be a bit of a nightmare. He had decided that on that particular day he did not want to be photographed and insisted on looking every which way but at the camera. Thanks to the patience of the young man operating the camera, suitable photos were eventually produced to go with the application.

She also bought some new clothes for him as he was growing rapidly. She wanted him to have easy-to-change outfits to make the travelling easier for them both. Mary enjoyed the search, and spent rather more than she had intended. 'What the hell,' she said to Alex. 'You're going to meet your Dad.'

Her emotions were like a roller coaster over the next few weeks. Sometimes counting the hours to going and at others dreading being disappointed by the whole episode.

It was during this period that Donald started behaving more strangely than he had before. Using her trip to France as a bargaining point, he inveigled her into changing her hair style.

225

'I think it would suit you much better short,' he said. 'You know, a kind of a bob style.'

Mary fought off the suggestion at first, but Donald's mood changed rapidly and what initially was just a suggestion became almost a demand. It was only in order to safeguard her visit to Ben that she eventually acquiesced, and asked the girls at the salon to do her master's bidding.

The girl who cut her hair seemed to know exactly what was needed. It was as if she had already been instructed. Before long, Mary's long tresses were consigned to the floor. When she looked in the mirror at the final result she could have cried. Her olive skinned face needed her flowing locks surrounding it. This new style was for somebody with a rounder face. But it was done, she had paid the price and her break in France was secured.

Georgina phoned her about a week later to tell her that they were going for the third weekend in February. She had booked the ferry and a cabin for the Wednesday so that they could go overnight.

'I thought it would be easier for Alex and you to be able to have a decent kip on the boat, and then we can drive straight down the following morning,' she said.

'Where, exactly are we going?' Mary asked, but Georgina still wasn't giving too much away.

'It's about a three hour drive, I think,' she teased, and would reveal no more than that.

They made arrangements as to when and where they would meet up, and Mary heard no more from her after that.

On the day of their departure she was up early to get herself and Alex ready, taking a taxi to meet up at Georgina's flat as planned.

Chapter 36

Dave's father, Mark Atkinson, was just settling in for the evening after a difficult and demanding day at work when the doorbell rang.

'Mr Atkinson?' the young man asked. 'I'm detective sergeant Protheroe, and this is a colleague from forensics. May we come in?'

Mark took them through to his spacious lounge, and they sat opposite him in separate chairs.

'I presume this has something to do with Dave?'

'I'm afraid so, sir. We have some news which might move our enquiries forward.'

Mark was told that a body had been discovered in Vloras, Albania, which might be that of his son.

The Albanian police, he was informed, had lost no time after the latest body had been found. The corpse had been taken to a temporary morgue and handed over to their forensic team in an effort to discover whose body it was. All the usual clues had been carefully removed from the man's body and clothing. Their diligence was rewarded when one of the team noticed that the size printed on the inner sole of his shoe was "10". It was neither European nor American, so they guessed that the shoes being worn had been bought in the UK.

The next step had been to check for UK based missing persons. From their examinations of the body, they estimated that he had been dead for approximately three months. It would be impossible to identify the body photographically as it was so badly decomposed.

There were three matches to their search but only one adult male.

A Nigel Westerman had been reported missing by the staff of Hotel Adriatix some three months previously. The police revisited the hotel where the luggage was still being held, and managed to take DNA samples from a toothbrush and hair found on a comb.

Within forty-eight hours this information had been sent to Interpol.

'We've come to see if there is a way that we can take DNA samples from here. Is there anything belonging to your son here?'

'Well, he still has his own room but it hasn't been used for a while. I'll take you upstairs. But if the body in Albania belongs to a Nigel Westerman, what's that got to do with my son?'

'We believe that whoever the person was, he was travelling with false documents. So, you see, it just might be your son's body that has been found. Do you know why he might have been travelling in Albania?'

'I have no idea what Dave was up to at any time. He could have been in Timbukto for all I knew.' The forensic policeman went up to Dave's room.

'You do know that we have located his wife, don't you?' the sergeant said.

'Katie? No. I presumed they were together. Where's Katie, then?'

'In France, apparently.'

'France? What the hell is she doing there?

Mark was told of Katie's capture, her rescue, and that she was living with an old boyfriend in the Loire Valley.

He was dumbstruck, his head spinning with a myriad of emotions. It was impossible to define how he felt about his son. Just a sense of shock. The only relief was that his son's beautiful young wife was safe. He could not differentiate between his natural paternal love and parental anger towards his son.

'We must point out, Mr Atkinson, that it is far from certain that this is your son in Albania, however we have to follow it up.'

'Yes, yes, of course,' Mark said. 'Does Katie know any of this?'

'No, sir. We will of course inform her once we have confirmed that this body is that of her husband. If, of course, it is.'

The forensic officer returned from Dave's room and said that he had found a number of small samples that may well be sufficient to determine the link between Dave and the body in Vloras.

'Will you be all right, sir?' Mark was asked. 'Have you got somebody who could be with you tonight?'

'I'll be OK,' Mark told them. 'If I do need somebody, I can make a few calls.'

'Well, we'll be off, then, sir. And we'll get back to you as soon as we have any more news.' As he left, the sergeant handed Mark a card with his contact details on.

Mark saw them to the front door, and watched as they drove away.

Returning to his lounge, he poured himself a large Famous Grouse, slumped back into his chair and burst into inconsolable tears.

Chapter 37

It was a blustery night when Mary and Georgina made their way to Portsmouth for the overnight ferry which would get them to France by early morning. Neither girl was looking forward to this part of the journey.

Luckily, the crossing was not as bad as they thought it might be. After a quick snack in one of the restaurants, they wandered through the labyrinth of passages to their cabin, spending the rest of the night in and out of sleep. The hum of the ship's engine and the rolling motion as it crossed the English Channel was not conducive to deep slumber. Mary hardly slept at all. She was trying to picture what Ben's reactions would be when he saw her. What his response would be when he learned that Alex was his son. Alex was the only one who seemed to take everything in his stride, and slept soundly until it was time to disembark at 6:45 French time.

It was barely light as they drove away from Caen. Georgina had studied the route thoroughly before setting out, but passed the map and details of the route to Mary as they drove away from the ferry port.

'Here you are,' she said. 'This should keep you awake. It's all down to you now.'

'Have you driven over here before?' Mary asked her friend who was looking a bit tense at the prospect.

'No. It's a first for me! You tell me where to go, and I'll try to keep on the right side of the road! If we go wrong, we go wrong. Don't worry too much.' Secretly, Georgina was dreading the thought of driving in France. At first her face was immovably fixed on the road, and her knuckles showed white where she was gripping the steering wheel so hard.

'I'll do my best. Can we stop somewhere fairly soon so that I can feed Alex?'

'Not just Alex,' Georgina said. 'I'm rather peckish myself. Keep a look out for somewhere that we can all have breakfast. By the way, how's your French? I hardly know any words except *"Oui"*, *"Non"* and *"Merde"*'

'*Merde*?' queried Mary. 'What's that mean?'

'I think it's the equivalent of our "Oh, shit!". I don't think the French have any other swear words. How can you live without swear words?'

The conversation went on in similar vein, Georgina relaxing now that she realised how straight and empty the French roads were, Mary trying to stay awake. As they watched the sun climb higher in the sky, they both had to admit that the panorama, set in the early morning sunshine with just a hint of frost on the fields, was lovely to see.

'This is beautiful isn't it?' Georgina declared.

Mary agreed until they needed to use a toilet in one of the small villages they were passing through. Georgina went first and came hurrying back.

'Bloody hell!' she exclaimed to Mary. 'I'd heard about their toilets but I never thought they still used things like that. That was quite disgusting. I think I'll keep my legs crossed from now on.'

'Is it that bad?' asked Mary innocently.

'See for yourself!' her friend retorted. 'You won't want to stay too long, that's all I can say.'

Mary made her way warily to the WC, soon realised that Georgina had not been exaggerating, and returned to the car almost immediately.

'See what you mean,' she said. 'Let's drive on!'

Other than that little episode, the journey was uneventful. Alex seemed to be enjoying himself throughout the journey, and

231

was taking everything in, looking out of the car window most of the time, and dozing off every now and then. They stopped for an early lunch, and found, to their relief, that the toilets in the busy little restaurant in the centre of a village the name of which neither girl could pronounce, were much more acceptable. They managed to select a meal from the menu with some help from the girl who served them.

As they drove further south the wintery sun bathed the countryside in its glow and the surrounding backdrop became even more alluring. Mary soon realised from reading the road signs that they were heading for Angers.

'I might have guessed where we were going,' she told Georgina. 'I should have known it was somewhere round Angers. He always loved it down here. So did I, come to that.'

'You've been here before?'

'Yes, just once, and we both had a wonderful time. It really was a bit special.'

'Well, let's hope it's a "bit special" this time, too,' Georgina said.

As they approached Angers, Georgina said, 'Now this is where it might get a bit hairy. I have driven to Angers with Ben from where he is living, but it did seem a bit complicated getting back from Angers. I think we'll have to go into the city first, and then I'll try to find my way out.'

After a few attempts, Georgina recognised the road to Sainte-Justine, and both girls, hearts in their mouths, drove the last few kilometres to Ben's new home in silence.

Chapter 38

There were just four days left before the big celebration. The cottages were looking pristine, and the garden in the front of them looked the best it could for this time of the year.

The old Parisian street lamp which Ben had placed in the middle of the flower bed in the centre of the driveway was now connected to the electricity supply and fitted with a sensor so that it lit up when anyone drove in. Initially, he had set the device to be too sensitive, and because of the amount of wildlife wandering in and out of the garden, the light was switching on and off for most of the night. He had managed to make it less responsive, and, other than the odd occasion, it now did as it was intended, and looked rather grand, a focal point as anyone arrived.

Katie had worked like a Trojan, cleaning and polishing just about everything in the cottages. Enough space for five or six cars had been created in the rear garden. Now they were concentrating on tidying up round the old barns to the rear of the cottages, trying to make them look less dilapidated than they actually were.

Ben had refurbished some of the original furniture that had been left from the previous tenancies. The major piece was a solid oak dining table, which he had lovingly sanded down and re-varnished, along with a number of chairs. Whilst they did not match each other, they offered a certain quality which reflected the overall aged impression he wanted to create.

Katie's state of mind had improved a great deal during these busy weeks, and Ben could see some of the sparkle coming back in her eyes. He noticed how she had started to eye up some of the local male residents when they ventured together into the village. She was even talking of joining the sports club so that she could use the gym.

Everyone who met her said how lovely she was, and it was being implied by a few that she and Ben were "an item". They both knew that was blatantly untrue. She had never once tried to flirt with him, other than the occasional hug, since her arrival, for which Ben was grateful. He wouldn't have known how to handle that. He still found her immensely attractive, and there had been times when he had found himself watching her "being useful" and started a little fantasy or two. He knew that any involvement would cause more problems than he wanted to deal with, and anyway, it was seemingly a totally unrequited lust.

They had decided to shelve the idea of providing English alternative foods. They talked at length about it, eventually deciding that putting Bangers and Mash alongside French cuisine would not be the wisest thing to do. They did, however, decide to offer a typical English pudding, and bought in the ingredients to make a large apple crumble to be served with good old English custard.

How many people are coming to this do? Ben wondered. He phoned François, fortunately found him in, and asked him if he had any idea of numbers.

'Not really, Ben,' he said. 'In this area, everyone thinks they are automatically invited to a celebration like this. And, of course, Madame Delphine has many friends and admirers, so I can't really tell you how many might come. Is that a problem?'

'Well, it's just that we don't have that much room, especially if it rains. I know we've got plenty of chairs and tables, but it's a matter of where do I put them all,' Ben said rather anxiously.

'Yes, I see. I had overlooked that. I will do my best to limit numbers. Let's just hope it all works out. That's all we can do, I'm afraid. I am arranging for Madame Delphine to arrive about six o'clock, is that O.K?'

Ben agreed that he was happy with that.

François then went on, 'So I will get her *Folies* friends to be there some time before that, so that they can be ready to greet her.'

The plan was that these ladies would come early and change into their costumes and be standing in the minstrel gallery in the dairy cottage awaiting her arrival.

Madame Delphine was being told that the party was a house warming, so she should have no reason to think that it was anything else. She would be taken into the smaller cottage, where there would be a small amount of wine and a taste of things to come; baby artichokes with anchovy sauce, *fougasse* with olives and a green salad with *aioli*, and then she would be asked if she would care to see what had been done to the dairy.

It was essential, therefore, that other guests did not come until a bit later. François and Michelina would be there early to help with the deception as would the builders and Jean-Pierre and his mother, and possibly, the Mayor, just to complete the image of the house warming.

It all seemed so simple and straightforward. 'Is this all going to work?' Ben asked.

'Of course, Ben. Don't lose any sleep over it. Anyway, even if our plans don't exactly come together, what does it matter? It will still be a lot of fun.'

'That's what I like about you French,' Ben admitted. 'You're so laid back about everything. I'll see you Saturday, if not before, then.'

By the Thursday Katie and Ben had done all they could. Everything else would have to wait until Friday or even Saturday to finalise.

Ben was looking forward to seeing Georgina again. He was wondering what she would think of the cottages now they were finished, and he was also eager to meet her new man. Ben tried to conjure up images of her chosen one but was at a loss to imagine who she had found who would be compatible with her life style. Someone with a great deal more courage than me, Ben thought. But he wouldn't have to wait much longer. Georgina had phoned to say that they would be there before midday.

Spot on half past eleven a car drove through the gate into the gravelled front garden.

Chapter 39

Ben saw the car arrive from the cottage, and ran out to greet Georgina.

He opened her door. 'Hi!' he said exuberantly. 'Great to see you again!'

Mary was too tired, too nervous to make a move. She sat and watched as Ben welcomed Georgina with a firm hug and a kiss.

It was only then that Mary looked over at the smaller of the two cottages and saw, to her horror, Katie emerging from the front door. She leaned over the driver's seat to grab Georgina and call her back.

'Georgina, get back in the car. Get me out of here. Take me home.'

Georgina climbed back into the car, completely stunned by Mary's reaction.

Mary's eyes were wild. She pointed to where Katie was standing.

'You might have told me *she* was here.'

Georgina glanced up to where Mary was pointing.

'Hold on,' she said. 'I had no idea Katie was here. Ben didn't tell me she was here.'

'No. I bet he didn't. I thought this was going to be a beautiful idea. Look at it now. How could you?'

Ben had walked round the car to the passenger side and he tried to open the door, but Mary had a tight grip, and refused to let go.

'Mary! It's you. I didn't recognise you. I was expecting, er, well I wasn't expecting you.'

'That's pretty obvious, isn't it,' she shouted back through the window. 'I'm probably the last person you expected or wanted to see. Seems you're cosy enough with that bitch.'

By this time Mary had floods of tears flowing down her face.

To be able to speak to her, Ben had to go round to the driver's side of the car and lean in over Georgina's lap.

'Mary, you've got to hear me out. It's not what it seems. Get out of the car and Katie and I will explain. I promise you, it's not what you think. Please, get out of the car and let us talk. You must believe me, I'm delighted, absolutely ecstatic to see you.'

'I feel a "but" coming on here somewhere,' Mary sniped at him. 'I don't think I want to hear your miserable explanations. All I know is that I've been looking forward to this moment for weeks, and now, the first thing I see is her.'

As Ben pulled himself out of the car Georgina said: 'Mary, I'm not going anywhere. Not just yet anyway. I desperately need a cup of tea and a pee in a decent toilet, so you can either sit here and wait, or get out of the car and join me. Let's just hear what they have to say.'

Still fuming and against her better judgement, Mary slowly got out from the car, reached into the back and brought out Alex in his carry cot. She slowly walked alongside Georgina into the cottage. Ben went over to speak to her only to receive the biggest brush off he had ever encountered.

'Don't even think about it!' he was told. 'At this moment I feel more inclined to kill than kiss.' And she walked away from him.

Katie didn't know what to make of the situation. She stepped to one side as Mary brushed past her with her baby, and then decided that she did not want to be involved in what was going on. She quietly made her way over to the dairy.

Once inside the cottage, Mary put Alex's carry-cot down on one of the sofas, and followed Georgina to the bathroom once again bursting into tears.

Georgina tried hard to comfort her without success. She was inconsolable. Mary was muttering as she cried, but her friend could not understand half of what she was saying.

Nor did Mary. All she knew was that, once again, the bottom seemed to have fallen out of her world, and this time it did seem that "winners take it all". Here he was, ready to show off everything he had achieved since breaking up from her. And here she was, hating the life she had, bringing his baby, his son, to meet him only to find that Katie, her arch-rival, had got there first.

Georgina decided to let her cry it out, and went back to find Ben. He was in the lounge, bending over the sleeping baby.'

'Why on earth didn't you tell me Katie was here?' she asked him.

'Why didn't you tell me you were bringing Mary?'

'It was meant to be a big surprise. How was I to know Katie had moved in?'

'It *was* a big surprise. The kind of surprise that dreams are made of. Look, let's not carry this on any further. I'll tell you briefly why Katie is here. I don't know that she'll thank me because I don't think she wants this shared with anyone else. I'll tell you just the basics, and then, if you feel able to, you can tell Mary, because she sure as hell won't listen to me at the moment. I can't really blame her. Everything looks wrong, but it isn't. Everything can easily be made right, beautifully right.'

Georgina tried to get her head round the situation. 'Ben, tell me there's nothing going on between you and Katie. It's taken so much persuasion on my part and even more courage on Mary's part to get here. It would be awful if...'

Ben interrupted her. 'When Katie told me she was marrying Dave Atkinson,' he continued, 'I told her that I thought she was making a big mistake, but you know what love can do, so she married him. At the same time I told her that if ever she needed me, she could contact me through my web site. Well she did contact me, about three months ago, through an Internet café in

Frankfurt. She had been kidnapped from outside Dave's house in Reading and taken to Germany. She had lost her credit cards, all of her money, everything. Anyway, thanks to the guys who ran the Internet café, we were able to get her out of there, and I brought her back here until we could sort out what to do. So here she is. No passport. Apparently she's never had one. And although things are, or were, improving, she's still a nervous wreck. Nobody, but nobody, other than the police, knows she's here, and that's the way it must stay until we know it is safe to make other arrangements.'

'Sounds like something from a Bond movie!' Georgina said. 'I'll leave Mary for a few minutes, and then see if I can get her to listen.'

During this discourse, Alex had decided to wake up, and was beginning to make his presence felt with his vocal chords.

'Guess he's hungry. I think there's a bottle made up for him in the car. I'll go and have a look,' Georgina announced. 'And while I'm doing that perhaps you would like to sort out his other end. Needs some fumigation, I think.'

'Why me?' Ben said.

'Because it's your prerogative as his...' Georgina bit her lip, 'because you're his host, of course.'

'Does that mean I'll have to change your nappy as well?'

Georgina looked back over her shoulder at his last remark, smiled, and walked out of the door.

Within minutes she reappeared, with a bag full of baby stuff, and handed it to Ben. 'There's a changing mattress there,' she said. 'Do you know what to do?'

'Not a clue,' Ben replied. 'But not much can go wrong can it?'

'There's only one way to find out. I'm going to have a word with Mary,' she announced, and made her way back to the bathroom.

Ben took the baby with him into the kitchen laying the changing mattress on the table. Carefully he picked Alex out of his carry cot and laid him on the mattress. Alex, however, had other ideas and immediately wriggled his way off the changing mat. Ben grabbed both baby and mattress and decided it might be safer to wrestle with the little lad on the floor. It was the first time he had really had a close look at him.

'You're a fine looking fellow,' he said. 'Let's see what we can do for you.'

While Ben searched around for a fresh nappy, wipes and powder, Alex looked up at him, watching his every move. Whether it was the different voice or something else that fascinated him, the crying and the wriggling stopped, and he started looking around, taking everything in. Ben struggled, eventually succeeding in undressing the baby's lower half, and discarding the offending nappy.

'Now that was really disgusting, young fellow,' Ben told him. 'I reckon you saved that one up just for me didn't you?' Ben cleaned the baby up and fought to get the clean nappy on him, all the time talking away to him. It seemed that the baby understood every word.

Having got everything back together, he continued the conversation.

'I bet you'll have all the girls after you, young man,' he said. 'They'll be chasing you all the time. Well, you just make the most of it, and take your time choosing the right one. Very easy to make mistakes. I should know. I wonder which girl will be your favourite. Someone like your mummy, eh? Now she *is* something special. You're a lucky man to have a mummy as lovely as her.'

He was surprised when he found himself having to hold back some tears.

Suddenly, he was aware of a presence behind him, looked round, and saw Mary standing in the doorway, eyes red from her tears and anger. Ben's mind went back over a year to when he saw Mary in this state when they had parted company.

'I seem to think we've been here before,' he said. Mary solemnly nodded her head.

'He's a lovely little man. I'm surprised you've come on your own with him. Won't he be missing his father? '

Mary sauntered over to Ben and Alex, kneeling down alongside them.

'He isn't *missing* his father.' she said softly into Ben's ear. 'He's only just *met* him!'

Chapter 40

Ben turned to look up at her, not understanding what she had just said. 'What do you mean he's only just met him?'

'He's yours, Ben. You're his father!'

There was a silence that seemed to last for ever.

'It's true, Ben,' she said quietly. 'He was conceived round about our last night together. I wanted so much to tell you earlier but I didn't know what to do. You had your life and I'd chosen mine. I didn't, couldn't find a way to tell you. I didn't know, still don't know, how you would react. So I tried to keep it to myself, until Georgina got involved, and it was her idea to bring me here to tell you face to face. She's just told me about poor Katie. I must go and apologise to her. I just didn't know...'

'Of course you didn't. Don't worry, I'll sort her out. I think she can probably cope with it now. But, I'm a dad? Really? I'm a daddy? This little fella is my son? Oh, my God. First I see you again, and now you bring me my son. Oh, Mary, Mary! How could you ever think I would react any other way? Have you any idea how much I've missed you? Have you any clue how many times I wanted to contact you? But like you, I thought you had chosen a new life, and I wasn't any part of it any more. What a pair of idiots we've been.'

The elation disappeared from his face for a moment.

'What about Donald, though? How's he dealt with this? I presume he knows he's not the father?'

'He's done his best I suppose, but he really has never come to terms with it. He's too much of a gentleman to throw me out on the streets - you know, "never darken my doorstep again" kind of thing - but he really can't deal with it. He has no interest

243

in our son at all. He's never even held him, not once since I brought him home. He's just a very moral man, and can't find his way through this nightmare.'

'Does he know you're here with me? Does he even know I'm the father?'

'Yes, he knows you're the father. I told him how it had come about, but he doesn't know I have come to see you. I told him I was going away with a friend, that's all.'

Only now did they hug each other. Only now did they kiss. Only now did they realise what a wild, wonderful, crazy life this was.

As they kissed, Mary looked over his shoulder, stiffened slightly and pulled away. Ben let her go, and she went over to the old original fireplace, and looked intently at a photograph standing on the mantelpiece. She picked it up.

It was a black and white picture of an elderly lady with silver curly hair, wearing spectacles.

'Who's this?' she asked as she brought it over to Ben.

'That's my mum,' he said. 'Why?'

Mary then told him all about her apparitions, and how the old lady, the same lady as in the photograph, had guided her slowly but surely into the situation they were in today.

'What was she like?' Mary asked.

'My mum?' replied Ben. 'She was a wonderful mum. The very best. She was always strict with me but in a quiet, unobtrusive way. I knew where I stood with her. You weren't aware of the fact that she always got her own way. She was wily, even devious sometimes, but I loved her to bits, and still do. Didn't know she was in contact with you, though. I don't even believe in things like that.'

'Nor did I,' Mary said, 'but I think I've changed my mind now.'

Mary went to feed Alex.

'Oh no!' Ben said. 'I've been missing out on this for far too long. It's my turn for that. Hey, I don't even know his name!'

'He's called Alex,' she said. 'Alex Benjamin.'

The embrace that followed said it all. There was no need for words.

Ben took the bottle from Mary, took Alex into his arms, went back into the lounge and sat down. Making himself comfortable with the baby on his lap, he proceeded to feed his son for the first time. Mary muttered something about no longer being needed and went out to the car to fetch her cases.

When Alex had been fed, Ben told Mary that he must go and find Katie, and try to put things straight with her. 'Tell her how terribly sorry I am,' said Mary.

'No,' Ben replied. 'You'll have to do that, Mary. It'll be much better coming from you. She'll be O.K., you'll see.'

Ben found Katie sitting in a corner of the living room in the dairy cottage. He put his arm round her, and slowly tried to untangle the mess that she felt she was in. Slowly, painfully slowly, Katie began to relax and accept the situation.

'But she called me a bitch,' she said. 'Even if she didn't know the truth, I'm still not a bitch. I quite liked her until now. And I've always known that you loved her, that's the only reason I let you get away.' A slight smile lit up her face.

'Shall I tell you why she came here?' Ben said.

'Well I guess it was to see you. Simple as that.'

'No. It's a lot more than that. This day was so important, not only for her, not only for me, but for the baby as well. You see, sweetheart, that baby is my son! He's mine. I'm a daddy. Can you see how important it was for Mary, now? It had to go right. And she thought that you'd ruined everything. All her painful plans gone out of the window.'

'OK, yes. But I'm still not a bitch, and she owes me a big apology, a really big, grovelling, over the top apology, before I can get over this.'

'And I think you'll get one. I've had to tell her how you came to be here. Hope you don't mind. I tell you, she must feel as guilty as you felt angry. Now, when you feel up to it, can we all get together in the cottage and make this the happy day that it was supposed to be?'

'I'll be over in a minute,' Katie said.

Later in the afternoon, everyone did get back together. It was like the old times, catching up on everybody's life. Ben phoned Madame Delphine, and booked a table for the evening.

As they drove away from *La Sanctuaire* Ben said:

'Don't tell anyone about me being a dad yet. I want to announce this on Saturday.'

'Saturday?' asked Mary. 'What's special about Saturday?'

'Oh, I should have told you, but I wanted it to be a surprise. I've arranged a special licence for us to get married, darling,' he said.

'What?' exclaimed Mary. 'You haven't even asked me. Don't start taking things for granted, Ben. I'm not someone you can just walk over. I have my own life as well, you know.'

Mary was getting irate, and the other two girls were open mouthed with the surprise at the sudden announcement. Ben let Mary rant on for a few more minutes before putting his hand firmly over her mouth and telling her that it was a joke.

'Some bloody joke!' Mary said, but now the other girls were laughing their heads off seeing the funny side of how easily Mary could be wound up.

'I take that as a no, then,' Ben said, looking Mary straight in the eyes, but Mary didn't answer.

Ben told the girls all about the party on Saturday, and gave them a potted history of Madame Delphine, and the plans that had been put together for celebrating her birthday.

'But as far as she is concerned,' he warned them, 'she thinks she's coming to my house warming party, nothing else. So don't go spilling any beans this evening, please.'

Arriving at the restaurant, Ben was greeted in the usual enthusiastic way by Madame Delphine.

'Oh my, Ben,' Madame Delphine smiled, 'not one pretty lady, but three! Introduce me, then.'

'Well, you've met Georgina before. This is Mary, and this is Katie.'

'Ah, yes. I have been told about Katie living at the cottage with you, but we haven't met before.' There were the mandatory kisses on the cheek, before Ben continued 'And this little man is Alex, Mary's son.'

'*Il n'est pas agréable?*' she replied, 'Oh, I'm sorry. I should speak English. Isn't he delightful? Such a pretty baby. Can I get anything for him? Heat a bottle or is he on baby food yet?'

Mary said it would be helpful if she could warm a bottle for him, and a waitress was called to look after the matter.

Madame Delphine continued to make a fuss over Alex.

'May I?' she asked making signs to indicate she wanted to pick him up. Mary nodded her approval and Alex was taken in Madame Delphine's arms to be introduced to just about everybody in the restaurant, guests and kitchen staff alike. Eventually he was returned to Mary along with a warmed bottle.

The meal was a great success and relieved all the tension from earlier in the day with one exception. As yet Ben was not aware that Katie had received her grand apology from Mary. He hoped it would happen soon, or things could revert to the hard feelings which were prevalent earlier.

As they were leaving, Madame Delphine came over to bid them good night with more kisses on the cheeks.

'I'm looking forward to seeing your new home on Saturday, Ben,' she said.

On the way home Georgina said, 'I reckon she really fancies you, Ben. You could see from the way she looked at you.'

'And he got a bigger kiss than any of us!' chipped in Katie. 'We'll have to keep an eye on them both on Saturday.'

'Yes, she might be planning a private showing of her can-can routine!' Georgina smirked. 'You could be her toy-boy if you play your cards right.'

Chapter 41

Friday was mostly taken up with plans for the party. It was good to have so much help in the kitchen and, much to Ben's relief, the girls seemed to be getting on well together now.

It wasn't until after lunch they all sat down to discuss other matters.

Katie had told Ben that she didn't mind her situation being known by Mary and Georgina, but she was adamant that it must not go any further and Ben made this clear to everybody when they got round to talking about the situations in hand.

'The problem is that Katie is, strictly speaking, here illegally at the moment. She has no passport, has never had one. The difficulty is I don't see how I can get one for her while we are still here, but I can't take her back to the UK because she hasn't got a passport. It's a bit of a catch 22 position,' he explained.

'Hey, I can help with that, can't I?' asked Georgina. 'I could get all the forms and so on, and if Katie can tell me where everything is, I should be able to put together all the bits and pieces they need. Obviously, you'll have to get the photograph done over here.'

'D'you think that could work, Katie?' Ben asked. 'The alternative is to see if the British Embassy in Paris can help us to get a passport. But we still have to answer the question of how Katie got here in the first place.'

'And I just don't want anybody to know where I am until I'm absolutely sure that I'm safe,' Katie added.

'As a first step, then, I suggest we nip over to Angers and get some passport photographs done for Katie,' Ben suggested.

'Then, if it's the right way to go, Georgina can take them back with her so that she can get them verified. Katie, can you give Georgina a name and address of somebody who can authorise the photographs. A policeman, your doctor, an M.P., you know the kind of person?'

'I'll think of someone. The only thing is, Georgina, I'm worried that someone might be watching the house. You must be careful. Always go during the day, and do it all in one visit if you can.'

'You have the keys, then?' Georgina asked.

'Yes, luckily enough I put them in a pocket, not in my bag when I was captured, and they didn't find them,' Katie told her.

'Look,' said Ben hurriedly. 'You two can talk about details later. I can get an application form and a list of documents that are required from the Internet.'

Ben and Katie went to Angers, and found a photographer who produced passport photographs while they waited. Then, after collecting a few more things for the following day, returned to the cottages.

When he had the opportunity, Ben took Mary to one side.

'And what about us?' he asked. 'I can't bear to lose you again. Can you stay?'

'I can't really, can I?' Mary replied. 'What about Donald? I'll have to go back so that I can at least tell him what has happened.'

'But you will come back, won't you?'

'Ben. This has all happened so suddenly. My head is in a complete whirl. I don't know what I really want at the moment. You've got a lovely place here, but I have only been to France for holidays in the past, and that's a lot different to living here. It's a bit different for you. You have always *wanted* to live here.'

'And you don't?'

'I don't know. There are things like the language. Obviously you have picked it up very well, but I've never been good at languages. And then there's the matter of schools and so on. I can't just say yes, can I?'

'Well, how about if you stay here for a couple of weeks, so that you can get the feel of the place, meet more people, see the schools, go shopping at the lovely markets and so on, and then see how you feel. You could get away with that with Donald, couldn't you?'

'But I haven't brought enough stuff for me or Alex to do that. I would have to go home to collect that kind of thing.'

'A week, then?'

'And how will I get home with Alex? Georgina is going back on Monday, and she can't stay another week.'

'I'll find a way of getting you back. I could even come with you if Katie feels comfortable staying here for a few days. That way, we could take the van and bring back everything you need in one go.'

'There you go again! You're presuming too much. I really don't know what I want to do. I am not even sure I want to live here. Let me ask you one thing. If you want us to be together, would you be prepared to come back to England?'

'That would be almost impossible. I've got a number of bookings now, so I couldn't come back now even if I wanted to.'

'So you're expecting me to come here to live with you, but if it were the other way round it would be a different matter.'

This was beginning to sound like an argument brewing, the last thing Ben needed. He hated confrontations of any kind, but with this girl, right here and now was something he definitely didn't want.

'OK,' he conceded, 'I see what you are saying. But I don't understand. Why did you come here? Why did you bring my son to me? Mary, I love you so much. I always have. And now there's a chance of us being together and that opportunity is being dashed in front of our eyes.'

'I came here because I thought I had to let you know about Alex. And, yes, I wanted to see you as well. I have the same feelings, too. Looking back, I think it was you I loved all the time, but at the time, neither of us would actually admit it because neither of us knew how the other one felt. But that doesn't really help me now.'

'Mary, I think you have got to take some time and consider the pros and cons of the two alternatives you have. I can't believe, from the little you've told me, that you really want to go back to Donald especially if he has no time at all for Alex. I know it's difficult for you, but I'm sure we could be good together again, all three of us!'

'I'm prepared to do that if you will as well. Let me know what the pros and cons are of living here. I won't know anyone, I can't speak the language, I won't have a job. It all looks pretty bleak to me. I'll do my list of cons if you'll do your list of pros showing why I *should* come to live here.'

'Fine. That's a deal, and we'll compare notes. Is that what you mean?'

'Done!' and with that she gave Ben a long lingering kiss. 'And now, about this party. I think you ought to have more English food for them to sample. How about if I make a couple of cakes, and could we serve good old English tea? Things like that?'

'Sounds brilliant. Can I leave that to you ladies? If you need ingredients you should find most of them in the kitchen. Anything else I'm sure we can get in the village. Actually, I'm beginning to get rather nervous about this "do". I've no idea how many people will be coming. François has told me hardly anything. I just hope he's got everything organised.'

Chapter 42

Everybody was up early on the big day.

The girls were busy in the kitchen producing cakes and a huge apple crumble to serve at the party. They were getting on well with each other. Mary had made her apologies to Katie, and they had been wholeheartedly accepted.

They talked of many things while they were cooking, and inevitably the subject of Mary and Ben came up.

'Have you made any plans, yet?' asked Georgina. 'Has he asked you to come and live with him?'

'Yes, he has,' Mary told them, 'but I have told him that I'm not sure it would be the right thing to do at the moment. There are so many things that seem to be problems. The language, my job, my friends. It goes on. What do you think?'

Katie and Georgina both went to answer together, but Georgina got in first. 'I don't understand,' she said. 'You were so excited about coming to see him.'

'Until you saw me here!' Katie interrupted.

'Yes, that's true. But you've managed to sort that out now haven't you? Surely you must be a bit tempted to get back together with him. He's so - I don't know the right word - so proud to be Alex's Dad,' said Georgina. 'I caught him outside last night with Alex in his arms, talking away to him. Telling him what a lovely world it is, showing him the moon and the stars, and saying that he was part of all of this. He didn't know I was there, but it was so touching, so beautiful, I almost cried.'

'Is that true?' asked Mary. 'I keep seeing him walking around with him, but I didn't know about that. Guess that's male bonding or something?'

'I'll tell you something, Mary,' Katie said. 'He's been really great with me. I knew he was out of his depth with me in the state I was in, but he was brilliant. He just let me take my time, and slowly but surely, he brought me through it and put me back together. *I* couldn't speak any French either, but every time we went out I would learn a few more words, and he would help me with pronunciation, and how to put sentences together, and now I can make myself understood reasonably well. It's when they answer me I still have the problems, but we're working on that, as well because they respect him for learning their language, they accept me as well. I have really enjoyed my time here, and I won't want to go back to England I can tell you.'

Mary asked, 'Do you know when you might be going home?'

'Don't worry, Mary. I won't be staying permanently, if that's what you mean,' Katie replied. 'Once I've got a passport, and I feel it's safe to go back, then I will, but all I'm saying is that I'll be sorry to leave this lovely place.' And then after a pause for thought, she added. 'But I'll tell you something else, Mary. If you decide to leave Ben, and go back to England to continue your life with Donald, then I'll happily take Ben for myself. I don't know how I've managed to keep my hands off him all this time. Just because of you I guess. I've never met anyone quite like him before. There aren't many men who have turned me down, but he did. And that was because of you.'

'I don't want to leave him. I just don't know whether I would be able to cope here.' Mary told her.

'Mary, I don't think you would have to "cope",' Georgina said quietly. 'I think he would do all the coping for you. Not in a bullying or forceful way, but because he really loves you. At least give it a chance, give it a try. If it really doesn't work out, then so be it. But I think you'll regret not giving it a go.'

'Oh, I don't know. Maybe you're both right,' Mary admitted. 'I'll give it some more thought. It's just that there is so little time. Everything is being rushed.'

'But you don't really have to come back with me on Monday, do you?' Georgina said. 'Why not stay a few more days and really give yourself a chance to make a rational decision?'

'Ben suggested that, but it isn't that easy. For one thing ...'

'Mary, I think you are looking for reasons *not* to stay. Try to think of reasons to be with Ben. Think of Alex. Think of some of the good things. You'll break Ben's heart if you leave him again, and you'll probably lose him for good.' Georgina chided. 'Like Katie said, you don't find many men like this one. And like Katie, I'd snap him up if I felt he had any feelings for me. But unfortunately he doesn't. Our friendship, sadly, has been a purely platonic one, but for all that, I've enjoyed knowing him.'

'Looks like I've got a lot of competition here!' Mary smiled.

'Too right you have!' Katie replied, looking Mary squarely in the eyes.

Mary continued her work much subdued, and deep in thought.

François called round late morning with Michelina.

'How's everything going?' he asked.

'Well, we're busy preparing some English food in the kitchen, and the cottages are clean and sparkly. But I really don't know how everything is going because I don't know what you have planned,' Ben replied, hoping it didn't sound too aggressive.

'I know that, Ben, but it will all work out, you'll see,' and then François filled him in with the arrangements. 'The first people to arrive will be the *Folies* ladies along with myself, Michelina, the Mayor and of course your good self and your friends. Ben, if you can take Madame Delphine into the cottage to show her what you have done to it, and then after a few minutes bring her over to the dairy, we will all be waiting.'

'And the food and wine?'

'The food will be kept warm in the cottage kitchen, if that's OK, and the wine will be served as soon as we are ready for it. You see, it's all organised, my friend.'

'Any other guests will be waiting for my text, and then they will come and join the festivities. So, Ben, other than being the perfect host for your "house warming" party, you really don't need to do anything. Just let it all happen. I don't doubt that something will go wrong somewhere. *Alors quoi*? I don't think it will matter.'

Ben was relieved. He was beginning to think that chaos was imminent, but he didn't have to worry. It was no longer his responsibility.

As they were speaking, Mary came running across the gravel driveway.

She stopped when she saw Ben was talking to François, and went to saunter away but Ben called her over.

'Mary, you haven't met François and Michelina, have you? This is Mary.'

'You do choose such beautiful girls for your friends,' François said in English looking intently at her.

Mary looked a bit embarrassed and then said to Ben, 'Where's Alex?'

'He's fast asleep in the cottage,' Ben replied. 'Nothing wrong is there?'

'No, nothing wrong. I simply wondered where he was. I'll go and take a look to make sure he's all right.'

Mary wandered off, and Ben excused himself and followed her into the cottage.

Alex was sound asleep.

Mary looked at Ben as he came into the room. 'It's you I wanted to see,' she told him. 'Have you done your pros yet?'

'Not exactly,' Ben said. 'Have you done your cons, then?'

'Yes, 'she said.

'Then let's see them,' Ben asked nervously.

Mary showed him a blank sheet of paper.

'There's nothing there!'

'I know. Let's see yours, then.'

'Hang on a second.'

Ben went off, found a scrap of paper and a pen, scribbled something on it and came back to Mary. He held the scrap of paper up for her to read. On it were the large, hastily scribbled words "I LOVE YOU".

Chapter 43

Madame Delphine had received her invitation weeks before but it had not been an easy thing for François to persuade her to come to Ben's "house warming" party.

'But it's my birthday,' she had spat back at François when he had mentioned it for the umpteenth time.

'But you *never* celebrate your birthday!' he had said. 'Ben would be so disappointed if you didn't come. He asked me especially to persuade you to come. He just wants to thank you for all your help. He's such a nice young man. You can't let him down.'

'But it's my *sixtieth* birthday!'

'And you want everybody to know that you are sixty? I don't believe you. You have deceived everyone about your age for years. Why do you want to admit, all of a sudden, that you are getting old?'

'I'm not getting old!' She was now getting cross with François, and at that point he had instinctively known that he had won the argument.

'You'll be amazed at what he has done up there,' he had told her, 'and he's gone to great lengths to get everything right for the party. You'll really enjoy yourself. I know you will.'

Ben, the three girls and Alex were there to greet her.

Madame Delphine looked absolutely stunning in a bright pink flowing dress with matching chiffon scarf, and went straight over to Ben and greeted him with the expected kisses to each of his cheeks, and then proceeded to do the same to the three girls as Ben introduced them to her once again.

'Ben, the cottages look wonderful. You have done so well here,' she enthused. 'Can I see inside please?'

Ben led the way into the cottage, and their visitor was given a guided tour. Starting in the living area Ben pointing out all the work that had been done. Madame Delphine took in all the details. She especially liked the drapes at the windows.

'I like those,' she said pointing at the drapes. 'And the way they match with everything else.'

'Mmm, 'Ben replied. 'They don't do anything. They're just for decoration. But it keeps a bit of England in here.'

From there they went into the dining area.

'Something smells good in here!' Madame Delphine observed. 'Have you been cooking?' she said, looking at the girls.

'Er,' Mary began to say, but Ben took the initiative and changed the subject by taking his guest to see the bedrooms. The smells were of a huge pot of *boeuf bourgignon,* brought in by the local chef, simmering slowly in kitchen. The combination of the bubbling beef and the *herbs Provençal* filled the cottage with a mouth-watering suggestion of things to come. Madame Delphine was inquisitive, walking in to each of the rooms and making comments about the décor, the quality of the work and the colour combinations that had been used, and once again, the drapes which matched the duvets in each room.

'A lot of the décor is down to Katie,' he told her. 'I'm just a bloke. I don't have much of a clue about these things.' He noticed Mary glance toward Katie but thought nothing of it.

Ben awaited his chance and said, 'But now you must see what we have done with the old dairy.'

'*Oui.* I've been told it is very clever what has been done,' Madame Delphine replied as she was taken over the gravel driveway to the other cottage. Ben insisted that the clever part was totally down to the builders.

'You're much too modest for an Englishman,' she said, smiling.

Arriving at the dairy cottage, he pushed open the front door, and ushered her in.

At first she did not notice the people up in the gallery. Her eyes were taking in what had been accomplished.

'Ben, this is amazing. It was just a shell before. I came up here once ...' It was only then that she looked up to the minstrel gallery to see five women, dressed up in their size-adjusted performance gowns, head dresses and all the finery that they used to wear all those years ago. Her eyes immediately filled with tears.

'*Oh non! Oh non!*' she cried. '*C'est merveilleux!*' and she ran up the few stairs to the minstrel gallery to hug and kiss her old acquaintances. These were not the mandatory kisses that were so easily imparted. These were extended hugs, and kisses of joy that were from the heart. The greetings went on for several minutes, and even Ben's eyes were filling with tears as he watched the utter joy and amazement in this reuniting of old friends.

François had slipped outside, returning after a few minutes with the champagne and the pre-dinner appetisers. He asked all the ladies to come down from the gallery and to celebrate Madame Delphine's sixtieth birthday with a few of her friends.

'You knew all along, François, didn't you? You all knew, didn't you? *Oh, quelle merveille, comment tout simplement merveilleux!*'

Madame Delphine was left with her friends from the past sharing memories and catching up with each other's lives while her hosts took the opportunity to go back outside to help with the other arrangements. What met their eyes was a mouth-watering feast being laid out before them.

Tables had been formed into a semi-circle following the line of the circular drive. By now the light was fading under the remnants of a spectacular sunset of pinks, reds and salmons. The

Victorian lamp in the centre of the garden, helped by the light coming from all of the windows of the cottage and the dairy, created a captivating atmosphere. The weather was a little chilly but a few gas heaters had been positioned between the tables.

On the tables, which were dressed in white with broad red ribbons, were earthenware dishes of country pressed *paté*. Platters of *charcuterie* were placed at random on the tables with a miscellany of French breads, and copious amounts of wine to cater for every palate.

Twenty or more people had arrived, and were told to keep the noise at a minimum, until the special lady appeared.

There was a hushed excitement in the garden as everyone waited for her to appear, but nobody wanted to hurry her. Everybody was aware that she thought, at that moment, she had seen the climax of her birthday celebration.

But eventually, it was Ben who went back into the cottage to interrupt her reminiscing.

'Madame Delphine, I'm sorry to intrude, but there is something I forgot to show you.'

So the six women followed Ben outside to find a throng of people who now, freed from their silence, cheered and clapped raising a volume of noise that had probably never been experienced in this place ever before.

There were enough chairs for everybody to be seated, and the eating, drinking, chatting and laughter began in earnest. In the background Madame Delphine's favourite composer, Chopin, was playing.

When the *paté* and *charcuterie* were devoured, the *boeuf bourgignon* was served. Judging by the faces of the congregation, and the dip in the volume of conversation, it was clear that it was appreciated. Finally a range of cheeses that was more likely to be seen at a *fromagerie* was brought to the table along with a selection of fruit and wine.

Later in the evening there were a few short speeches from François, the Mayor, and one or two other people who Ben did not recognise. The builders were congratulated on doing such a marvellous job, and Ben for instigating such imagination, and of course many references to Madame Delphine and her colourful past.

The whole evening was a huge success, and Ben kept himself in the background feeling honoured to be just a small part of it.

It was getting late when Ben disappeared from view.

By now clouds were scudding across the night sky, creating doodles of pale light around the cottages where the moon occasionally shone through.

A few minutes later he reappeared carrying in his arms a sleepy Alex. He grabbed Mary's hand, and walked to the front of the dairy cottage from where he could address the party.

'*Mesdames et Messieurs*,' he started, now confident in his French, 'Madame Delphine thought that today she was coming here to celebrate our house warming, but she was of course deceived. Then she thought that she was here to celebrate her birthday, and, of course, this time she was right. But we have not finished with celebrations just yet.'

Everyone stopped their chatting and eating and waited for him to continue. He glanced over at François and saw the look of surprise on his face. Ben then beckoned Mary over to join him.

'No, ladies and gentlemen. I want you to join me in celebrating something more. I want to introduce you all to my son! I only met him a few days ago, but this little fellow is my son! His name is Alex.' He paused again to let the applause calm down. 'And this beautiful young lady here is Mary, who is Alex's mother, and she is going to move here with me so that we can all be together.' More applause. 'And, if I play my cards right, I think she might even agree to marry me one day.'

Ben knew the French were renowned for being romantics, but he was not expecting what happened next. Chairs were knocked to the floor as people rushed to where he, Mary and

Alex were standing. People pushed and shoved to be able to get near enough to shake hands, hug, kiss or merely touch them. It was overwhelming. It seemed that everyone wanted to see Alex. This was something he could never have imagined.

When he had a chance, he turned to Mary and whispered, 'I think they like you!'

A few remaining bottles of Champagne were brought out, corks popped and glasses raised to toast them, and to welcome them to their new home.

Katie and Georgina simply looked on in disbelief. 'Well, Katie,' said Georgina, 'I think that puts an end to any romantic thoughts we may have had for Ben.'

'Yeah. It's a pity, really,' Katie replied, 'but I'm so happy for them all.'

In the early hours of the morning the party slowly but surely, drew to its close.

As they made their way back into the cottage Georgina suddenly stopped in her tracks.

'You know what?' she said. 'We didn't serve up our English grub after all!'

'Anyone for apple crumble, then?' Katie shouted.

Chapter 44

Ben was up first on Sunday morning to take care of Alex.

As usual he could be heard chatting away to his son while the others were still asleep.

'That was some do last night, eh? You're a star my lad, there's no doubt about that. They all loved you. You'll be really happy living here. There's so much to do, so much to show you. And all this fresh air. You'll be so fit and strong. And you can grow up with the animals as well. You know, I want some chickens, and perhaps a goat or two. That'll be fun, won't it?'

He was just about to give Alex his breakfast when he heard the sound of a car arriving at the front of the cottage. He put Alex in his baby chair, and went to investigate.

In the drive was a smart blue-liveried police car. Two gendarmes got out from the car and approached him.

'*Bonjour, monsieur. Nous sommes à la recherche de Madame Atkinson.*'

'Mrs Atkinson? I think she's still asleep. I'll go and get her for you. Come inside. Can I ask what it's about?' Ben asked.

'It's about her husband, Dave Atkinson. We need to ask her some questions. The police in Thames Valley have asked us to call.'

'I'm glad you speak English,' Ben said, 'or we might have had a few problems. Mrs Atkinson speaks very little French'

Ben went to wake Katie, but discovered that she was already up and dressed. He told her the police had arrived and saw her tense up at the news.

'Don't worry, Katie. I'll be there with you if you want.'

263

'Too right, Ben. I need you right there. Do you know why they're here?'

'They said it's about Dave, but I don't know any more than that.'

'So it's not about the Germany business then?'

'Don't think so.'

'Well, come on then. Let's go and get it over with.'

Together they went downstairs to where the gendarmes were waiting for them. The policemen rose from their seats.

'Madame,' they said sombrely, 'I'm afraid we have some very bad news.'

'About Dave? Have you found him?'

'No, not exactly, Madame. But we have located his body...'

Katie slumped into a chair. 'Body? You mean he's...'

'Yes, Madame. He's been killed. In Albania. A town called Vloras.'

'Killed? Who by? You mean murdered?'

'We're sure that is the case. He had been shot three times and his body was not found until recently. We have confirmed that it is his body by DNA matching. There is no doubt.'

'But why would anybody kill him?'

'We don't know that yet, but the police in Albania are trying their best to find his killers. Have you any idea what he might have been doing in Albania?'

'If I knew where he was and what he was doing I wouldn't be here. I wouldn't have been kidnapped and taken to Germany by those horrible men.' Katie replied acidly.

'Yes, we have been asked to get more information about that. You reported everything to the police in Frankfurt, we understand. Have you heard any more from them?

Ben could see that Katie was getting agitated, so he answered the last question: 'Not a thing,' he said. 'I'm surprised. I know that they arrested the man who was holding Katie – er, Mrs Atkinson – in Frankfurt, but we haven't heard anything else.'

'The man in Frankfurt. Was he one of the men who abducted you? They asked Katie.

'No, he was just a guy – Romanian – who was told to look after me. Look after! What a joke. He was foul. The place was like a pigsty. It was awful.' Ben thought she would be crying at any moment.

'Look,' Ben said. 'There must be a connection between all of this - Dave being killed in Albania, Katie's kidnappers and the Romanian guy in Frankfurt.'

'Yes, everybody agrees on that. It is like a jig-saw puzzle. There are a few pieces missing, but the police in Germany, Albania and England are working together with Interpol to try to find the missing pieces. It may take some time, but hopefully...'

'But we are near to catching the men who abducted you.' the second officer interjected. 'The police in England have discovered some CCTV footage which should help, and they think they have the number of at least one of the vehicles. So we are hopeful.'

As they were talking, Mary and Georgina appeared at the doorway. No words were spoken, but in answer to Mary's questioning look, Ben waved them away. Katie had not even looked up, and he could see her becoming distressed.

'Is there anything else you want to know, or anything else you need to tell us?' Ben asked. 'I think Mrs Atkinson has had enough for now.'

'No, monsieur, I think that is all for now. We are sorry to have to bring such bad news, but given time, I am sure the police forces that are working on the case will find these felons and bring them to justice.'

They rose from their seats, said good-bye to Katie and walked to the door with Ben.

'We will probably need to speak with her again. We are being instructed by the police in Thames Valley.'

'Of course,' Ben said. 'I understand, and thank you.'

265

He watched as they drove away, then walked back into the cottage. Katie had gone.

The girls came back into the lounge.

'What was all that about?' they said in unison.

'They've found Dave. Or, at least, they've found his body. He's been murdered in Albania.'

'Albania? What the hell was he doing there?' Mary said.
'Nothing nice, I guess,'

'Look, can one of you go and see if Katie's OK. I'll carry on where I left off with Alex.'

Ben found Alex asleep in his chair, his head fallen forward, and looking most uncomfortable. Ben let him sleep on while he prepared the little man's breakfast and then gently woke him and fed him with a few spoonfuls of cereal followed by his bottle of milk. Alex loved his food, and seemed to savour every mouthful.

'I think she needs *you*, Ben,' Mary said as she entered the room. 'She just isn't responding to me or Georgina. So I'll take over here while you use your charms and try to get through to her.'

Ben thought he detected something in her voice but did not react, making his way up to Katie's room. Georgina looked up as he came in and shrugged her shoulders which said more than words about the situation. Ben sat down on Katie's bed as Georgina left the room.

'Do you want to talk?' Ben whispered, 'or would you rather sleep, or be on your own?'

Katie opened her eyes. They were reddened, but not from crying. They were dry and looked sore. There were no signs of tears.

'I can talk to you,' she said. 'It's just that the other two don't know the half of it do they? They can't begin to understand what I'm feeling right now.'

'And what are you feeling?'

'I'm feeling like a total idiot, that's what. I'm furious with myself for getting myself into this position.' She looked up at

Ben, straight into his eyes. 'Why didn't I listen to you? You told me this would happen, didn't you? Why did I ever get involved with that man?'

'You were in love, Katie. And we both know how powerful that is, don't we? It's something we have in common. Come on, girl. We've got through everything else together. We can find a way through this, no problem.'

'Sure. I know that, but I am beginning to feel guilty because I should be sobbing my heart out knowing that Dave's dead. But I'm not. I'm feeling relieved, almost glad that he's out of my life. The "not knowing" has gone and it feels so good. So bloody good.' She sat up and leaned toward Ben and they hugged tightly.

'You've been so good to me, Ben. So strong yet so gentle. You know me better than I know myself, I think. So, yes. I know we can get through this together. The only problem I can see is that now Dave's out of my life, I might...'

'Might what?'

'Doesn't matter. Just leave it.'

Ben was aware of the phone ringing downstairs and heard Mary answer it.

'Who was that?' he shouted down the stairs.

'It was Dave's father. He's coming over to see Katie.'

Katie released herself from Ben.

'When?' she shouted.

'Tomorrow,' Mary replied. 'He'll call us with time of arrival when he knows it.'

Chapter 45

Georgina returned to England on Monday, leaving Ben, Mary, Alex and Katie behind.

'I'm really sad to be leaving,' she told them. 'I don't think I will ever experience anything like these last few days ever again. I've really enjoyed myself, and I wish you all happy times here. I'll be back to see you as soon as I can.'

Georgina had taken with her everything she needed to put together Katie's passport application.

'Do be careful, Georgina,' Katie said as she was driving away. 'Thanks for doing this for me, but don't take any risks. '

Georgina didn't answer, drove slowly out of the wooden gate, turning left down the track on her way back to Reading. The others stood at the gate and waved her on her way.

'What a wonderful girl she is,' Mary said. 'I don't think any of this would ever have happened if it hadn't been for her.'

It was Ben who took the phone call from Mark Atkinson later in the morning.

'Hi, Ben,' he said. 'Just to let you know I will be arriving at Angers train station at about quarter to three. Can you pick me up?'

'Of course, no problem,' Ben told him, and thought that was the end of the conversation, but it wasn't.

'Ben, I've got to tell you. I have the most awful news for Katie. I won't beat about the bush. Dave has been murdered in Albania. I've just had it confirmed by the police after a DNA test. I don't know how I'm going to tell her. I've never had to do anything like this before. I hope I can count on you to support me – and Katie.'

'Of course you can. But as it happens, she already knows. The French police were asked through Interpol to break the news to her yesterday morning. I've got to admit, Mark, that this hasn't come as much of a surprise to me, and I don't think it has to Katie either. She's been unusually introvert since she heard. Now she knows the facts I don't know how it will affect her. She's such a great girl. She really doesn't deserve this, especially after all she has gone through already.'

'Tell me about it!' Mark said. 'I feel so responsible for what has happened. It's almost as if I had done these things to her myself. How could a son of mine cause so much pain? It's just beyond belief.'

And with that he was gone.

Picking up his hand luggage, Mark made his way toward the gate to start his journey to Southampton Airport.

Aboard the aircraft he wasn't listening to the instructions being given by the hostess. He automatically buckled himself into his seat as tears started welling up in his eyes.

How is it, he thought, that a son of mine can cause such a disaster, hurt so many people, fail everybody who has ever loved him and yet make me cry?

The tears were starting to roll down his cheeks and he tried to hide them by casually wiping his face with a tissue.

'Would you like a drink, sir?'

He looked up at a pretty girl, so smart in her FlyBe uniform.

'A Scotch would be nice. Thanks.'

The drink was downed in just two gulps. Needing a distraction from the pain he was feeling, he put on his headphones and tuned to a classical channel. Rachmaninov's second piano concerto was playing, the melancholy of which sat easily with his own frame of mind. He wallowed in its pensive beauty.

Before he knew it he had landed at Orly airport, and was taken by the shuttle bus to Charles de Gaulle airport where he boarded the train to Angers. As the train got nearer to its destination, so he got closer to desperation trying to plan how he could find the right words with which to approach Katie.

Ben went on his own to meet Mark Atkinson.

They had never met before, and although Katie had given a good description of him, Ben had decided to make sure of meeting the right person by writing "ATKINSON" on a piece of card which he could hold up for people alighting from the train to see.

It worked.

'Ben? I'm Mark Atkinson. Thanks for coming to meet me.'

'No problem,' Ben replied. 'My car's parked just round the corner.'

The two men walked together to Ben's car without speaking, and loaded Mark's luggage into the boot.

On the short journey back to the cottage, they spoke only of Katie.

'I must warn you, Mark,' Ben confided, 'She's really shaken up by this. And she's extremely volatile. I don't know what kind of a welcome you'll get. She's been through one hell of a lot in the last few months, and now this. It's as much as anybody could take.'

Mark told Ben that he, too, was trying to sort his mind out over his feelings.

'As yet, I haven't told any of the family. I just don't know how to, but it will have to be done, it will have to be near the top of my "to do" list when I get back. Oh, my word, this is nice!' he said as they drove through the gates at *La Sanctuaire*.

Ben ushered Mark into the cottage and introduced him to Mary.

'Where's Katie?' Ben whispered to Mary.

'She's upstairs in her room.'

Mark heard what was being said.

'Don't worry,' he said to Mary. 'She'll probably come down when she's ready.'

Mary offered Mark a drink. 'A decent cup of tea would go down well,' he said.

Much later, when they were about to sit down to eat, Katie appeared. There were no signs that she had been crying, just a vacant look to her face, especially her eyes. Dave did not come into the conversation while they enjoyed their meal.

Whether it was the wine that brought about Katie's tirade or not, nobody knew, but the majority of it was directed straight at Mark, who had thought the time had come to broach the subject of Dave.

Katie just let fly at him, damning him for raising such a monster, allowing her to get involved with him, wondering just how he could live with himself, sleep nights. And it ended with her screaming at him: 'Do you know something? The only thing you're son was really any good at was fucking. And now he's fucking dead!'

The room went silent.

Nobody knew what to do or say.

It was Ben who got up from the table, went round to Katie, knelt down beside her and cradled her in his arms. He expected tears, but none came. She felt tense in his arms, but after just a few seconds, seemed to uncoil and returned his embrace while everybody looked on. They both stayed in each other's arms for what seemed an eternity, not speaking, not looking at anybody. Just two bodies entwined.

Eventually, Katie broke away from Ben.

'Sorry, everybody. It had to be said, and I'm not apologising for what I said, just the embarrassment I caused. I think I'll go back to my room now, if you don't mind. Maybe I can be more civil in the morning, Mark.'

When she had walked through the lounge, up the narrow stairs to her bedroom, and had closed the door behind her Mark said: 'Wow! What a girl!'

'Isn't she just?' Mary said glancing at Ben.

'I've got to say you handled that well, Ben,' said Mark.

'Mmmm. Didn't he!' Mary said

Chapter 46

During the few days that Mary stayed in France, Ben spent every minute of their time together trying to impress upon her that she had made the right decision. The one thing that convinced her more than any other was the quality and design of French children's clothes. Mary must have visited every shop in Angers that sold kids' fashion – *Chipie, Enfance, Catamini* – and fell in love with all of them.

'I'll be spending a lot of Euros on this stuff,' she said. 'It's a pity Alex isn't a girl, though. The girls' clothes are absolutely beautiful.'

When Mary went to see the *Ecole Maternelle,* the nursery school in the village, she received a warm welcome and, accompanied by Alex in his pushchair, was shown around every part of the building. She smiled when she saw so many happy faces, enjoying a variety of activities. She saw some of the older children in the miniature kitchen, preparing and cooking food, much of which was being grown in the nursery's garden where, although it was only the end of February, the little ones were busy tending cabbages and other vegetables to be used in the kitchen.

'Impressed?' Ben asked.

'Oh, yes,' she replied. 'What a difference to the nurseries back home.'

'Exactly. And, you know, this difference goes right across the French education system. I'm not sure why, but I made a study of schools around here before I came, and there are top-rated schools at every level right on our doorstep.'

Ben introduced Mary to many of his new friends at the *tabac* and the *centre sportif,* enjoyed showing her around the village and the city of Angers and, day-by-day, Mary became more and more convinced that the conclusion she had arrived at was the right one.

'Ben,' Mary said on their last evening at *La Sanctuaire,* 'Will you be absolutely honest with me?'

'Of course,' Ben replied, apprehensive of what was coming next.

'It's about Katie. Well about you and Katie, to be precise.'

'Yes?'

'What do you really feel for her? I've seen you with her the last few days, and I have to wonder whether...'

'Wonder what?'

'Well, I still think she's a threat.'

'You're joking – I hope.'

'No. The way you hugged her the other day, the way she would only talk to you about Dave. It just makes me wonder if...'

'If there's something going on? No there isn't.'

'So you don't love her?'

'Ah, that awful word "love". It covers a multitude of things doesn't it? Yes, I do "love" her, but in a completely different way than I love you. I think the French do better on this matter. They have more than one word for love. For my love for you I would say *"Je t'adore",* for Katie I would say *"Je t'aime"* but I'd also say that about pizza! In English they both translate as "I love you", but only one means I *really* love you. My love for Katie is as it might be for a sister. I care about her. I have shared her ordeals with her. And she with me. Of course I love her.'

'Don't get cross with me. I just had to know.'

'So now you do.'

'It's just that when we were preparing the food for the party, we were all talking, and Katie blatantly said that if I left you and went back to England that she would willingly take my place. And she meant it, Ben. I know she did.'

'So, is that what made you decide to stay? You couldn't bear the thought of me and her?'

'No. It wasn't. I decided to stay because I love you, and want to share my life and Alex's life with you. How could you think that?

'And how could you think that Katie and I have anything going? We've been together here for months. The only thing we've shared is the occasional hug and the even rarer kiss.'

Mary looked bashfully at Ben and couldn't find the words to speak.

'So, can we stop this silliness, then?' Ben continued. 'There is no threat to us from Katie, but that doesn't mean that when she needs one, I won't give her a hug. Mary, no words in any language can tell you how much I love you, but we have to trust each other. If we can't, then there is little future for us.'

Mary was once again taken aback by Ben's assertiveness, something she didn't remember from their previous relationship. He was so much stronger now and wasn't afraid to say exactly what he meant. This was more the man she wanted.

'Ben, I'm sorry. I just had to know. You're absolutely right. If we can't trust each other...'

'OK. Subject closed. Agreed?'

'Agreed,' Mary said, feeling for once in her life that Katie would not be a thorn in her side. She might even become a friend.

There were remarkable changes in Katie as well. Once Dave's father had returned to England, she seemed more relaxed. She had turned down Mark's suggestion that she return with him.

'There will be a lot to sort out,' he had said, but she had stated firmly that she would return as and when she felt able to, and not before. Mark, of course, did not know of the passport problem and she didn't want to enlighten him.

'Well, I will just have to try to sort things out from here, Mark. I'm not coming back to England until I know that I will be safe.'

Two days before Ben, Mary and Alex were leaving to meet up with Donald, she awoke almost a new person. She felt extricated, unshackled from everything to do with Dave. She felt alive and free for the first time in months.

She studied herself carefully in the bathroom mirror and shook her head.

'This just will not do, girl,' she said out loud to herself. 'What have you done to yourself?'

She ran to her bedroom, found a note pad and pen and started to make a list. Hair colouring, nail varnish, lipstick, mascara, eye-liner, the list went on. She felt guilty that once again she would be using Ben's credit card. But this was an emergency. Katie was about to be born again.

On the day they left, she waved them good-bye as they drove off in Ben's white Transit van then went back indoors. Later, grabbing her list, she strolled into the village to catch the bus to Angers. She had been there several times with Ben, but this was the first time on her own. She knew exactly where she was going.

The medley of perfumes as she entered *Boutique Gaëlle* filled her head. She had looked in at the shop on one of her trips with Ben and had vowed to return one day. Now she entered the store and had never seen anything like this before; the range of perfumes, the lights and colours of the individual displays. It was like being in a fairground, almost too much to take in. As she made her way from one manufacturer's stand to the next, she was offered samples of creams, potions and perfumes, each of which seemed to out-do the previous one. How was a girl to choose? She asked herself.

'Puis-je vous aider?' A young man's voice spoke softly beside her.

'Pardon?' she retorted.

'Oh, you are English?'

'Yes'

'Sorry, I presumed...'

'No problem,' Katie said, somewhat surprised to be approached by a young guy in such a feminine environment.

'Please don't take this the wrong way, *Mademoiselle*,' he said. 'I just wondered whether you would allow me to make some suggestions for you?'

'What kind of suggestions are we talking about, here?' Katie said, smiling.

'Well, if you could spare the time, I would like to introduce you to some products that I think would most suit your beautiful complexion. I think you would call it a making-over?'

'Make-over,' she corrected him. 'And how much would that cost me?'

'Nothing *Mademoiselle*. But if you wish to purchase some of the products after you have seen what they can do for you, that is all I ask.'

'Yeah?'

'*Oui* Mademoiselle. There is no catch, I promise you.'

'Then, I've got the time,' Katie joked, and she was taken by the young man to a comfortable anti-room behind the sales area.

Katie was expecting, now, to be handed over to a beautician – a lady beautician – but to her surprise, she found that her young man was going to perform the miracles.

She was there for almost an hour, trying this, trying that, until finally she saw the finished product. And she was impressed. She thanked her artist friend.

'*J'ai le plaisir, Mademoiselle*,' he said. 'I had such a lovely face to work with in the first place.'

Katie almost blushed. She bought most of the products that he had used on her and walked out into the bustling Rue St. Denis to make her way home. She felt like a film star at the Cannes Festival.

Back at *La Sanctuaire*, she took a leaf out of Ben's book, poured herself a large glass of red wine and went down to the patio at the far end of the garden. She felt happier today than she had done for a long time, and simply sat taking in the sights and sounds of the stream and the surrounding countryside.

Much later she went indoors, dressed herself in tight-fitting jeans and a peacock blue top which reflected the colour of her eyes, and took a final look at herself in the mirror.

'Look out, boys.' she shouted into the mirror. 'Katie Forrester is back. And she's on the prowl!' Minutes later she was on her way to the sports centre.

As Mary, Ben and Alex made their way to Caen and thence to England, Mary was becoming more and more apprehensive. She was dreading having to face Donald with the news that she was moving to France with Ben, afraid that he could become violent. He wasn't used to not getting his own way.

'But don't you think he might be relieved?' Ben suggested. 'He might not have said that you had to go, but you know that he can't deal with the situation with Alex. He might be happy that you have made this decision to save him having to.'

'I wish I could think that, but as crazy as it seems, I'm certain he will do everything in his power to keep me there. I don't understand it, but he seems determined that I should not leave him. God knows why after what I've done to him, but that's how it is.'

Ben was trying his best to reassure her that everything would be OK, but he wasn't succeeding.

The best, the only thing Mary could do was to keep her fingers crossed that the meeting with Donald would not be as bad as she was anticipating.

If you have enjoyed reading Sanctuary and

want to know what happens next,

here's the first chapter of the sequel

from Glyn Smith-Wild:

Repercussions

To be published shortly.

Chapter 1

Ben was ushered, or more precisely, propelled into a large room.

Trying to stop himself from overbalancing, his hands landed on the olive green leather surface of a giant antique desk. Slowly, he lifted his head to take in his surroundings.

The place resembled something from a period drama. The lower part of the walls was clad in a wood, as rich in colour as he had ever seen. Donald, who was responsible for Ben's sudden arrival in the room, saw him looking.

'South African Cherry,' he said. 'I had it imported specially. Sit down, Ben.'

Ben ignored the request, and continued to look around the study. The ceilings were bordered by extravagantly carved cornices depicting vine leaves and bunches of grapes, and surrounding the two sparkling chandeliers were matching carved roses. The upper parts of the walls were clad in a deep cherry red flock wall covering with intricate gold relief.

Before he could absorb any more, he once more felt a firm hand on his shoulder.

'I asked you to seet down.'

Until now Donald's voice had been that of a country gentleman, a calm, almost velvet voice. Suddenly, there was the strong trace of a South African accent, something that had always, even under normal circumstances, sounded somewhat menacing in Ben's mind.

Ben moved backwards and sank into a cream leather sofa. Donald positioned himself on the corner of the desk.

'Thank you.' Donald sneered slowly, no longer attempting to conceal his South African background. 'Now I don't know exactly who you think you are, young man. But to calmly walk into my house and announce that you are taking Mary away with you is, to me, the very height of audacity.'

'I'm not exactly taking her away. As I told you it was her decision …'

'I'm not terribly interested in the technicalities, Ben. All I'm telling you is that there is no way she is leaving. She belongs here with me, and that, my friend, is how it is going to be. So I suggest that you just act sensibly, and get the hell out of my house!'

Donald remained where he was, fixing his stare into Ben's eyes. Ben stayed put as well. He desperately needed time. He had to get to grips with the situation. At the far end of the study there were two large computer screens, looking strangely incongruous in the historic opulence of the room. Their flickering screens appeared to be displaying financial information similar to the ones that he had seen on television in stock exchanges, a mass of flickering numbers edged with red or blue.

'Is that what you are into?' Ben asked, hoping it would give him the seconds or minutes he required to adjust to the imminent scenario.

'Yes, but I don't see that is any of your business.'

'Probably not, but it is just that Mary didn't seem to know much about what you did.'

'Eez that so? Oh, dear. That's such a shame.' Donald's voice was quiet, overflowing with sarcasm but immediately changed back to his normal, sharp, clipped South African inflection. 'Well that is just how I intended it to be. Finance is something that should not involve women at all. It's nothing to do with her, and it has even less to do with you.'

Ben was using the time to look around again. The door through which they had entered was now behind Donald, and to Ben's right there were two sets of French doors looking out onto the substantial area of lawns to the rear of the house. He had to squander more time here.

He and Mary had agreed before they arrived that whatever transpired, she should just concentrate on collecting as much as she could of her and the baby's things, putting them in Ben's van which was parked on the front drive. She would then take her car and drive herself and the baby and wait for Ben in the car park of the flat in Reading where they once both lived. He would catch up with her in the van. It was imperative, therefore, that Ben gave her as much time as he could.

He pulled himself out of the sofa and went to walk away from Donald.

'Well!' Donald roared. 'What are you waiting for? Just go!'

'I'm just trying to think. If I leave now, what I would tell Mary.'

'You don't have to tell her anything. I'll do that for you. I can tell her that I paid you to leave her here. Yes, that would be a nice touch. I could say that you were only too eager to take the money.'

'Well, she'll know that isn't true. She knows I don't need money. You'll have to do a bit better than that. Anyway, now she knows where I live, she will be away from here at the very first opportunity. Unless, of course, you intend to imprison her here.'

'There is no way she would leave here without my consent I can assure you.' Donald now bore a cynical smile on his face. 'One click on my central control panel, and every door and window of this place is locked. Nobody comes and nobody goes out unless I let them.'

Ben was beginning to feel very uncomfortable, and the palms of his hands were becoming sweaty. He was way outside his comfort zone.

'Now, I think you're going to be sensible and take the easy way out of this.' Donald's voice took on that soft but sinister tone again.

'Well, I'm not so sure about that,' Ben bluffed. 'I need to know what's going to happen to my son. According to Mary, you have shown no interest in him at all. How will he fit into all this?'

'The brat? You can take him with you. Yes, that would be a very good idea. He's yours. You take him. It would make things so much simpler for me. I'll go and get him if you like, then you can just leave Mary here, and go.'

Ben was frantically trying to plan an escape. Then he looked again at Donald, something new dawning on his mind.

'I think we've met previously somewhere, haven't we? I've just realised that I've seen you before. I just can't remember where or when.' As he spoke he moved little by little, trying to get himself between Donald and the door. Donald had realised very quickly what was happening and had moved backwards to the door, taking a key from his pocket, turning it in the lock, and replacing the key in his jacket pocket.

'Now, I'm losing patience with you, Ben,' he said. 'I don't like stupid men, and I especially don't like them if they interfere in my plans. So I will ask you again to be sensible, and just get the fuck out of here, with or without the baby. I just want you off my property. Now.'

'And if I decide not to?'

To Ben's horror, Donald looked round behind him and grabbed one of the many polished swords that hung on the wall behind him, removed the blade from its sheath and came towards him, the shiny curved blade high over his right shoulder glinting from the sunlight from one of the French windows.

'Decide not to? Decide not to? I make all the decisions here. You won't decide one way or the other, Ben. The decision is already made.'

The man was now standing facing Ben. In his eyes a look of pure evil.

It all happened in a flash. Donald brought forward his arm

4

with the sword. Ben acted instinctively, picked up the nearest thing, a chair which was much heavier than he was expecting it to be, and swung at the man, knocking him flying over the desk and onto the floor the other side. Donald came towards him again. Ben grabbed the chair a second time, this time letting it fly from his grasp catching the man full in his stomach. This time he stumbled and caught his foot on the sword's sheath which had lain on the floor. He fell heavily backwards catching his head on the corner of an antique dresser which was situated near the door. Ben moved slowly round the desk, half expecting him to rise up again. Donald remained supine on the floor. Gently, he fumbled in the man's pocket, found the key where it had been secreted, and quietly let himself out of the study without a backward glance, locking the door behind him.

Turning right down the hallway, Ben made his way to the front entrance of the house. As he arrived in the atrium, he saw Mary making her way down the impressive curved staircase, which dominated the entrance to the house, her arms full of clothes and baby equipment.

'What's going on?' she asked.

'Never mind what's going on. I'll tell you later. For now we just need to get out of here. Is there much more to take?'

'No this is about it, I think. I just need one more trip upstairs, and I'll be done.'

'Great. Where's Alex?'

'Alex is fast asleep in my car.'

Mary continued out to Ben's van to unload her bundles and quickly returned to the house to collect the final load of belongings, Ben chasing her up the stairs.

'Mary,' he called after her, 'have you got any photographs of Donald?'

'There will be one or two on my camera,' she replied.

'And you have your camera with you?'

'Yes. It's amongst the stuff I've put in the van. Why? Is it important?'

'I think so. I'm pretty certain that I've met Donald before. I just can't remember where or when.'

Mary was busy collecting the final things she wanted to take, and passed an armful to Ben.

As they hurried their way down the stairs, Ben thought he heard knocking sounds coming from the study.

'Come on, girl,' he shouted to Mary. 'Have you got your car keys?'

'Yes, of course I have.'

'Then let's get out of here!'